TARGETED

SHADOWS LANDING: THE TOWNSENDS,
BOOK #2

KATHLEEN BROOKS

ALSO BY KATHLEEN BROOKS

Forever Driven

Forever Secret

Forever Surprised

Forever Concealed

Forever Devoted

Forever Hunted

Forever Guarded

Forever Notorious

Forever Ventured

Forever Freed

Forever Saved

Forever Bold

Forever Thrown

Forever Lies

Forever Protected

Forever Paired

Forever Connected

Forever Covert

Forever Burning (coming August/September 2024)

Shadows Landing Series

Saving Shadows

Sunken Shadows

Lasting Shadows

Fierce Shadows

Broken Shadows

Framed Shadows

PROLOGUE

Junior year of high school . . .

Hunter Townsend opened the mailbox and grabbed the mail. Bill. Bill. Bill. Another college interest letter for his younger sister, Olivia, who was a year younger than he was. Some more bills. And another recruitment letter from a college hockey team for his older brother, Stone, who was a senior. And then there it was. The letter from the college standardized testing group with his scores. There was also one for Olivia since she'd decided to take it "for fun."

Everyone kept asking Hunter about college since his older brother, Stone, was going to be the first in the family to go to college on a hockey scholarship. Then Olivia, the fourth of nine Townsend children, was already getting interest from colleges because she was a genius. But Hunter wasn't sure what he wanted to do.

He was good at strategy, not English literature. He'd grown up playing Battleship with his older brothers, Damon and Stone. As they all got older, the game moved to chess.

He loved military history, not art history, which was why he was very worried about this test. Hunter was good in math, but not fantastic. English was his weakest spot. Hunter tore open the envelope and frowned. Yup, a big weak spot.

Hunter shoved the rest of the mail back in the box, crumpled up his standardized test scores, and marched back toward town. It was two miles away, their house was outside their small town in upstate New York, but he needed the walk. What the hell was he going to do now? Community college probably. With Stone getting offers from all these major universities and Olivia already getting interest from colleges, Hunter felt left out, adrift, and stupid.

The noise of a radio, the sound of metal on metal, and the bay full of men working on cars and motorcycles reached him. Hunter had ended up at the mechanic shop where Damon, the eldest of the Townsend nine, worked.

Damon looked up from where he was working on a motorcycle and frowned. Not that Damon smiled often. Instead, his oldest brother seemed to have the weight of the world on him. Apparently, working on motorcycles was stressful.

"What's wrong?" Damon asked as he looked back down at the motorcycle.

Hunter shoved his hands in his jeans and pulled out the crumpled piece of paper. Damon looked back up and took it from Hunter's hands. He worked to get the wrinkles out and then read the scores.

"Well, now you have a starting point. I've heard there are books we can buy to help you learn how to take these types of tests."

"That's BS. I have a 3.4 grade point average, but

according to this, I'm stupid." Damn, it hurt more than Hunter realized.

"You're not stupid. You just have strengths and weaknesses like everyone else." Damon handed him the test scores back and stood from where he'd been sitting on an overturned bucket. "You're a smart guy, Hunter. You have a freaky ability to strategize. You'll find something that allows you to play to your strengths. We'll come up with a plan after you process the scores and realize they don't represent your intelligence. Then, when you're clear-headed, we'll talk it over and find a solution."

Hunter tried to think more objectively but it was hard. However, he knew Damon would help him. He always had. It was Damon who showed up at every school play, every basketball game, and half of the parent-teacher conferences. Not because their parents were bad parents—they were great. However, nine kids in under fifteen years were expensive and time-consuming. Their father worked twelve-hour shifts and picked up every extra job he could to help pay for everything. Their mother had her hands full with all the younger kids. The Townsends were their own village and looked out for each other. Hunter did the same for his younger siblings, too.

"Hey," Damon said, reaching into his back pocket and pulling out his wallet. "Can you go get us two milkshakes?" Damon handed him some cash. "Then you can help me fix this bike."

Hunter took the cash only because he knew Damon would have him work it off. He wouldn't ask Hunter to repay him, but Damon knew Hunter would have insisted. This way, they both got milkshakes and Hunter didn't feel like he was mooching off his older brother.

· · ·

Hunter was halfway to the ice cream parlor when he saw a friend from high school. Sarah was a senior. She was a cheerleader, homecoming queen, prom queen, and, well, just a queen. She was incredibly nice and beautiful, but she had a jerk of a boyfriend.

Hunter had his fair share of girlfriends. He wasn't blond like his younger twin brothers, Rowan and Forrest, his next younger brother, Kane, or his sister Olivia. Instead, Hunter had inherited the same black hair Damon, Stone, Penelope, and his younger brother, Wilder, had. The Townsends were either blond or black haired with either blue or varying shades of grey eyes. They were a jumble of their parents in every way. While they could look as if they were complete opposites—blond hair, blue eyes versus black hair and gray eyes—there was no denying they were all related.

"Hi, Hunter," Sarah said with a kind smile. "I heard Stone is being recruited in Massachusetts and Minnesota. That's so cool. Tell him I'm so happy for him."

The door to the store she was standing in front of opened and Brock, her boyfriend, strode out, glaring at them. "I leave you one minute and you're out here flirting with this douche. I told you Slutty Sarah was the perfect nickname for you."

Sarah didn't fight back. Olivia would have ripped the guy's nuts off. Instead, Sarah hung her head. "I wasn't flirting, Brock. I was telling Hunter to congratulate Stone for us."

"Don't disrespect me like that, Slutty Sarah!" Brock's hand raised as if he were going to hit her.

It wasn't a secret that Brock was rough with his girlfriend, but Hunter had never seen it in person. He saw the times when it was hot out and Sarah wore a turtleneck or a scarf. He saw the times she wore long sleeves when everyone else on the cheer team wore sleeveless tops. Hunter and the rest of the school, teachers included, knew what was happening even if they didn't see it. However, Sarah always smiled and never asked for help. But maybe she was too scared to, and right now Hunter was seeing it firsthand. He'd kill a man who treated his mother or sisters like this. Guilt and shame slammed into Hunter. He could have stopped this a long time ago if he'd just spoken up.

Brock outweighed Hunter by fifty pounds. Hunter was six foot two and one sixty, but he wasn't as strong as Damon. He still looked scrawny while Brock was close to two hundred and twenty pounds, just as tall as Hunter, but he had muscles everywhere.

That didn't stop Hunter from grabbing Brock's hand midair and turning Brock's wrath from Sarah onto him. "Not today, Brock. Don't you dare lay a hand on her, you asshole."

Brock yanked his arm free and sneered. "You gonna do something about it?" Brock shoved Hunter and sent him stumbling backward.

Here's the thing though. Hunter was the third out of nine children, and seven of them were boys. Hunter could fight. But thanks to Olivia's insane obsession with the law, Hunter also knew about restraint and the difference between assault and self-defense.

Hunter moved to stand in front of Sarah, even as she begged Hunter to leave it alone and then begged Brock to leave with her. Hunter kept his eyes on Brock, but reached behind him for Sarah. Hunter was careful to speak in a calm voice, "Sarah, go to my brother Damon's garage. He'll take care of you."

Sarah didn't move at first, but when Brock sneered at her, she finally moved. She ran. "Slutty Sarah! Running straight to another man," Brock taunted.

"I don't want to fight you, Brock. God knows you deserve to have your ass beaten for what you've done to Sarah, but I'm giving you a chance to act like a man for the first time in your life and walk away," Hunter said calmly.

"How's this for being a man?" Brock swung and his fist connected with Hunter's face. Hunter didn't move a muscle as he took the hit. Then he smiled. Hello self-defense.

Hunter swung, smashing his fist into Brock's face, then ducked instantly to avoid Brock's punch. The fight, such as it was, didn't take long. Bullies were rarely able to live up to their own hype. Four punches and Brock was on the ground, bleeding from his eyebrow, nose, and lip.

A man put his hand on Hunter's arm. It wasn't aggressive, but it was sure and strong. Hunter turned to see a man in camouflage. "At ease. I've called the cops." Brock went to get up, but the man put his boot on Brock's chest to keep him down. "I don't think so. Stay," he snapped at Brock before looking up at Hunter. "You're a smart fighter. You don't see that every day."

"Thanks," Hunter said, still not taking his eyes off Brock. "He was going to hurt her."

"I know. I was on my way over from my recruitment office to stop it, but you beat me to it. Ever thought of joining the Army?"

"Hunter!" Damon called out as he ran down the sidewalk. Sarah was hovering at the shop door, flanked by two large men holding giant wrenches to protect her.

The soldier held out a card and Hunter took it. "Stop by for a chat sometime if you want to learn more."

∽

"Townsend!" Hunter jumped up from his bunk at basic training and stood at attention. "The commander wants to see you. Now."

Hunter strode from the barracks. He'd done really well in Army basic training and was one day away from graduation. He'd trained with Damon and Stone to get Stone ready for a career as a pro hockey player. Olivia had helped him study for the military entrance test. The Army's test was a lot easier than the college standardized test simply because it covered things Hunter was interested in. It didn't matter what the author was thinking when they wrote about the curtains being blue. There was math, mechanics, and more. Hunter had aced it.

Basic had been hard, sure, but he was in such great shape after helping Stone that he'd easily finished first in each training exercise. He didn't want to brag, but this was his thing, and he excelled.

Hunter knocked on his commander's door and waited to enter until he heard the command. "You wanted to see me, sir?"

Commander Olander looked up from the papers on his desk. "Have a seat. I've been looking over your recruiter's letter, your test scores, and your high school report cards. What do you think of basic training?"

Was this a trick question? "It's going well, sir."

The commander smiled. "Going well? You're first in every training exercise. Sometimes by a large margin. You're running the courses and hitting marks Special Forces do." Hunter didn't know that. That was pretty cool. "Your recruiter thinks you would be the ideal candidate for Special Forces. Your tests show you are ideal for it too. You're a top marksman and I want to send you to marksman training to really hone that. Do you speak a foreign language?"

"I've never had anything more than two years of Spanish in high school. My sister took French, so I picked that up too. But I wouldn't say I was fluent. I didn't think that was a requirement for the Army."

"It's not for the Army, but it's very helpful if you plan to climb the ranks in Special Forces. And if I've ever seen someone perfect for Special Forces, it's you. It's going to be a lot of work for the next couple of years. Are you up for it, Townsend?"

"Yes, sir!"

～

"Where are you?" Damon asked.

"Can't tell you," Hunter said as he looked out at the foreign soldiers his Special Forces team was training to protect themselves from the neighboring country that wanted to invade them. "What's so important you got through to me somehow when I'm on a mission?"

"I think Olivia's in trouble. She's moving to Shadows Landing," Damon said.

"Doesn't that billionaire she works with, Ryker Faulkner, live there?"

"Exactly. I won't let him take advantage of our sister."

Hunter understood. Olivia was a badass lawyer, but she was their sister and they would look after her. "I'll meet you in Shadows Landing as soon as I can, but it might be a while."

～

Hunter stepped off the military cargo plane at the Charleston Air Force Base with a new job and a new base. He found Damon leaning against his car, waiting for him. "Does it feel like you're in enemy territory?" Damon asked as airmen and naval personnel walked by.

"Joint base, my ass. They left out the best branch of the military," Hunter smirked before hugging his brother. "It's good to see you."

"It's been too long. I appreciate you coming."

Hunter nodded and tossed his duffle into the back of the car. "So, the billionaire wasn't an issue. I heard he's married now. But tell me about this guy trying to date our sister and why haven't you been able to run him off like the others?"

"Granger Fox is the sheriff and doesn't scare easily. I'll give him credit for that. Olivia swears she's not seeing him, but I don't believe her. The man is constantly watching her, and she him."

"Any man who wants our sister has to prove himself worthy. Now, tell me about Shadows Landing," Hunter said as they drove out of the base.

"It's not too far from here. Nice little town. Quirky. The plus side is everyone I've met seems to really care for Olivia." Damon paused, his lips turning down into a frown. "I've been so busy building my business. I haven't been there for you all like I was when you were growing up. It's time I change that."

Hunter looked at his older brother in disbelief. "Damon, you've always been there for us. When I was injured and transported to Ramstein, who was there when I got out of surgery?"

"Me," Damon said after a moment.

"When Olivia got that huge legal win, who was there to celebrate with her?"

"Me," Damon admitted.

"When Wilder opened his first nightclub, who was there?"

"Me," Damon said with a little chuckle.

"When Kane made it into the FBI, who was there at his ceremony?"

"Okay, I get your point," Damon said with a smile.

"When Forrest graduated with his master's and when Rowan had that horrible case that absolutely wrecked him and almost made him quit pediatric surgery, and when Penelope ran off to Europe . . . who was there for them?"

"Okay, okay, I get it." Damon shook his head, but his frown returned. "But when was the last time we were all together?"

Now it was Hunter's time to frown. "Too long."

"Exactly. And now our sister is looking at a man in a new way and he's looking at her in that same way. It's time to settle down. I'm surprised at how much I like Shadows Landing. I bought a house there. Stone and Kane did as well."

"You *what*?" Hunter almost shouted.

"Plus, Stone is looking to see if he can get transferred to the hockey team in Charleston."

Hunter was stunned. "I don't know what to say."

"You could come work for me in Shadows Landing if you like it here. You were always a good mechanic."

"Leave the Army?"

"Just think about it." Damon nodded up ahead. "That is my house. We need to change quickly. We have a wedding to crash."

"Does Olivia know I'm coming?" Hunter asked as he took in the small town. The courthouse, the treasure museum, the barbecue joints, and the busy Main Street.

"I thought it could be a surprise," Damon said with a little smirk that made Hunter laugh. It wasn't a reunion. It was an ambush, and Hunter was all for it.

Hunter hated suits. He could tolerate his dress uniform, but his muscled neck always seemed too big for dress shirts and ties made him feel as if he were being strangled. They missed the wedding of someone local named Edie, but Hunter had to admit the groom sounded interesting. Tristan had been with the Millevian military. Hunter had spent some time there before, not that the Millevia government or military knew about it. He'd been laying the groundwork for a possible military coup, which had just been averted, apparently with the help of the groom.

Hunter was a creature of habit and that meant observing a situation before he walked into it. Damon went to get Stone and Kane as Hunter took in the reception from the shadows.

Instead of focusing on his sister, Hunter's focus was on the woman walking toward him with a giant smile on her face. Her strawberry blonde hair was in loose waves around her exposed shoulders and rested against full breasts. She wore a pink and green dress, pink lipstick, and sparkling white cowboy boots. Her eyes matched the green of her dress to a T, and the dress hugged her curves just as well. This woman was all curves and happiness. And she had high maintenance written all over her.

"Another Townsend. Welcome to Shadows Landing," she said in a soft, Southern voice. She flashed a killer smile at him and Hunter didn't know what to do. He would have picked her up if he were on leave, have a few fun nights, and then never talk to her again. But this was someplace he would be visiting more than once. He had to watch himself, but his attraction to her was off the charts. Juicy was the only way he could describe the woman standing in front of him. And man, did he want to take a bite. "I'm Maggie Bell," she said, holding out her hand to him.

"Hunter Townsend," Hunter said, closing his large hand over her soft, small one. Jesus, she even smelled good enough to eat.

"It's nice to meet you, Hunter. Welcome to Shadows Landing."

1

"Magnum Bell," the announcer called as Maggie walked onto the range to take her position. She was ranked number one in the United States in the 50m rifle three-position event and had easily qualified for the Olympics in not only that event but also in the 25m rifle. However, this year, she was also trying to qualify for the Olympics in trap shooting, rifle, and shotgun. It wasn't done much, but she had mastered Trap and turned to Rifle three years ago. This Olympics she really wanted to compete in mixed trap with her brother, Gage. Gage had qualified earlier for trap. Now, it was up to her.

Recently, she'd been using indoor arenas for rifle practice, but Maggie had grown up shooting trap and skeet with her brother and parents, not to mention winning a silver medal at the last Olympics. She hadn't been actively competing as much as she worked to master Rifle. Shooting had always been a family activity. They regularly held family shooting competitions to see who would clean up after dinner or who got to choose the movie for family night. And just like then, her whole family was here to support her and Gage.

Maggie took her position outdoors in the warm June sun. It was refreshing as the sun heated her skin and the breeze ruffled her hair. Her mother had taught her long ago that she could use her long hair to know how to adjust for the wind during a shot. She used that knowledge now as she lifted her shotgun and took a deep breath.

She's too high-maintenance for me. I need a real woman, not a girly-girl.

Hunter Townsend's words he'd said to his brother, Kane, right after she'd introduced herself to Hunter at Edie's wedding, ran through Maggie's mind. She'd been hoping for a dance from the ruggedly handsome man, but instead, she was insulted when he didn't think she could hear him. Maggie should have given him another chance. Shown him she wasn't high-maintenance just because she liked pretty colors and wore her grandmother's pearls. However, she hadn't. Even though she still found him frustratingly sexy, they now had a relationship more akin to rivals than friends.

The clay target flew through the air. Maggie sighted it, pulled the trigger, absorbed the recoil, and felt immense satisfaction as the target exploded. How's that for a girly-girl? Ha! In the back of her head, she realized her annoyance at Hunter's judgment had given her the best year of her life in terms of professional shooting. Not that she'd *ever* give him any credit for it.

～

The drive back to Shadows Landing was a family celebration. Gage had qualified in trap, and she in rifle and trap. Brother and sister were headed to the Olympics together.

"Good thing we already bought all our tickets in anticipation," her father, Clark, said as they drove into Shadows Landing.

"And reserved six houses since so many people said they wanted to come," her mother, Suze, added.

"Mom, it's in Italy. They're not going to come," Maggie said from the backseat.

"Are you sure about that?" her mother asked and then pointed out the front windshield.

The entire town was lined up on the sidewalk, holding signs that read: *Congratulations Maggie and Gage. Italy, here we come!*

Her father pulled over at Harper's Bar, and Kane Townsend opened the door for her. Cheers went up as she and Gage stepped out. Tears filled her eyes as everyone ran forward to hug them.

Four years ago, Maggie had made her first appearance in the Olympics. She'd been too nervous to tell anyone she was going. But now they all knew. And they all supported her.

Lydia Langston and her eight kids were the first to hug her. Miss Winnie and Miss Ruby, two matriarchs of Shadows Landing and complete opposites in every way, were next. The smell of apple pie wafted up from a basket Miss Winnie was holding in her pale, thin, frail-looking arm. However, she was surprisingly strong for an old lady who resembled nothing so much as a boiled chicken. Miss Ruby, taller, rounder, and with her natural black hair turning silver instead of Miss Winnie's stark white, reached into the basket and pulled out two pies.

"To celebrate. We're so proud of you both!" Miss Ruby handed the pies to her and Gage and hugged them both.

"Oh God. I'm shook!" Timmons, who worked at Maggie's parents' bed & breakfast and wedding venue, said, looking as if he were about to pass out. Timmons was only a year older than Maggie's twenty-eight years, but you'd think they were from different generations. Timmons only spoke millennial, but now that his younger brother, Kyler, had been visiting, Gen Z was slipping in.

"We are so proud of you," Ryker Faulkner said as his wife, Kenzie, gave her a hug.

"We streamed it at the bar so everyone could watch it," Harper Faulkner Reigns, who owned the bar, told her.

The entire town took time to celebrate. Gator, named so because he was an alligator removal expert, unhooked his thumbs from his overalls, wrapped her in a bear hug, and lifted her three feet off the ground. "We're right proud of you two."

"Thanks guys," Gage said, shaking Turtle's hand.

"Anne Bonny said you're the best shot she's ever seen." Skeeter knew the most about Shadows Landing's pirate history. The town had been founded by pirates who'd hidden their stolen treasure beneath the church. Skeeter also said he talked to the pirate ghosts who founded the town. Maggie had wanted to dismiss it, but Bell Landing, their house, had its own ghost. Every old house or building down there did. Too many cold breezes, creaky sounds, and bumps in the night to dismiss.

"Thanks Skeeter. I was trying to make Anne and the others proud."

"As much as I don't want to believe in ghosts," Damon Townsend said, "I'm sure they're proud. We all are. You're truly magnificent to watch in action."

"It really was poetry in motion," Forrest told her.

"I've never seen someone move from shot to shot so smoothly," Kane added as he patted her shoulder like a proud brother.

"Wow, thanks guys." Maggie had worried for a while that Hunter's low opinion of her would be matched by his brothers, but that hadn't been the case. They'd all been lovely to her.

Rowan Townsend chuckled to himself and then looked at his brothers. Stone similarly grinned. "You thinking of Hunter?" Stone asked.

"He's going to have to eat so much crow when he finally opens his eyes and sees how talented our Maggie is," Rowan said more to them than to her.

Maggie had already noticed that only one Townsend was missing. "Where is Hunter? I thought he'd want to give me crap that my competition rifle is pink." Maggie scanned the crowd and saw Edie Durand talking with some of the Faulkner family. She looked worried, so Maggie scanned the crowd for Edie's husband, Tristan. "And where's Tristian? Is he on duty tonight?" she asked of the deputy sheriff.

The smiles of the Townsend brothers slipped. Damon cleared his throat. "Hunter was called away yesterday for a mission. We don't know the details, but Tristan went with him."

"Oh." The familiar weight of worry slammed into her. She might want to hate Hunter, but she never wanted him hurt. She held her breath for every mission until he came home. Usually, she had enough notice to wish him a safe return, but not this time and that worried her. They had their routine. They'd take swipes at each other, but then she'd tell him to be safe. She didn't like not being able to whisper the little prayer for his protection when she waved goodbye to him. It didn't matter they'd banter and tease each other a moment before. Maggie always made sure Hunter knew she wished him safely home.

Maggie followed the crowd into the bar. The celebration raged around them. The Faulkner family was one of the largest in town. Same with the Townsends. Inside the bar, they were all mingling together and making sure to come by and spend time with both her and Gage.

Maggie was friends with them all, but it was Georgie, the former bartender, who she was closest to. When Georgie came to Shadows Landing, innocent of the world and down on her luck, the designer jeans gave her away. But Maggie knew Georgie would tell her truth in her own time. Turned out she was from a family with old money, big drama, drugging, and a kidnapping thrown in for good measure. Georgie had finally broken free from them with the help of her now-husband, Kord King, and her grandfather. A bartender no more, she was now in charge of her family's investment conglomerate. Apparently, the investments were large enough that managing them was a full-time job. You still wouldn't know it though. Georgie mostly dressed as if she were still a bartender.

"Tinsley looks like she's going to pop," Georgie said as she joined Maggie at the table.

"She's due at the end of the month, right?" Maggie asked about Tinsley Faulkner Kendry.

"Yes, and look at Paxton. The man is hovering more than Bubba when a packet of jerky is opened." Maggie laughed because Tinsley's husband really did look like the town's alligator trying to chase down his favorite treat. But then

Georgie turned to her and took her hand. "You look sad. Is it because Hunter left and you couldn't say goodbye?"

Maggie rolled her eyes. "It's stupid, G. He hates me and I can't stand him. But I feel as if something is going to go wrong since I didn't do my little ritual to send him off. Please don't say anything. I don't want people to get the wrong idea."

Georgie looked amused as she took a sip of her drink before sitting it back down. "You mean the fine line between hate and love is eroding, or never actually existed in the first place?"

"That's not true! Okay," Maggie said in a whisper, "maybe there's some truth to it. But he's such a big, dumb jerk to me. He's not to others. Just to me."

"Look, I won't deny that. I also won't say it's his way of flirting because that's messed up. I think he made an incorrect judgment about you and is too stubborn to open his eyes and reassess. When he gets home, it'll be right in his face. Then we'll see what Hunter Townsend is made of. He's man enough for the military. But is he man enough to admit he was wrong and apologize?"

"I wouldn't bet on it," Maggie said, and they both laughed.

The rest of the night was a blur of people talking about the Olympics being held next month and celebration. There was only one person left that Maggie wanted to see and that was Edie. Her first husband had been killed in action, so knowing Tristan was on a mission with Hunter had all kinds of warning bells going off. This was serious, and if Tristan, the government assassin from the small country of Millevia located on the coast between France and Italy, was with the US Army the mission was probably there.

Maggie searched and found her near the back of the bar. Edie looked miserable and Maggie didn't say anything. She simply wrapped the kind woman up in a hug.

"Are you okay, Edie?" Edie shook her head, placed her hand to her mouth, and darted to the bathroom. Maggie followed and wet a paper towel as Edie threw up. "Here you go," Maggie said, handing it to her. "I'm sure you're scared to death."

"It's not that. Well, it's not just that. See, when Tristan told me he was going with Hunter and he couldn't tell me anything more . . . he knew I would be upset. But I know the drill. My late husband and my brother were Navy SEALs. Everything was always 'classified' on every mission. As much as I was dying inside at the idea of Tristan leaving, I knew better than to do anything but smile, hug him, and tell him how much I love him. The second he left, I threw up. Then again today. So, I went to see Gavin and Kenzie at the clinic. I thought I had the stomach bug," Edie told her as tears began to form behind her eyelids and threatened to spill.

"Are you sick?"

Edie shook her head, and the first tear fell. "I'm pregnant. I didn't think I could get pregnant. I'm older. My gynecologist called my uterus 'geriatric.' I tried to call Tristan, but they've gone dark. I can't even tell my husband we're going to have a baby, and I'm scared to death because now it's not just me. I've been a widow. I could be a widow again. But now a baby might never know their father."

Maggie caught Edie as she flung herself into Maggie's arms and sobbed. Maggie held her, telling her they'd be safe, telling her Hunter and Tristan would be back in no time and how happy Tristan would be to become a father.

All the words were hollow because fear dominated how she felt right now. Fear for Hunter, fear for Tristan, and fear for Edie. If they'd gone dark, they were walking into the thick of the mission.

2

Millevia . . .

"Thanks for coming with us, Tris. I know it was hard to leave Edie behind," Hunter told Tristan as the Special Forces battalion walked off the plane and onto Millevia's military base. Well, Hunter's team was labeled as Special Forces, but they were really a small mixed group of men. Some from the Army, some from the Air Force, and a couple of Marines. Special Forces had many strengths, but sometimes things needed to be done quickly and with precision. No time to embed and learn the culture and cultivate contacts. This test team was somewhere between Special Forces and Delta Force/DEVGRU and it seemed to work well so far. Each military branch had its own strengths and weaknesses, so they made a team composed of multiple branches, and suddenly, you have an expert in every situation you might come across.

When Hunter had told his commander he needed to get to Charleston, his commander had told him about a joint operations group that was starting up under the Army's control, and Hunter had been tapped for it. His team went all over the world, but usually for no more than a week at a time. They were a mix of special operators and worked well together doing the secret in-and-out missions. While Hunter was the overall team leader, each mission had its own leader based on what the mission entailed and who had the expertise to run it.

"It's hard leaving her. I never want her to worry about a husband again," Tristan said about his wife. "But when I learned my best friend, David, was a possible hostage along with the American Marine Raider team, I couldn't sit back. I know these mountains. I know these people. I want to help."

The whole team was in full dark mode the second they were off the plane. Phones were turned off and left on the plane. They had a rescue mission to execute and everyone was focused on their objective.

"Tristan!" The commander thumped Tristan on the back. "Thank you for coming and bringing your friends. Sergeant First Class Townsend, Captain Francis Bonetti." Hunter shook his hand.

"Captain. My team is ready to assist in any way you need us." It was time to get to work.

Captain Bonetti took them to a command station where they met the Millevian team that would be working with them. Between Hunter's Spanish, Italian, and French, he was able to follow along in their native language, but they made sure to switch to English when it was time for Hunter to fill his crew in.

"An American Marine Raider team based out of North Carolina was called in to assist the Millevian military group that had gotten word of a potential terror group. Information on this new group is sparse. A concerned farmer called in that all of his fertilizer had been stolen. That by itself wouldn't be a big deal, but five other farms across Millevia also had all their fertilizer stolen and several construction sites across the country had some cast boosters stolen," Hunter told them.

"They're building bombs," Tristan said flatly.

"Seems like it," Captain Bonetti confirmed. "We don't know the target or who this group is. Nothing is on our radar. That's why we called the Americans."

"The only thing Naval intelligence found tied to stolen fertilizer was a commercial ship filled with fertilizer had been hijacked, pilfered, and then let go, but that was three years ago," Hunter told the teams. "If it's the same group, then they are now well-supplied. However, military intelligence couldn't find any chatter about an attack. All the usual suspects came back clean. Surveillance has shown no increased activity, which we should see if they were preparing for an attack." Hunter's team nodded. That was unusual. "That leads us to believe it's a new terror group. Captain Bonetti worked with local farmers in the regions that were being hit. He stationed soldiers as farmhands. One witnessed the stealing of fertilizer and followed them into the mountains near the Italian border with Millevia. With that information, the Navy sent a Marine Raider team. They went into the Maritime Alps together but they didn't come back down."

Captain Bonetti frowned. "Drones were sent, but they used lasers to blind them. Satellite images came through and there are bodies. However, it appears this group's camp is hidden inside the mountains. These mountains have been mined for almost two thousand years. The mining really picked up during the fifteen hundreds and peaked in the sixteen and seventeen hundreds, and then again after

WWII. However, now most of the mines are closed, leaving behind many miles of abandoned tunnels. We believe this new group is using the tunnels as their base of operations."

"Which means you can be looking at where they went into the mountains and miss when and where they come out," Tristan pointed out.

"Exactly," Captain Bonetti said. "We asked Tristan to join us because he's familiar with these tunnels."

"Show us the tunnels," Hunter ordered.

Two hours later, the team was fully briefed and plans laid out. The team ate, mentally prepared, and then at one in the morning they loaded onto two helicopters and headed into the night.

"Go!" Hunter ordered as he tapped the night helmet of every operator on the way down the fast ropes and onto the mountainside beneath them. Tristan was doing the same with the team from Millevia in the helicopter a mile away from him. Hunter grabbed the rope and slid down with his night-vision goggles on and his rifle over his shoulder. He landed in the small clearing of the forest to find his team had already secured the area.

The helicopters flew off as the teams trekked through the thick forest trees toward the top of the mountain where the satellite images showed bodies. Hunter's team moved silently, approaching their target from seven o'clock while Tristan and his team approached from five o'clock.

"Satellite imagery shows no movement up ahead," Captain Bonetti told the teams from where he was monitoring the mission at base.

They were a mile from the target, and even though they were moving uphill through the forest, they moved steadily, thanks to years of training. The problem was the trees were starting to thin, and soon they'd be at a high enough altitude that the trees would end, leaving them exposed.

"Team Alpha at tree line," Hunter reported.

"Team Beta at tree line," Tristan called in thirty seconds later.

"You have about four hundred meters to reach the target. All imagery is clear," Captain Bonetti informed them.

"At the ready, two by two, fanned out," Hunter instructed. "Let's move."

Hunter raised his rifle and moved up the steep incline. It was the perfect location for an ambush. He'd made it almost two hundred yards when they came across the first body. The team medic moved forward and examined the Millevian soldier. "He's dead. Shot in the back as he ran away."

Hunter called in the news, which was then followed by similar news from Tristan's team, now in view of each other. By the time they reached the entrance to the old mine, they had recovered the bodies of two Americans and six Millevian soldiers. Not a single body had a comms device on it. Weapons had also been taken.

Hunter used hand signals as they surrounded the entrance. Hunter took one side, Tristan the other. Their team dropped into high and low positions and two stayed behind to guard the entrance.

With a move of Hunter's hands, they entered the old mine.

Night vision made the mine even eerier. Then there were the bodies. Each had to be checked to make sure there were none alive. Most were terrorists. Some were soldiers.

Hunter held up his hand, halting them. Up ahead, he could see the mine opened up, but he also saw old mining carts mixed with new tables and chairs. Tables that had been turned over to connect with the mining carts to provide a barrier.

They were still missing soldiers. This wasn't an offensive setup. It was defensive. Hunter had a decision to make. They could attempt a surprise attack or they could announce their presence. The point wasn't a kill mission, but a rescue and intelligence gathering one.

"US and Millevian Military. Put down your weapons and stand up slowly," Hunter called out.

Tristan immediately repeated the order in both French and Italian.

"What's your command?" a clearly American voice called out.

"12th Special Forces Group."

"There is no 12th group," the voice called back quickly.

"We're nicknamed The Deadly Dozen and I assure you it's real. It's just not well known. I'm Sergeant First Class Hunter Townsend from Charleston. We were sent to aid Millevia to rescue a group of Marine Raiders out of North Carolina. Don't worry, son, the better Carolina is here now."

"Well shit, you're probably a Gamecocks fan," the voice grumbled and Hunter smiled in the dark. "Come on back. We need help. Hope you have some medics."

Hunter and Tristan were the first to broach the barricade. Help was right. Hunter did a quick count. Ten Americans, but only four of them seemed capable of holding a weapon. The rest were in various degrees of medical crisis. Five Millevians were also there, but only two were holding weapons although severely injured, one of which was Tristan's friend, David. The others were unconscious. There were only two guns between them. One knife, and the rest were holding rocks, pens, or chair legs. All of them looked ready to pass out.

"Call it in," Hunter ordered Tristan. The Millevian medic rushed to help along with the American medic. "What's your name, Tarheel?"

"Petty Officer Brayden Lewis, sir. But you need to help our Master Sergeant. He saved us all."

"Helos are five minutes out," Tristan called as the medic raced to Hunter's side and began to work on the Marine.

"What happened here?" Hunter asked.

"We didn't see anything or anyone but followed the soldier who had seen the men coming in here. We watched it for hours, with no movement. We thought it was empty. We approached in tandem, breached the entrance, and made it here. They were lined against the walls waiting for us. It was an ambush. Some men were able to escape. Did they tell you where we were?" Petty Officer Lewis asked. The man was probably only twenty-five but looked as if he'd seen as much as Hunter had, which was most likely true. Special operations had a way of aging a person.

"They didn't make it. They were taken down in the tunnels or chased outside and taken down. I'm sorry," Hunter told the Marine. He nodded sadly but didn't break. He kept sitting there and looked down at his legs. It was then Hunter noticed the blood. "What happened?"

"One leg broken, another one shot in the knee. I can't walk. I tried, but since I was still able to use my upper body, I refused to leave my team behind. I can at least shoot." Petty Officer Lewis took a deep breath and then ran down the events. "Master Sergeant Langston killed I don't know how many of them and went after the leader. He was shot twice, yet he managed to fight hand to hand with the leader after Langston ran out of ammo. But the leader didn't die. He shot

Langston and then ran. There's an exit that way," Lewis pointed. "We surrendered when it was clear we were so badly hurt that we couldn't fight back or leave. We thought it was our only choice. They took our coms, our personal effects, not that we had many, and our weapons. Then they began to shoot. It was like it was fun wounding us. They made a mistake though. They turned their back on the Master Sergeant. Even badly injured, Langston took down one of the men by snapping his neck, grabbed his gun, and shot the other. Then he organized this defense and passed out."

Hunter organized a joint team to guard the tunnels that most likely led to an exit so no one could sneak up on them before turning to the medic. "How is he?" Hunter asked.

"Heart is barely beating. He needs blood badly and he's most likely septic. It'll be a miracle if he lives."

"Can we move him?"

"Not right now. I'm surprised he's even breathing."

Dammit. "What do we need to do so we can move him?"

"He needs blood."

Hunter rolled up his sleeve. "I'm O neg. Do it."

The medic didn't need to be told twice. He grabbed the field transfusion kit and got to work.

"Helos are here," Tristan said as Hunter's blood began to flow into the man passed out on the floor.

"Evacuate them all, but we stay behind. They can come back and get us and it'll give us time to check out the tunnel they used to escape and gather any evidence we can."

The evacuation was complete except for the Master Sergeant. "See what you can find while I finish this transfusion and we wait for the helicopters. We'll watch your back from here."

The team headed down the tunnel and Hunter could finally look at the man he was giving blood to. He was probably in his mid to late thirties. The medic was working on the bullet wounds the best he could, but it was clear the man needed surgery. Morphine and a huge dose of antibiotics were administered and the medic sighed and stood up. "I'm going to call into the hospital. If he actually makes it to town, he needs the best surgeon Millevia has."

The medic stepped a couple of feet away and made the call right as Hunter heard movement from the escape tunnel. Hunter held up his weapon and saw the medic move to cover the injured and hold up his own gun.

"It's us," Tristan called out. Hunter didn't lower his weapon until the entire team was back and there was no sign of anyone following them.

"There's a larger room about four hundred yards deeper into the mountain. Another tunnel leads deeper and also a tunnel that looks newly built, leading up and out of the mountain about a half a mile from the cave's entrance on the north side," Tristan reported. "Found a good amount of spilled fertilizer and bomb materials. However, there are deep tire marks indicating they were able to load up a lot of the material and drive it out of here."

"Let's see what we can find out about the dead terrorist," Hunter said as the medic nodded into the phone and hung up.

"I've already taken photos and sent them off to both the Americans and Millevian military for identification," Tristan told him.

"Medical transport will be here in five minutes. Let's get

him ready," the medic told them. "Is anyone else O negative?"

"I am," Tristan said.

"You two, on the medical helo with me. He needs more blood than Townsend can give."

"Come on, men, let's get him moved," Hunter said as he grasped the Master Sergeant's hand to keep the transfusion flowing as they maneuvered him onto the table they'd broken the legs off to form a gurney.

When they moved him, the man groaned. His eyelids fluttered. "I got you, Langston. We're getting you out of here."

"Team?" he managed to ask as the medic poured something into a water bottle and then shoved it at his mouth and ordered him to drink.

"You lost four, but the rest are already evacuated. Now it's time to get your ass home. You did a good job saving your men. I'm Hunter Townsend. What's your name, Langston?"

"Landry. Landry Langston. Get me home to my family, Townsend." Then the man closed his eyes again.

3

"I got him some protein and electrolytes in that drink and now the morphine is really kicking in. He probably won't wake up for a while. The transfusion is working. We'll switch in the helicopter. Let's go," the medic said, but Hunter was staring at Tristan even as they lifted Langston and began to carry him out.

"It can't be Lydia's husband, can it?" Hunter asked Tristan, a feeling of dread settling over him.

"How many Landry Langstons can there be?" Tristan stared with shock at the man whose life was hanging on by a thread.

One. There was only one, God help them all.

"Listen to me," Hunter ordered the second they got loaded into the helicopter. "Go straight to the hospital as fast as you can. We have to save him. We know his family."

The medic's jaw tightened, and as they lifted into the air, he unhooked the transfusion needle from Hunter's arm. He changed needles and then inserted it into Tristan's arm. "This is giving him the best chance he's got."

Hunter leaned down and kept his hand over Landry's.

"Hang on Landry. I'm from Shadows Landing. I know Lydia. She'll raise you from the dead and then kill you again herself if you die now. Landry Junior is getting big, man. He's surfing with Granger and thinking of trying to compete. Lacy, wow, what a spitfire she is. Just like you are. You should see how she wields a rapier." That got the medic's attention. "It's a Shadows Landing thing," Hunter told the medic.

"Hey Landry. I'm Tristan Durand. I'm Edie's husband. I'm from Shadows Landing, too. Edie has classes at the church with Lydia, Lacy, and now Leah since she turned ten. You must be so proud of them. You have a great wife and super kids. Did you know they alligator surf? Apparently, you used to do that too. At least that's what they say when they're yelled at for surfing."

Hunter leaned forward next. "I bet if you live Miss Ruby and Miss Winnie will make you so many apple pies you'll never run out. So, fight, Landry. Fight for your family. Fight for your wife. Fight for those apple pies."

～

Maggie sliced through the stuffed dummy and felt her stress melt away. The long sword she was using was heavy and she felt her muscles flex as she pulled it free. Not only could Maggie shoot 18th century firearms with breathtaking accuracy, but she could also wield a rapier, a dagger, a sword, and a cutlass with ease, thanks to the women's only church group.

Shadows Landing was founded by pirates. The clergyman who founded this church was a pirate. The town was filled with the families the pirates had when they chose the location to be a safe place for them to settle down.

However, that didn't mean it was safe for the women when the pirates went off to plunder.

The Carolinas were still very much a frontier as the colonies were growing. British soldiers could be a problem. Thieves could be a problem, too. So, the pirates installed one of their own as the pastor of the church who, along with others who were too old to plunder, taught the women of Shadows Landing how to defend themselves. That tradition carried on through the Revolutionary War, the Civil War, both World Wars, and to today. As soon as a girl turned ten years old, she could learn the ways of the Shadows Landing women.

"Very good, Leah!" Lydia clapped as her fourth oldest and second oldest daughter stabbed a dummy with her small dagger. Leah had just turned ten a couple of months ago and was so excited to come to class with her mother and her older sister, Lacy.

Lacy, now a teen, moved from a dagger to a rapier and was something to behold. She'd joined the fencing club at school and it was almost comical how fast she won matches.

Here, Reverend Winston taught them, encouraged them, and pushed them to their max, just like his father had, and his grandfather had before him. The Winstons had led the women of Shadows Landing in more than prayer for generations.

"Very good, Melinda," Reverend Winston said proudly. Reverend Melinda had come to Shadows Landing three months ago as a pastor in training from Key West. Her warm, tawny brown skin seemed to glow with sweat as she worked with the dagger. She'd taken to the classes as if born for it. Considering that Key West had its own pirate history, maybe she had been.

Maggie's sun-kissed skin was not glowing. It was

dripping in sweat. Melinda somehow still looked put together after an hour of training, while Maggie felt she could scare Anne Bonny if she floated in right now.

"How are you doing, Edie?" Maggie asked in a whisper. Edie had confided that she hadn't told anyone yet about the pregnancy and asked Maggie to keep it quiet.

"So sick, but Kenzie said exercise is good for me, so here I am. Thanks for not telling anyone yet."

"Telling anyone what?" Lydia asked as she joined them. She kept her eye on her two girls, but here bickering wasn't allowed. Instead, Lacy was helping Leah. It was really sweet to watch.

"That Edie is trying to figure out Miss Ruby and Miss Winnie's secret apple pie recipe," Maggie answered.

"Ha! Good luck. It's all right here," Miss Winnie called out, tapping her head.

They laughed, and then Lydia's smile fell. "I know you and Hunter aren't together, but I also know you care for him. I see how you make sure he knows we're all waiting for him to return home when he goes on a mission. And you, Edie, bless your heart. How are you two holding up with both Tristan and Hunter gone?"

Edie's eyes began to shine with unshed tears. Maggie reached out and took her hand in hers. "It's hard. How do you do it? Landry is gone for a year at a time, back for a short bit, then off again."

Lydia nodded. "In just two more years, he'll be thirty-eight and he'll have twenty years in service. The plan is for him to come home then and work out of the Charleston base maybe. Luckily, he's in communications so I don't have to worry about him going out on missions like Hunter does. He goes with them to a certain point and sets up their comms. So many times, he's unreachable and it's all top secret, but at least I know he's safe."

"Hello?"

Reverend Winston heard the voice from the church's entry and stepped from the room as Lydia told them about Levi's improvement with hockey since Stone was helping him.

The door opened and Edie gasped. She reached out and gripped Maggie's hand so tight that Maggie flinched. But then she saw why. Reverend Winston was looking serious as a military chaplain stood next to him.

Edie screamed such a primal, guttural sound of pure pain as the chaplain's gaze met hers. She fell to the ground, but his eyes didn't follow. They moved to Maggie's next. Hunter? But he'd tell Olivia . . . who was standing just behind Maggie and was now rushing to Edie, which was where he was looking.

Maggie's heart broke. In that moment, it shattered and fell like boulders into her stomach. Was it Hunter? Maggie had lost love before she ever had it. She should have told Hunter she liked him. She should not have taunted him to teach him a lesson. She should have told him so many things. But now it was too late.

"Mitzi," Reverend Winton said softly to the elderly woman wearing a T-shirt with cats in ninja suits on it. "Would you take Lacy and Leah to get a piece of pie across the street at the diner for their good work today?"

The girls began to protest. "Yes, you did such a good job. We're going to say a prayer, then I'll join you," Lydia said with a determined smile, trying not to frighten the children.

Edie stopped crying and stared wide-eyed at the chaplain as the girls left and Reverend Winston closed the door behind them. "Okay. I'm ready. Tell me," Edie said as she stood with an inner strength that had Maggie in awe of her.

"Lydia Langston, your husband is Landry Langston. Is that correct?" the chaplain asked, turning to Lydia.

Edie gasped and instantly grabbed one of Lydia's hands as Maggie took her other to prevent her from falling down as Lydia swayed with shock. The entire class came to give their silent and their physical support. "That's correct. I'm Mrs. Langston."

"I'm sorry to inform you that your husband has been gravely injured. He's not expected to make it. I've come to give you our support during this difficult time," the chaplain said gently.

Lydia shook her head. "You have the wrong person. My husband is a comms man. There's no way he's injured."

The chaplain hid his surprised expression quickly with a comforting look. "Your husband was on a mission overseas. His team was ambushed, but he has been rescued. He's unconscious and has been transported to the hospital, but he's not expected to live. I'm here to orchestrate a secure video feed so that you can see him and say your goodbyes."

Maggie could feel Lydia's body shaking. "I don't understand. I know he works on top secret communications, but how could he be ambushed? It's not Landry. It just can't be."

Reverend Winston placed his hand on her shoulder and turned to the chaplain. "Could you shed more light on this situation?"

"Ma'am, your husband wasn't in communications. He was the team leader of the Marine Raiders."

Lydia froze, then straightened. Her jaw tightened and her nostrils flared. "If that ambush doesn't kill him, I will! We discussed that and decided it was too dangerous! And bless his dumbass heart, he thinks he's going to die on me before I kill him for lying to me for eighteen years? Well, he has another thing coming. Where is my husband?"

"I'm sorry, that's confidential." The chaplain looked a little nervous.

Then he looked scared when Lydia growled and turned to Olivia and pointed at her. "Find my husband. I know you can. Do it and do it now."

Then Lydia stormed from the church, leaving the slam of the large front doors echoing in her wake.

4

"They're planning a terrorist attack," Emily Gastaud, President of Millevia, said with a frown. "Do we know the target?"

"No ma'am," Hunter answered. "And the terrorists we've identified do not belong with a known terror group. This appears to be a new terror cell. We're working on finding connections between the dead terrorists now to try to find how they met and their philosophies so we can identify potential targets."

"Captain Bonetti, notify all high-value locations in Millevia to increase their security. Call in the reserves. I want this country and our citizens protected," President Gastaud ordered.

"Yes, ma'am." The captain hurried from the room and the president ordered everyone else out as well.

"Thank you for coming back, Tristan. And please thank Edie for me. I know it was a sacrifice for you both. How is David? I'm heading over as soon as I have things in order here." Emily and Tristan were old friends, and thanks to Tristan, Emily was now in power and righting the wrongs of the past several years of leadership. She and David had also started dating.

"He's in surgery. I was hoping to be dismissed and head to the hospital and then I can send you another update. Also, we know the American team leader who is also in surgery," Tristan told her.

Emily looked at Hunter with sad eyes but a backbone of steel. "Please accept my condolences on the loss of your brothers in arms. Both of you, go to the hospital and send me updates. I have to call President Stratton and plan our next steps. The American president has offered his full support."

Hunter followed Tristan from the president's office. It had to be hard for Emily to focus on work when the man she loved was in surgery. However, that was what being a leader was about—making the hard calls.

Tristan walked as if he knew every inch of the town and the country. Hunter wondered if he missed it here. He and Edie came back twice a year for a visit from what Hunter understood.

"I'll drive," Tristan said to the soldier preparing to escort them to the hospital. Tristan took the keys and jumped into the SUV. "Hang on. David should be getting out of surgery soon, and I want to be there when he does."

Hunter had to grab the door a couple of times as Tristan maneuvered the narrow cobblestone streets for what he swore was a shortcut. He slammed on the brakes at the front of the hospital less than five minutes later.

"You miss this, don't you?" Hunter asked as they strode inside, people getting out of their way since Tristan was clearly in power mode. He stood tall and walked, knowing people would move.

"I don't even realize I fall right back into military talk and action. I miss the mental strategy, but I don't miss the death. I enjoy waking up to my wife every day, having friends, and having a life that's outside the military. You'll understand when you finally open your eyes and fall for the right woman," Tristan said as he punched the elevator button and stood back, waiting for it to arrive.

"No woman will force me to leave the military," Hunter said with a roll of his eyes as a mental picture of a smiling Maggie Bell popped into his head.

Tristan shook his head as the door opened and they walked inside. "Edie didn't make me leave the military. Hell, she didn't even ask me to. You'll want to leave it after a while because the person you love is at home and you're not. I miss her. I miss the quiet. I miss the peace that holding her in my arms has on soothing my battle-tested heart. Not all men will leave. Look at Landry. I'm only saying it gets harder when you have someone you love at home."

"Speaking of which," Hunter said as they stepped out onto the floor with all the wounded soldiers on it, "you better call Edie. She's probably worried about you."

Tristan nodded as they approached the nurse's desk. "I'm from the president's office. How is David Parcodi doing?"

The nurse typed the name into her computer and nodded. "He's out of surgery and did well. He's in recovery. He'll be transferred to room 409 in about an hour."

"Landry Langston?" Hunter asked.

More typing and another nod. "He's just been moved to room 428 from surgery recovery. It's touch and go," she said.

They began to walk away but military police stopped

them. "You have to turn in all weapons," he said, pointing to another military policeman sitting behind the nurse. "They'll be locked up and only you will have the key."

Hunter handed over his weapon, as did Tristan. "I'm going to call Edie, let Emily know about David, and I'll meet you in Landry's room," Tristan said.

Hunter headed down the long hallway until he saw another nurse's station. This one wasn't informational but was full of nurses checking on patients, going over charts, and getting medications ready.

Hunter saw that Landry's room was directly across from the station, which was good. That meant they were keeping a close eye on him. Hunter walked into the room. The lights were off except for a reading light over his bed. Music was playing softly as a doctor and a nurse worked.

"How is he doing?" Hunter asked quietly.

The doctor looked up from the chart and quickly took in the fatigues. "It's a miracle he's alive. How do you know him?"

"We're from the same small town and I'm friends with his wife and eight children." Hunter wanted the doctor to see Landry as more than a soldier. Landry had a lot to fight for, and he wanted the doctor to fight for it too.

"I'm Doctor Fissore. I'll be taking care of Sgt. Langston now post-surgery. The surgeon removed three bullets, a section of his intestines, a shard of a rib that was cracked off, and a section of his arm muscle that had an infection from one of the bullets. He's also septic. We're giving him fluids and heavy doses of antibiotics. I heard he had two blood transfusions before he even got here. They saved his life." The doctor's eyes went to the slight bruise on Hunter's elbow. "You saved his life. Without that transfusion, he wouldn't have made it. Now we wait. Wait to see if he's strong enough to fight the infection that's raging in his body. I'll be back every hour to check on him. If anything changes, press that red button and we'll come running. We leave the music on to give his brain stimulation and to hopefully fire up with will to fight, but if it bothers you, you can turn it off. I'll give you some time with him."

Hunter pulled up a chair and reached across the bed to take Landry's hand in his. "Hey Landry. It's Hunter Townsend again. I'm Olivia's brother. I can't wait for you to wake up so I can take you back to Shadows Landing. Tinsley is pregnant and due at the end of the month. You can bet Miss Ruby and Miss Winnie will bake her an apple pie. That alone is enough to make me want a baby. Speaking of babies, your little Lennie is so adorable. Her hair has these sweet little wispy curls and she has everyone wrapped around her little finger, even Landry Junior, and you know how hard it is to impress a teenage boy. Lindsey stopped wearing pigtails last week. She told me she was too big for pigtails and wanted these fancy braids. She asked me to braid her hair. Let's just say, she'll never ask me to do that again. Not sure how but somehow, I made her look like Pippi Longstocking got electrocuted."

Hunter heard heavy footsteps rushing down the hall and turned, putting himself between Landry and the door. He relaxed when he saw Tristan rush in, but the look on Tristan's face made Hunter go on alert again. "What is it?"

"You need to call Lydia. I'll stay with Landry."

Maggie and the town rushed after Lydia. She'd gone straight to Harper's Bar, ordered a shot of tequila, tossed it back, and then began talking to herself. Maggie found her stomping from one end of the bar to the other. Marching in one direction, she'd cry. The other, she raged.

"What can we do, Lydia?" Maggie asked.

"He better not die. What will happen if he dies? How will I tell the children? *What* will I tell the children?"

"You'll tell them the truth," Harper said gently. "Always tell them the truth. That way, you can face it together."

"Call Georgie and have them bring the kids here," Lydia said before motioning Harper for another shot.

"Ryker's working on getting you all the information you need," Olivia said, joining the bar that was quickly filling with people as word spread.

Miss Ruby and Miss Winnie were already organizing a food train and a babysitting train. The town was filing in the door and signing up at both tables to help the entire Langston family.

"I can take the kids anytime you need, Lydia," Damon said after joining them.

"If Landry is in a war-torn country or a politically unstable country, I can get you to him. I have contacts," Kane added. Maggie knew he was some kind of private contractor, but she wasn't really sure what that meant. Kane didn't talk much about it but took quite a few work trips. Some short, some long. Apparently, they took him to countries others might not travel to.

"Stone and I can take the kids too. I'm so sorry, Lydia," Natalie, Stone's new wife, hugged Lydia and quickly got out of the way as Gator, Skeeter, and Turtle rushed into the bar.

Gator wrapped her up and lifted her into a tight hug, leaving Lydia's feet dangling. "I'll help you kill him after he recovers," Gator said and Lydia burst into tears.

"Mommy!" Lacy yelled as she and Leah raced into the bar with Miss Mitzi hurrying after them. Not far behind them were Georgie and Kord with the rest of the Langston children.

"What happened?" Landry Jr. looked so scared but stood stoically. Gator put Lydia down as her children rushed to surround her. Except for Landry Jr. "Mom? Is it Dad?"

Lydia nodded. "Daddy's been hurt at work. I don't know anything else at the moment."

The kids began to cry as the town embraced them. Gator held on to little Leo as Georgie rocked Lennie, who was too young to understand what was going on. Skeeter put a supportive hand on Lyle's shoulder as Stone wrapped an arm around Levi. Lydia comforted Lindsey while Maggie pulled a sobbing Lacy to her and hugged her tight.

Only Landry Junior wasn't crying. Until Granger bent down and whispered into his ear. Landry nodded and bit his lip, trying not to cry, but he gripped Granger's hand tight. As the town banded together, a phone rang. It took Maggie a moment to realize it was hers.

She looked down at it and frowned, not knowing the number. She declined the call and it immediately began ringing again. This spammer was calling at the wrong time.

"Stop calling, asshole," she hissed the second she answered it.

"Maggie, it's Hunter."

Maggie shot up from where she was hugging Lacy. Ellery, Dr. Gavin Faulkner's wife, came over to hug Lacy so Maggie could walk away from the group. "Hunter, it's not a good time. Something's happened. Something bad," she whispered.

"I know. That's why I'm calling. I'm with Landry."

That stopped Maggie in her tracks. Oh God, was Hunter hurt too? He was there. He was in danger. All she wanted to do was to protect him. "Are you hurt?"

"No. Tristan just got off the phone with Edie and told me that someone notified Lydia. Dammit, they should have waited. He's a fighter, Mags. He should have died, but he's out of surgery and still alive. I tried calling Lydia. Hell, I tried calling the whole town, but no one answered their phones. I need to talk to Lydia and give her the chance to talk to Landry."

"I'll get her now. Just tell me one thing. Are you safe?" Maggie asked.

"Don't look now, Mags, but you're making me think you actually care."

Maggie smiled into the phone. "I was just going to ask Damon if I could buy your gun if you died. That's all."

"As if you could even figure out how to use it. The narrow end goes *pew pew* when you pull the trigger." Hunter was quiet for a moment, his voice softening. "I'm safe. How is Lydia?"

"Not good. She just told her kids that Daddy was hurt." Maggie had to look up and hold her breath to not cry.

"Damn. Okay, let me talk to her."

Maggie took a deep breath and turned back to the crowd. "Lydia, phone call."

"Not now," she began to say but Maggie's look told her to take it. "Let Mommy take this call. I'll be right back." Lydia came over to Maggie and tried to take the phone, but her hands were shaking so badly she dropped the phone. Maggie caught it and held it back up. "Can you put it on speaker?" Lydia asked.

"Here she is, Hunter," Maggie said.

"Lydia, it's Hunter. I'm with Landry."

Lydia gasped and grabbed onto Maggie's arm so hard Maggie would have a bruise. "Is he alive?"

Hunter's voice was so different. It was soft and soothing,

yet strong enough that you took whatever he said as fact.
"He is. He's tough as nails, Lydia." Hunter gave her a
rundown of Landry's injuries and surgery. "Now they're
battling sepsis. I've been talking to him since I found him."

"*You* found him?" Lydia snapped. "Hunter, just what the
hell is my husband up to?"

Hunter cleared his throat. "I don't know why you didn't
know that he was a Marine Raider, but he was leading a
joint team to investigate a possible terrorist plot when the
team was ambushed. Landry saved most of his team after
being shot and left for dead. He's a hero, Lydia, and I'll stay
with him until I can bring him home. I thought you might
want to talk to him."

Lydia could only nod, so Maggie had to answer him.
"She'd like that. The kids are here too. Do you think it
would help to hear their voices?"

Lydia nodded again and took a deep breath. "Let them
talk to their daddy. It might be the last time."

"I'm telling you, Lydia, your husband is tough. He won't
go without a fight. He'll fight for you. He'll fight for his
family."

"Kids," Maggie called out. "Come here, please." The kids
slowly walked over as they wiped at tear-streaked faces.

"Mr. Hunter is on the phone," Lydia said, trying so hard
not to cry. "He's with Daddy, but Daddy is still sleeping.
However, Mr. Hunter thought you might want to tell Daddy
that you love him before we go to bed."

"Just like we do at home?" Lyle asked.

"Just like at home, but this time Daddy can't say
goodnight back. But Mr. Hunter will tell him everything
each of you said all over again as soon as he wakes up, right
Mr. Hunter?" Lydia said in her mom voice.

"I promise to tell him every word you say. Your dad woke

up once and the first thing he did was talk about you all. He'll be so excited to know you called him. Leo, why don't you go first? Do you want to tell your dad about soccer?" Hunter asked so kindly that Maggie felt like crying.

One by one, each child talked to their father. Each one got harder and harder as they went by age. Lacy and Landry were the only ones left. The others talked to their daddy and then were embraced by the town once again.

Lacy went next. She held her mother's hand and told her dad about summer break, swimming in the river, and weapons class. "Come home, Daddy. Please."

Then she ran away in tears, straight into Miss Ruby's arms.

"Don't worry, Dad. I'll take care of Mom and all my brothers and sisters. I'm a man now. I'm fourteen and Mr. Gil said I could work at the gas station this summer, so don't worry about anything. I'll take care of everybody until you come home." Landry didn't cry. He didn't move. Instead, Maggie could see the literal weight of the world come down and settle on the boy's shoulders.

"Thank you, Landry. You're a great big brother and son," Lydia said with a sad smile. "Let me talk to Dad now, okay?"

"I'll check on the little ones," Landry said, turning stiffly and walking back to his brothers and sisters.

"Landry, you *fight*. Fight with every fiber of your body to live. Your whole family needs you and loves you. I love you, Land. Hunter, bring my husband home."

"I will," Hunter said with a promise in his voice that Maggie knew, dead or alive, Hunter wouldn't return to Shadows Landing without Landry.

5

"Lydia," Ryker said gently, which the public wouldn't believe, since the grumpy billionaire tended to be known only for this ruthlessness in the boardroom. But in Shadows Landing, their home, he was just Ryker, the loyal friend. "I have all the information on Landry."

Lydia reached out and grabbed Maggie's hand as Edie joined them. It had been ten minutes since they'd hung up with Hunter and everyone was still reeling. "Okay, tell me everything."

Ryker nodded and glanced down at his phone. "Internal reports show that right after you had Landry Junior, Landry joined the Marine Raiders. The pay was considerably higher. He hasn't exactly been on deployment the whole time either. He had training and is now stationed in North Carolina. However, he did ask for extended deployments because of the increase in bonuses. Bonuses that he put into educational accounts for the children. It also looks as if he's been taking every advancement he can get to bank on the higher pension. Two years until he's been in the Marines for twenty years and can retire at full pension."

Lydia sank down into the nearest chair. "He didn't tell me because I didn't want him in danger. But everything he did was to give us a better life. But how is life ever supposed to be better if I don't have him in it?"

"Come on, Lydia. Let me take you home. I'll stay the night with you if you'd like," Edie offered. Lydia just nodded as if all the fight had drained out of her.

"Thank you all," Lydia mumbled as Edie rounded everyone up. Georgie, Kord, and Edie helped get everyone home as Maggie watched them shuffle from the bar.

It broke her heart to watch. Military families might not be shot at or in danger, but they served and sacrificed as much as the soldiers did. Maggie's thoughts instantly went to Hunter. He seemed so big, so strong, so invincible, but he was just a man. A very sexy, infuriating man, but flesh and blood. He'd gone into an obviously dangerous situation and rescued Landry. Then turned around and was so kind and gentle with Lydia and her kids.

"Maggie," Olivia said, interrupting Maggie's thoughts of Hunter. "Gage took your car to help drive some of Lydia's kids home. I told him I'd give you a ride home."

"Thanks," Maggie said, her mind still not with Olivia but with Hunter as she got into the car.

"You actually really like my brother, don't you?" Olivia asked kindly but with a bit of surprise in her voice.

"What? No," Maggie instantly denied.

"He doesn't deserve you," Olivia said, ignoring Maggie's denial. "But he'd be really lucky to have you."

"He won't have me because he hates me. And I can't stand him," Maggie added, then felt guilty for saying it out loud when Hunter had just saved Landry.

Olivia chuckled. "We both know he aggravates you, but

you don't hate him and he doesn't hate you. He just hasn't looked beyond the pretty package to see what's inside. Yet, he's drawn to you. He still argues with you. He seeks you out every chance he gets. I think you're a puzzle to him. He's used to women flocking to him. You don't. You give it back to him just as much as he dishes it out and women don't do that with him."

"You do that with him," Maggie pointed out.

"Exactly. I'm the only one. He doesn't know what to do when it's someone who he's attracted to. And before you try to deny it, my brother stares at you as if you're an oasis in the desert."

"Natalie told me you put her through it when she started dating Stone. I wouldn't think you'd want me to try to get together with Hunter."

Olivia rolled her eyes as she pulled into Bell Landing. "I didn't put Natalie through it. I put Stone through it. And you can bet your silver medal I'll put Hunter through it. Payback as a bitch but nothing compared to payback as a cockblocked sister." Olivia turned to Maggie, serious once again. "I'm not saying to throw yourself at my brother. I'm telling you to make him grovel when he finally sees you, but know I have your back. You're the first woman to keep her wits around him. You're strong enough to handle Hunter and the job he comes with. I know today was hard. It's hard every time Hunter leaves. But we also know you wouldn't try to stop him from doing his job. You'd support him. When he finally falls for you, you better watch out because Hunter is the most loyal man you'll ever meet. There would be nothing in this world to stop him from getting to you if you needed him."

Maggie sat, looking at her house for a moment, taking it all in. "I'm not saying I like him, but I will say I'm drawn to him." Maggie opened the door and got out, but Olivia rolled down the window, stopping her.

"It's a start. Remember, hold strong until he's groveled. Don't be distracted by the muscles. Make him use them as he crawls to you, begging forgiveness for being such a dumbass."

Then with a wave, Olivia left Maggie standing on the driveway, wondering if what Olivia had said was true. Could Hunter actually want her? How did that make her feel? Maggie would have the entire sleepless night to think about it because until Landry, Hunter, and Tristan were safe at home, she didn't know if she'd sleep again.

~

Hunter was exhausted, but military training taught him to never give in to the exhaustion. There had been no change in Landry's condition. He was no better, but also no worse. The doctor said his body was using all its energy to fight off the infection. Dr. Fissore told them at midnight he was going to sleep in the physicians' lounge with the promise to be back at six in the morning to re-evaluate Landry's condition. He instructed the nurse to wake him if Landry needed anything. Tomorrow, they should have a better idea if the treatment was working.

The door opened and shut some time later as Tristan walked into the dimly lit room with two cups of coffee. "Thought we could use these. I had to sweet-talk a nurse into getting them for us. The cafeteria and the coffee shop aren't open at three in the morning."

"Thanks, Tris." Hunter took the offered cup and smelled the sweet, sweet caffeine.

The door opened once again and a doctor walked in. He

stopped, surprised to see them in the room. "Oh," the doctor said. "I didn't realize anyone was inside. You startled me."

"We have that effect on people," Hunter said, eying the new doc. "What can we do for you?"

"I'm here to examine Mr. Langston and administer his medication. If you don't mind, could you step out while I look Mr. Langston over?"

Tristan frowned, but Hunter nodded. "Let's top off our coffee."

"But," Tristan began to say.

"But we'll have to sweet-talk the nurses, I know. One of them is pretty cute. It won't be a hardship. Let's go." Hunter didn't feel the nonchalance he was portraying. Dr. Fissore was very clear that he was the lead doctor on this case. That, and the man standing with a clipboard had the wrong hospital ID on. The photos didn't match and he was very quick to turn the ID around to hide the photo the second he realized he wasn't alone.

Hunter got up, pushed the privacy curtain halfway open, and made sure Tristan followed him out of the room. Hunter didn't close the door all the way as they left. He stopped at the guard stationed outside Landry's room and leaned over to him. "Go get hospital security and the MPs. Quietly, but very quickly," Hunter whispered.

The man nodded and ran off.

"Hunter," Tristan whispered.

Hunter put his finger to his lips and motioned for them to creep back into the room. The half-closed privacy curtain hid their entrance to the room. Hunter watched as the doctor patted down Landry's body. This wasn't an exam. It was a search. Next, he searched the drawers, the closet, and the bathroom. He was moving quickly, knowing Tristan and

Hunter wouldn't be gone long. But it was also clear he didn't find what he was looking for.

"Now there'll be no evidence," he whispered to Landry as he pulled a syringe from his pocket. "All your fighting and you still lose."

"Protect Landry," Hunter whispered right before he made his move. He knew Tristan would back him up. Hunter didn't charge. He slipped into the room, moving as quickly and quietly as he could. The movement was deliberate as the man pretending to be a doctor pulled the cap from the needle. "What's that, Doc?" Hunter asked as he stepped from the shadows close to the bathroom across from the bed.

The doctor didn't jump, which meant he was trained, but Hunter's plan worked. The doctor had to turn around and that meant he lost sight of Landry. Tristan slipped into the room, pushed the bed lock off, and was wheeling Landry out of the room in less than two seconds.

The fake doctor turned to leap at Landry and Tristan, but that gave Hunter the opening he needed to charge the doctor. Hunter slammed into him harder than any linebacker. They crashed into the wall as Tristan shoved Landry, bed and all, out of the room with the IV stand trailing behind like a tail whipping from side to side.

Hunter wanted to ask so many questions, but there wasn't time. The man had recovered and was trying to stab Hunter with the needle he had in his hand. Hunter blocked the jab and slammed his hand into the man's nose. The man kicked out, hitting Hunter in the knee, sending him stumbling back.

Shouts were heard in the corridor as the man advanced on Hunter. The fighting came hard and fast. Punches, stabs, and kicks so fast Hunter didn't have time to think. He acted purely on muscle memory from years of training. Block, block, punch. He took some hits and he gave some hits but it was all so fast none of it registered. The man was trying to stab him with the needle when someone yelled from the door. The man paused long enough for Hunter to grab his hand, turn it sharply so he heard the wrist snap, and jam the needle into the man's neck.

He held it there, not injecting it as the room filled. "Who are you? What do you want?"

The man smiled. There was no fear in his eyes. Hunter knew that look. He'd seen it on suicide bombers before. "You'll never stop us. We'll take back what is ours and all the glory with it."

The man smiled, reached up, and shoved Hunter's thumb onto the plunger of the syringe, sending the injection straight into his own body.

The man's eyes closed and he keeled over with the needle still in his neck. Nurses and doctors ran into the room as Hunter stared down at the dead man. They tried to resuscitate him, but Hunter could have told them to save their efforts. The man was dead and now there were more questions than ever before.

"Where's Landry?" Hunter asked the MPs, now also filling the room.

"Two doors down," one of them answered. "Follow me."

Hunter followed the military police officer to the room where nurses were checking Landry for injuries and hooking him back up to oxygen. Tristan stood guard watching them while also watching the door.

"Dead?" Tristan asked. Hunter nodded. "What do they think Landry has and why is it worth killing over?"

"I don't know, but Landry isn't safe here. We need to move him."

Dr. Fissore raced into the room in wrinkled scrubs. "I just heard." He immediately began to examine Landry.

"He's no longer safe here, Doc. We need to move him. What will it take?" Hunter asked.

"Run a full blood panel on him, nurse," Dr. Fissore ordered. "If he's stable, I'd say an ambulance, a doctor, and a nurse. But I don't know where you can take him. There are only three hospitals in Millevia. It won't be hard to track him down."

"Military plane?" Tristan asked.

"I only want people we know and trust." Hunter paused and then looked at the doctor. "What if you had two doctors, an ER nurse practitioner, and a private plane?" Hunter asked.

The doctor's eyebrows rose, but he nodded. "If I can get him stabilized enough. I'll give you a list of everything they'll need."

"No need, you're coming with us to meet them."

Hunter pulled out his phone as he walked away after the doctor nodded his agreement. "Ryker. It's Hunter. Mind if we borrow your plane?"

6

It took twenty-four hours to get Landry stabilized enough to move. Hunter and Tristan took shifts with only Hunter's team and Tristan's personal friends as guards. Either Tristan or Hunter was awake at all times. Tristan had spent some of his "off" time with his friend, David, who was going to make a full recovery.

Landry had started to talk in his sleep about five hours ago. After a full day on antibiotics, IV fluids, and several wound cleansings later, he'd batted his eyes open, asked for Lydia, and fell back asleep. His fever broke at the same time that Ryker's plane landed in nearby Monaco.

"We can move him now," a similarly exhausted looking Dr. Fissore said after looking at the latest blood panels. "How are we going to get him out of here?"

"We got that covered. Hope you're not claustrophobic, Doc," Hunter told him.

They wrapped Landry up in a dark sheet, swaddling him like a baby before covering his head with the sheet. Hunter and his team then carefully laid Landry in an industrial rug, like the kind you walk on when you enter the lobby, and covered him with the ends. The same was done to the doctor, Tristan, and finally Hunter.

Then, a mix of Hunter and Tristan's team dressed as rug cleaners, loaded them on carts, pushed them to the back entrance, and hefted them into a box van that belonged to the rug cleaner used by the hospital. Inside the van, the two men who had lifted the rugs into the back of the van and the driver were part of Hunter's team. They were unwrapped, and Landry was moved back onto a hospital gurney where Dr. Fissore reattached his IV and monitored him on the drive to Monaco.

"Did anyone try to follow us?" Tristan asked as they neared the private airfield of the rich and famous. No one would expect a soldier to fly private.

"No, sir. Captain Bonetti monitored us from homebase and said we were in the clear. What do we do about security?" the soldier asked as they approached the gated entrance.

Hunter looked out and saw Ryker Faulkner, in full billionaire mode, striding toward the gate as if he owned the airfield. "I don't think we'll need to worry about it." Ryker handed the man a wad of cash and the gate opened. They were never stopped as they drove onto the private airfield.

Ryker pointed to the closest hangar and the soldier drove the van into it. The hangar doors closed as soon as Ryker had joined them. Only then did Hunter open the back of the van.

"Thanks for the plane," Hunter said as he climbed out. "This is bigger than your other plane. Is it new?"

"Borrowed from a friend. I brought everything you asked for. How's Landry?"

"His fever broke this morning. Doctor Fissore thinks he'll pull through," Hunter said, nodding to the doctor who was issuing orders on how to move Landry to the soldiers. "I didn't know you were going to be joining us," Hunter said to Ryker.

"I thought you could use the cover and I know who to bribe so it was as if you were never here. Plus, I wasn't going to let my wife come alone when danger is clearly following you. I also brought company." Ryker nodded to the plane.

The steps were lowered and Lydia raced down them with Edie a step behind her. Tristan instantly ran to his wife and wrapped her up in a tight hug. Hunter looked to the plane, hoping to see Maggie for some reason, but instead saw a couple of his brothers.

"I understand Rowan—he's a doctor—but Kane?" Hunter asked as his brothers walked down the stairs, followed by Dr. Gavin Faulkner and Ryker's wife, Kenzie, who was a nurse practitioner and former ER nurse.

"How do you think you got access to the rugs and that truck? That was all Kane. Your brother has more questionable contacts than I do. When sneaking out of a country, those are the contacts you need," Ryker said. "Also, why didn't you tell me Kane owned KAT Insurance?"

"You just learned that now? I thought you'd have hostage and kidnapping insurance," Hunter said as he watched Lydia running to the van.

"I thought KAT stood for Kidnap Abduction and Transactions, which is all over the website."

"Or Kane Allen Townsend."

Ryker rolled his eyes. "What is it with your family and their initials? Anyway, turns out I do have insurance through Kane's company. I thought he might be valuable in this situation."

Hunter's attention was taken away from Ryker as Lydia stopped when they lowered Landry's stretcher out of the van. "Landry, I'm here, baby. I'm here. I love you so much." Lydia kissed his face and held his hand. "I've missed you so much. Wake up so I can kill you again for lying to me." Lydia then gasped, tears flowing from her eyes. "He just squeezed my hand! Landry! Do you hear me?"

Dr. Fissore, Gavin, and Rowan all rushed forward as Kenzie was pulling out her stethoscope. They surrounded Landry. For the first time since Hunter had met Dr. Fissore, the man smiled.

Kane approached Hunter then, frowning. "They know Landry's been moved. They're trying to find him."

"Who?" Hunter asked as Tristan stepped away from Edie to join them.

"I don't know. Some . . . men in Millevia. Feelers have gone out to the underworld for information on American soldiers leaving the country. Money is being offered so there's not much time until we are found out."

"Can't we monitor their communication or something?" Hunter asked.

Kane shook his head. "This is old school, bro. All word of mouth. Nothing in writing, nothing on the Internet. It's being done through a known intermediary. I can stay and have a word with him if you want. I've worked with him before and I can usually pay him off."

"How confident are you that you can get information from him and not have it turn around and bite us in the ass?" Hunter asked.

Kane didn't react. He simply looked at Hunter impassively. "This is my job and I'm good at it. I'll get you the information you need, but it'll cost me."

"I'll cover the cost. I know the US government won't.

Their stance is technically to not negotiate," Ryker said in the same serious tone as Kane. "Will five million be enough?"

"They usually ask for ten million, but I've never had to pay more than a million. Most of the time, I end up down to six hundred thousand, but that takes a lot of time." Kane answered. Hunter realized his little brother did a lot more than Hunter realized. "It'll take time. I have to work my contacts."

"Do it," Hunter said as he watched Lydia clinging to her husband.

With a nod, Kane walked back into the plane. A moment later, he came down with a backpack and left.

"That's what Kane does?" Rowan, the youngest brother of the Townsend family, asked. "I thought he just worked in an office selling insurance."

"Isn't this patient a little big for you?" Hunter asked. Rowan was a pediatric surgeon and Landry was no child.

"Parts are parts, you know. Plus, it's easier to see the organs when they're so big," Rowan joked. "But seriously, I'm here in case we have to do emergency surgery. You said only people we could trust. We couldn't take any risks with any other surgeons."

"Thanks, Row. Now, let's get out of here. The sooner we're on American soil, the better I'll feel."

Dr. Fissore filled the new medical team and Lydia in before leaving. He recounted the events since Landry first arrived at the hospital and then they worked to keep Landry comfortable before the plane took off. Landry had a whole section of the plane as they moved him to a couch where they were able to strap him in.

"You know what to do?" Hunter asked the doctor.

"Yes. I must admit I'm not looking forward to this bit, but

when it's over, I'll report to the hospital that I was attacked in the room and knocked unconscious. When I woke up, Landry was gone."

Hunter nodded. "You're a good man. We couldn't have done this without you, Doc." Then Hunter punched him several times. He felt horrible about it, but it had to be done.

Hunter reached out and helped the doctor up where Hunter's team was ready to smuggle him back into the hospital. "Sorry about that."

"It needed to be done. Take care of him. And if you have a chance, let me know how he's doing."

Hunter was the last to board the plane. Only after everyone had boarded and the door was shut did the pilots get clearance to leave and the hangar doors opened.

"I'm guessing you didn't eat much," Edie said, her hand never leaving Tristan's.

"Not really," Tristan told her.

"I can fix that," Ryker said, standing up and headed to the kitchen on the plane.

"You look pale. Are you okay?" Tristan asked his wife.

She didn't look okay. She looked sick to her stomach and worried.

"Yes, we've just been a mess since we found out about Landry. I was worried to death about you, Maggie about Hunter, and then poor Lydia . . ."

"Wait," Hunter said, interrupting her. "Maggie was worried about me?"

"You are so smart, yet so freaking dumb," Rowan muttered.

Hunter turned to ask Edie about Maggie, but Edie suddenly jumped up and ran to the bathroom. Tristan frowned and hurried after her. A moment later, that was a shout from the bathroom. "You're pregnant?!"

Hunter and everyone else looked back to where Tristan emerged, looking elated. "I'm going to be a father."

Hugs were given and as the others celebrated, Hunter heard his name being called.

"Hunter," the soft voice said, drawing his attention to Lydia, who took the seat across from him. "I heard what you did for Landry." Lydia bit her lip as she reached out and took his hand in hers. "I don't know how I can ever thank you enough. The only thing I can do is this." Lydia stood up and smacked the back of Hunter's head hard. "Open your eyes, for crying out loud." Then she hugged him tightly as she cried. "Then maybe you can find someone to love as much as I love Landry."

7

For the first time in days, Hunter slept. Even in his sleep, he heard the murmurs of the medical team as they kept a close eye on Landry. He heard the way Edie ran to the bathroom several times. Then he heard when the flaps changed and the landing gear was activated and opened his eyes.

It was strange not landing at the Air Force Base, but instead at a private airfield where an ambulance was waiting for them. "You called an ambulance?" Hunter questioned.

Kenzie nodded. "It's all good. I know all the EMTs. That's my friend and he's one hell of an EMT. He's not on duty. Technically the vehicle is going to get serviced, so there's no log of him picking anyone up."

"You are so sexy when you're sneaky," Ryker whispered to her before placing a kiss on her cheek. "And I've called the president of the hospital and they know the situation. Landry will be entered into the hospital under a fake name. We'll claim John Doe status until Landry is safe. I also hired private security."

"Ryker, that's too much," Lydia said. "I can't pay for this."

"Lydia, I'm not asking you to, nor would I even allow you

to. All I want you to do is focus on Landry. The town is taking care of the children and we'll bring them to visit when the coast is clear."

Hunter worked with Ryker, Gavin, Rowan, Tristan, and the EMT who had been introduced as Charlie to move Landry onto the ambulance. Hunter sat in the front seat ready to protect them as the medical team drove to the hospital with Ryker, Edie, and Lydia in the SUV directly behind them.

"I've got this part," Kenzie said as they went into the employee parking garage. "Stop here, Charlie." Kenzie jumped out, knocked on the door, and waited. A moment later, a nurse opened the door. "Thanks, Jen."

"Take him to the Faulkner suite," Jen ordered as she placed a mask and a hair net over Landry's head as if taking him to surgery. "Goodness," Jen said, looking up at Hunter after the medical team and Lydia hurried into the hospital. "We need to be careful of you."

"Me? Why?"

"You're obviously a Townsend and the nurses have a pool going on who can nab one. You'll have nurses stopping by to flirt constantly." Jen looked back at Ryker, who was now the only person left with him. "You need to bring Olivia if you bring one of the Townsend brothers. She's the only person scary enough to keep them at bay."

"Noted," Ryker said proudly. Hunter hadn't appreciated that about Ryker when they'd thought Ryker was dating Olivia. However, now he did. The man had given their sister a chance when others wouldn't hire a female attorney. Not only that, but Ryker fully enjoyed and appreciated the badassery of their sister. He was very much like them—a proud brother.

"Just try not to draw attention to yourself," Jen huffed

and then muttered to herself about impossibly sexy Townsends ruining her shifts as they took the stairs up to the Faulkner suite. It was a hospital room that was large enough to hold the Faulkner family that Ryker had paid for with one of his donations.

The medical team already had Landry hooked up by the time they made it to the room. "We're going to take eight-hour shifts," Gavin told them, "Jen, Kenzie, and I. Kenzie, you're on in sixteen. Jen's on now and I'll stay on tonight but will sleep in the room for the next eight hours."

Hunter felt the change in the room without turning around. Someone had quietly joined them. Hunter moved fast and had a knife to their throat before anyone could say anything.

"You're getting slow. I got a good eight feet into the room," the woman teased.

"Thanks for coming, Blythe," Ryker said, no one seeming to care about the knife to the woman's throat.

Hunter dropped the knife and smiled at the petite bodyguard. "Good to see you again. That leaping scissor hold to the neck flip thing you taught me saved my ass a couple of months ago."

"Glad I could help. So, this is the special man I'm to protect? I read his record. He's one hell of a hero."

"Thank you for coming," Lydia said from the chair at the side of Landry's bed. She hadn't let go of her husband's hand since Hunter had entered the room. "I feel much better with you here watching out for him."

It took about an hour, but everyone settled in. Rowan took Ryker, Kenzie, Edie, and Tristan home as Hunter hunkered down to talk with Blythe. He told her everything they knew so she'd know what to be on the lookout for.

Gavin fell asleep on the couch within a minute. Apparently, it was a doctor thing. They could sleep anywhere, anytime. Just like soldiers. Jen did one last check-up on how Landry was, and while still not fully awake, he was squeezing Lydia's hand when asked to.

Lights were dimmed and Blythe moved to the chair on Landry's other side—the one that faced the door. They both looked toward the door when they heard footsteps approaching.

"That's not Jen," Blythe whispered, slowly pulling a gun and hiding it under the blanket by Landry's hip.

"I know. Female though," Hunter whispered back, moving into the shadows of the room.

There was a soft knock on the door and then it was slowly pushed open. The familiar scent of food hit first, then the sweet floral scent that was embedded in his brain. Hunter put his gun away and opened the door, surprising Maggie. Her loose hair was in waves down her back, held back by a pearl encrusted headband. Her pink dress hugged a figure that Hunter could only dream of.

"Hunter!" she smiled up at him and his heart did this strange flip thing. "It amazes me every time you come back. I didn't think your ego could fit on a plane."

Hunter laughed, but his stomach betrayed him and grumbled before he could zing one back at her. Her lips frowned as she reached into the purple and teal paisley monogrammed carry case she had and pulled out a to-go box and handed it to him. "I made fried green tomato and pimento cheese po'boys. I figured y'all would be hungry."

"Oh my gosh. You're the best. Thank you so much," Lydia said with a smile and a sigh. "I think I can finally eat now that I have Landry home. It's been almost two days since I've had anything. And Maggie, he's squeezing my hand now!"

Maggie walked past Hunter, leaving the smell of her light floral perfume to haunt him. "That's such good news. And Blythe, I have something for you too. And I'll put this one over here for Gavin when he gets up. I also made a pecan pie for everyone to share and some sweet tea."

"Is that a Mary Poppins bag?" Hunter asked as he watched Maggie pull item after item out of the large rectangular monogrammed monstrosity with two metal handles.

Maggie rolled her eyes and ignored him as she gave a rundown on how Georgie and Kord were doing taking care of the kids. Landry Jr. and Lacy were stepping up in a big way and had helped to put all the kids to bed.

"Landry," Maggie finally said after she emptied her bag. "I'm so glad you're home. I made your favorite, pecan pie. You can have a slice as soon as you wake up and Gavin allows it."

Lydia beamed up at her. "He squeezed my hand again."

"Dear Lord, what are you trying to do?" Jen asked as she rushed into the room. "First was the rumor of a Townsend sighting and now whatever that is you made smells so freaking good. Hungry nurses are like zombies out for brains. They're all trying to find the source, and if they find Hunter here . . . well, he'll be put out to stud."

"Is it Tuesday already? That is what he does, after all," Maggie said snarkily, even as she said it with a smile.

"How nice that you think I can pleasure the entire nursing staff at once. You must have been thinking about me sexually to come up with that." Hunter loved that Maggie blushed and sputtered. "If you think I can do that, imagine what I could do if it was just you and me?"

"Live to flirt another day," Jen said, grabbing his arm. "You need to leave."

"I don't have a car. I can handle a couple of nurses."

Jen looked at him as if he were dumb. "They're hungry, starting the night shift, and horny. You wouldn't survive three minutes."

Maggie sighed. "I'll take you home."

Maggie hugged Lydia and then, at Jen's urging, hurried from the room with Hunter hot on her heels. Damn, the man looked fine as hell, even if he looked exhausted. She wanted to feed him and tuck him into bed. Although, he was eating and making the most erotic groans as he ate her po'boy while they took the stairs to the parking garage.

"That was really good. Where did you get it?" Hunter asked as they walked into the garage.

"I made it," Maggie said as she used her key fob to unlock her car.

"It was really good. I thought you just ordered take-out." He paused and looked at her truck. "You drive a pickup truck? I thought this was your brother's."

"No, it's mine, but he borrows it a lot."

"It's not pink."

Maggie looked over her shoulder and stared daggers at him. "Why do you think so little of me? Yes, I like pink. Yes, I like to feel pretty in cute dresses. Yes, I cook. Yes, I drive a truck. Yes, I shoot. Why can't I do all of that and do it well?"

Hunter glanced into the back of her truck and frowned. She knew what he saw. She had a locked gun safe back there. It was bolted to the frame of her truck. The one she took to competitions or out on hunts with her family. He probably thought it was to protect her dresses.

Hunter climbed into the truck and was quiet for a moment. "I'm not used to women being all those things. I've had my share of women like you—you know, into pretty, frilly things—in my life before, but the moment things get tough, they cry. I have to leave, they cry. I can't afford huge diamonds, they cry. I miss their birthday because I'm on a mission, they cry. I don't spend every minute of the day fawning over them, and they cry."

"Are you serious?" Maggie asked incredulously. "You literally read the book by the cover and never looked inside. Have you *ever* seen me cry? Have you ever heard me ask anyone for diamonds or anything? I can afford my own diamonds, my own fancy clothes, and my own rifles, thank you very much. I don't need a man to buy them for me. I'm secure in who I am, Hunter. If your fragile male mind can't fathom a woman being multidimensional, that's on you. Not me."

"I'm beginning to see that," Hunter said, looking at her with such intensity it made it hard to focus on driving. "But, don't tell me you never do the same?"

"Of course, I don't."

Hunter raised an eyebrow. "Okay then. Who was the worst boyfriend you ever had?"

"Cooper Vandersmith. Met him freshman year of college. Total frat boy type. All he cared about was knocking back drinks and partying."

"Why did you break up?" Hunter asked.

"He believed if he was drunk and slept with other women, it wasn't cheating because it was the alcohol's fault," Maggie said dryly. She'd broken up with him right away and never looked back.

"Did you ever date anyone like him again?" Hunter asked as if he were interested.

"No," Maggie paused. "I see what you're doing. It's not the same."

"How is it not the same?"

"I would like to think I would look beyond first impressions if I was interested in a man."

Hunter raised an eyebrow. "You mean, in the ten years since freshman year, you never came across a guy who liked to party and tried to get to know him more?"

Okay, so when she saw guys super drunk at bars and they hit on her, she always said no. It was a giant red flag. But wearing pink wasn't a red flag . . . it was a pink one. For Hunter, who had gone through the same type of thing as she had—a broken heart. "So, you're saying you've given women like me a chance but, while not cheating on you, they've hurt you, and I remind you of them?"

"Exactly. Do you know how hard it is to go off on a mission and not have support back home? You're leaving to tears and *why can't you be more like my ex who works in finance?* When I leave, I need my mind focused. It's literally life and death. I see how I took out that past pain on you, and for that, I am sorry."

Maggie felt her anger begin to ebb. Cooper had done a number on her too, and her life didn't hang in the balance. She remembered Edie throwing up, finding out she was pregnant, and refusing to tell Tristan since he needed his head in the mission. "I'm sorry too. I guess everyone has a history. Sometimes we can get over it, and other times it stays with us."

Maggie pulled onto Main Street in Shadows Landing. They were both quiet until Hunter looked at his phone. "My family wants to meet me at Harper's. Can you drop me off there?"

Maggie nodded and pulled over across the street from Harper's Bar. "I'm going to go check on Kord and Georgie. I'm sure they're overwhelmed with all the kids."

Hunter put his hand on the door handle but didn't open it. He turned around and, for once, looked introspective. "Thanks for the ride, Mags. And the talk. I never told anyone about that before."

"It's easier to take a bullet than be vulnerable, isn't it?"

"I know one will hurt, but the other can destroy you." Hunter shrugged and got out of the truck. "Thanks again, Mags. I'll see you soon."

Hunter closed the door and stood on the sidewalk across from the bar, waiting for her to leave. Maggie pulled a U-turn, and as she drove away, she looked in the rearview mirror to see a man had joined Hunter as they watched her drive away.

8

Hunter had just closed the door when he sensed he wasn't alone. It was nine at night, and downtown was still busy with people finishing up dinner, but this was different. He glanced around but didn't see anyone as Maggie pulled a U-turn. Hunter turned to watch her drive off, not believing he'd shared his dating past with her when a man he didn't know strode from The Pink Pig.

Hunter was about to turn to get a good look at him when he felt the gun to his back. "Don't warn anyone or I'll kill you and then them. Do you understand?" he asked in a deep, conversational tone with a hint of an accent that Hunter couldn't exactly place other than it being Eastern European.

"Yes," Hunter said, already looking around him, cataloging who was where and ways to disarm the man so as to not put anyone else in danger.

"Hand it over."

That got Hunter's attention. "Hand what over?" What also got Hunter's attention was Damon stopping at Harper's Bar door. Damon turned and looked right at him.

Damon glanced down the street and Hunter's gaze followed. FBI Agent Peter Castle walked toward Damon. Next to Peter was Hunter's brother-in-law, Sheriff Granger Fox.

Damon caught Hunter's eye and, in a way only close brothers could do, Hunter passed a message. Damon looked away as he pulled out his phone. An SOS was going out and Hunter knew he had limited time to get as much information as possible from this man before he was taken down, either by Hunter or by one of his friends.

"Hand what that soldier gave you. Don't act stupid. Where is it?"

Hunter was actually confused. What did they think he had? "What soldier? Because I wasn't given anything."

"The soldier you managed to sneak out of the hospital. Why would you do that unless you knew what he'd found?"

Landry. Landry had something the terrorists wanted. That's why they tried to kill him. "That guy wasn't snuck out. He died and I came home. Mission over," Hunter told him.

"Bullshit. I believe he has a wife here. And you're here. Can't be a coincidence. If he didn't give you anything, you're useless to me. So, I'll ask you one more time to hand it over." The gun pressed deeper into his back. Hunter glanced at Damon and gave the smallest nod.

The man dropped before the report of a bullet reached Hunter's ears. The man whose gun had been jammed into Hunter's back dropped to the ground. It was a perfect kill shot to the head.

"Are you hurt?" Damon asked, running to him. He was the first one to reach him. He didn't bother to look to see if someone was still shooting. He was going to protect his little brother and Hunter loved him for it.

"I'm good. Nice shot, Granger. I guess I can't tease you

anymore," Hunter said, looking to where Granger and everyone else were running toward them.

"I didn't shoot him," Granger said, looking around the street.

"Well, then great shot, Peter," Hunter said, holding out his hand for the FBI agent.

"Wasn't me," Peter said, similarly looking around.

Dare, part of the ATF, hurried from the bar with his gun in hand. "Thanks for saving my ass, Dare," Hunter called out.

"Wasn't me. I heard the shot and came out to investigate," Dare said.

Hunter frowned. Then laughed. "Hell of a shot, Tristan! Where are you?"

Hunter turned around in a circle and then saw someone walking toward him from the direction of the courthouse. The sound of cowboy boots echoed off the street as everyone turned to stare.

Hunter felt his mouth open as the pink dress swirled around Maggie's thighs. Her pearl necklace and pearl headband stood out in the moon's light. Maggie could take his breath away on any given day with her natural beauty, but what was robbing Hunter's speech right now was the pink rifle she had leaning up against her shoulder as she strode toward them.

Damon, to his side, snickered. Granger outright smothered a laugh. Dare was biting his lip and breathing really hard. Peter's shoulders were shaking with suppressed laughter.

Hunter moved to block the body from her view. She shouldn't have to see a dead man that Tristan killed, but then Maggie stopped right in front of him. She leaned around him and looked down. She didn't cry. She didn't throw up. Instead, she frowned. Here it came. The hysterics.

"Hmph. I was about a half a millimeter off center."

Hunter snapped his gaze to the shot in the man's forehead and then to the pink rifle she had leaning against her shoulder. "Okay, the gag's up. Funny prank, Tristan."

The guys burst out laughing and Maggie rolled her eyes at him. She turned on one booted heel and spun around, sending the skirt fluttering and giving him a very tempting view of her upper thigh.

Maggie strode away, but right before she disappeared from sight, she called out over her shoulder, "You're welcome for saving your life."

Hunter was still looking around for Tristan when Damon smacked the back of his head so hard that Hunter stumbled forward.

"What was that for?" Hunter asked.

"I'm trying to knock some sense into you."

"What for?" Hunter asked.

"Maggie just saved your life and didn't shoot you when you said Tristan did it and was pranking you."

Hunter chuckled, but then Damon hit him again. "Ow, stop."

"I'll stop once you look her up online."

"I got a dead guy here who knows about Landry, I can't—"

Smack. "Do it. Now."

"I'm—"

Smack.

"Okay, okay. Shouldn't we clear the dead guy from the street first though?"

"Here!" Harper called out as she ran toward them with an empty potato sack. "Just cover him with this. We're not here looking at him anyway. We're waiting for you to finally use your phone and look Maggie up."

Hunter glanced around and noticed that there were a large number of people gathering on the street, and they were in fact, staring at him, not the dead guy.

"Fine." Hunter pulled out his phone, opened his browser, and typed in Maggie's name and Shadows Landing because the search results surely needed to be narrowed down. What would Maggie be on the internet for?

Maggie Bell, Five Time World Trap Shooting Champion, Takes Aim at Rifle

Maggie Bell Silver Medal Olympian from Small Town

Maggie Bell World Rifle Champion for Three Years Straight

Maggie Bell Wins Again

Maggie Bell, World's Best Shot, Makes Rifle Shooting History

Maggie Bell Qualifies for Second Olympics in Rifle and Trap

The Bells go to Italy: Siblings, Gage and Magnum Bell, both Qualify for the Olympic Shooting Team.

Hunter felt his mouth drop open as a sinking feeling filled him. "Oh boy, I've really screwed this one up."

"Finally!" everyone called out, tossing their hands into the air.

Damon waited until Hunter looked up and held up his hand, wiggling his fingers to make sure Hunter looked at them. "Smart." Damon lifted one finger. "Funny." Damon lifted another finger. "Beautiful." Another finger. "Tough." Another finger. "Independent." Damon held up one full hand before lifting his other hand. "Doesn't scare easily." Damon raised his sixth finger. "And finally, can hit a bullseye from 400 yards." Damon looked down at the man and then up the street. "Although, I'd say she hit it at 800 yards. Hmm, now that's a woman worth marrying. Now, where did I hear that?"

Damon turned around and strode off, offering to buy people a drink at the bar for putting up with his dumbass brother for so long.

Hunter looked down at his fingers where he'd been silently checking off the boxed as Damon said them. Maggie fit every single thing he said he wanted in a woman and then some. She was understanding. She was compassionate. She made him feel like no other woman ever had, and he'd been a huge jerk to her.

Maybe she's been right in front of you this whole time. Son of a bitch. Damon and the entire town had been telling him all along that Maggie was the one for him, and he'd been too arrogant to listen. Meanwhile, she'd just sat back and let him keep putting his foot in his mouth.

Hunter smiled. Damned if that didn't make him like her even more. Now he really needed to find a way to make it up to her. Because while he might be slow to realize it, he was smart enough to know not to let the woman of his dreams walk away one more time.

9

Maggie stalked back to her car, secured her long-range rifle in the safe, and got into her truck. *Unbelievable.* She literally just saved Hunter's life, and he thought it was Tristan.

"That's *it.* I don't care how hot he is. Or how nice he is to the kids in town. Or how much he loves his family. I'm *done.* Over him for good," Maggie swore to herself as she drove to Kord and Georgie's house. She was done with Hunter Townsend. There was a banker in Charleston, Charles Wicksmith, who had asked her out several times. It was time to say yes and move on.

The upstairs lights were off, so Maggie tapped lightly on the front door, not wanting to wake the younger children.

Kord opened the door with a grin. "So, Hunter finally got his comeuppance? I would have loved to be there. Although, from what I heard, there's no way I would have made that shot."

"News travels fast," Maggie grumbled as Kord opened the door.

"You know that. You're the one who taught me that,"

Georgie said, patting the sofa. "Now sit and tell me everything."

Maggie sat down on the couch and shook her head. "It's over. I'm over him. He thought it was Tristan. Didn't believe me when I walked up, *still holding the rifle*."

"How did you know he was in trouble?" Kord asked.

Maggie took a deep breath and closed her eyes for just a second. She saw the memory as if she were watching it live. "I dropped him off and made a U-turn to come here. As I was driving away, I might have looked back at my rearview mirror and saw him watching me. I might not have looked away because I was hoping he was watching me because he was ready to see the real me. But then I saw the man approach him. I didn't know him, but I saw him pull a gun from under his shirt.

"I drove off, parked, and got my rifle. I used the scope to watch what was happening. I saw the moment the man's face changed and the moment Hunter looked to Damon for help. So, I fired."

Kord looked down at his phone as she talked. She didn't take it personally. She was sure her own phone was blowing up with texts. "Granger says the man wanted something from Landry and he thought he'd given it to Hunter. The man had decided to kill Hunter the second before you fired. You saved his life for sure."

"I'm sure he still thinks it's Tristan." Maggie rolled her eyes.

"No, he doesn't," Lacy said, coming around the corner. It was clear she'd been listening the whole time. Great. Now Maggie was going to be judged by a thirteen-year-old girl.

"How do you know?" Georgie asked her. "And you shouldn't be eavesdropping. You should always make yourself known."

More movement and Landry Jr. walked out. "Hi, but Lacy is right. Hunter knows it was you. He finally looked you up. It's all everyone is talking about."

"It won't matter. He probably thinks the articles are lying," Maggie said sarcastically.

Lacy sat cross-legged on the floor and nodded. "Boys are so stupid, Miss Maggie."

"Hey, we're not stupid," Landry protested.

"Dense. Dumber than a fence post. Can't see what's right in front of them. Can see a deer or a gator a mile off, but can't see the *girl* standing right in front of you," Lacy said savagely to her older brother. Maggie couldn't correct her though. She felt the same.

Landry and Lacy began to argue, until Lacy dropped the bomb. "How did you find out all this information?" she asked her brother.

"Kyra," Landry said with a shrug.

Lacy smiled victoriously and then turned to the adults. "As you know, Kyra is Quad's younger sister, who happens to be in Landry's grade, and who has a massive crush on him. So, she's feeding him information in hopes that he'll talk to her more."

"Whoa," Landry said with shock written all over his face. "Kyra is just a friend. And where did you hear that she likes me?"

Lacy crossed her eyes and looked very much like her mother right now. "See," she said to the grownups. "Boys are stupid. Can't see what's right in front of them. Kyra's told practically the whole school she has a crush on Landry and look . . . he has no clue."

Landry looked angry for a second, but then he blushed. "Does she really have a crush on me?"

Lacy ignored her brother and looked at Maggie with

more sympathy than a thirteen year old should have. "Good luck with Mr. Hunter. I would give him another chance if he stops being stupid. He's really nice, and he and Mr. Damon are the best at getting Lennie to stop crying when they rock her to sleep. Any man whom babies or dogs feel safe with is a good man. Now, I need to get to bed. Tomorrow Miss Georgie and Mr. Kord are letting Landry and me go see our dad."

Lacy left the room with her brother trailing after her, asking her over and over again about Kyra.

"Did I just get schooled on romance by a thirteen-year-old?" Maggie asked.

"Yes, and she wasn't wrong. The question is, will you forgive Hunter if he comes begging for forgiveness?" Georgie asked her.

That was the question. Would Hunter care enough to offer an apology? And even if he did, would it change anything? Maybe it was time to let go of the teenage crush she had on Hunter and grow up.

Maggie's whole family was waiting for her when she got home. Gage and her father were cleaning their guns and grumbling about disrespectful men. Her mother was smiling and baking at eleven at night. Timmons was filming himself doing a choreographed dance for social media.

Gage saw her first. "I'm going to kill him."

"Who?" Maggie asked.

"You saved his life and he doesn't even thank you? That arrogant ass needs to be taken down a peg or two," Gage replied.

"No man treats my baby like that. I've let it go on long

enough, but no longer," her father said, clicking the shotgun back into place.

"Oh God, it was fire. I saw the shot you made and I was shook AF."

"Shook about what?" her mother asked, coming into the room with a fresh baked pie.

"Word was Hunter would be low-key salty upon finding out Maggie was a better shot than him, but I'm hearing he doesn't want to drag her anymore. He wants to apologize."

"No cap?" Gage asked Timmons.

"Bet."

Her mother rolled her eyes and set the pie on the table. "The question is: what does Maggie want? Does she want to forgive him or not?"

"It's been a big yikes for Hunter, but it hits different when it's fam." Timmons nodded his head and her mother's brow creased. Then she shook her head and decided to just ignore the mix of Timmons's Gen Z and millennial slang.

"I'll kill him and then Mags won't have to decide if she forgives him or not," Gage said with a smile that had Maggie worried.

"No," her mother said, "or no pie. We don't kill people unless it's with kindness." Her mother looked to Maggie and paused, "Or with a perfect shot to the head."

Gage smiled. "See? I have options."

"What do you want, Magnum? We've all known you like him or you would have cussed him up one side and down the other when he questioned your ability to shoot. But I also know you might have had enough. The decision is yours," her father told her.

Maggie took a slice of pie and sat back on the comfortable couch. "I don't know exactly what I want to do,

Dad. Give me time to figure it out. And Gage, if anyone ends up shooting Hunter, it's gonna be me."

~

Maggie knew it was a mistake the second she hung up with Charles Wicksmith. She'd accepted the date he'd invited her to on a voicemail two weeks ago. She'd never called him back, but she thought she had to have a date with someone else before she knew how she felt for sure about Hunter.

If the strange feeling she had when she talked to him didn't tell her, her gut screaming at her to leave the dinner immediately sure did. Charles had come off as kind, confident, and intelligent when they'd met.

If this dinner had taught her anything, it was that he was a narcissist.

It had started off well enough. Charles was in his late twenties, clean cut with perfectly cut professional hair, and was wearing a suit. He took her to Port, a very nice restaurant that Ryker Faulkner favored quite often. They started off with polite chit-chat as they got to know each other. He enjoyed those tough-man competitions where they ran through fields and mud. He'd gone to an Ivy League college. He recently bought his first condo in one of the new upper-class modern developments that overlooked the water. He was a private banker for the large bank in town and felt free to tell her how much money he made. He worked with a lot of wealthy people and he loved to name-drop. Maggie was the opposite. She didn't like to talk about money, and certainly not about other people's money.

Then Charles had ordered his third gin in thirty minutes. The veneer of politeness fell away with each sip he took.

"I bet you feel stupid now," Charles said before taking another sip of his gin.

Honestly, Maggie had zoned out when he discussed his 401K and had a moment of panic being thrust back into the conversation, which had been solely about him for the past ten minutes. "How so?"

"For taking so long to go on a date with me. Women are like that. Shallow." Charles took another sip. "All they care about is money. I open my wallet, and they open their legs."

Maggie gasped, shocked at the sheer crudity of it. This came out of nowhere and now she was done. Maggie set her napkin down on the table, thankful that she drove herself to dinner, and stood up.

"Hey, where are you going?" Charles demanded.

"I'm sorry, I don't think this is going to work." Maggie placed a fifty on the table, feeling sorry that she'd already ordered her meal and didn't want the staff to get stiffed.

"No one walks out on Charles Wicksmith," he hissed. "What? Is my investment portfolio not big enough to get your panties wet?"

Maggie wanted to rage. She wanted to throw his gin in his face. But, she was a woman. Sadly, her first reaction was to say she was sorry again and try to avoid creating a scene or she might be labeled problematic. "No. I just need to leave. Goodbye."

Charles smirked and tossed back his drink. "I see what this is."

Maggie didn't stick around to ask what he meant. She hurried from the restaurant and didn't breathe until the door closed behind her.

Mumbling to herself about stupid men, Maggie walked through the lamp-lit parking lot to her car. She was reaching for the handle when she heard it. The footsteps were closer than she realized. Charles had somehow silently followed her.

Maggie whirled around to find him smirking no more than a couple feet from her. "I got your message," he said, his words slurring.

"What message?"

"In a hurry to get out of there so we could screw. Good thing you're wearing that skirt."

Maggie wanted to argue, but he was there, shoving her back against her car. Fear rocketed through every inch of her body. However, she wasn't one to freeze. Her weapons class at church taught her that.

"No. Don't touch me!" Maggie placed her hands on his chest and shoved. Charles stumbled back, but it wasn't far enough.

Charles grabbed her wrist as he stumbled, yanking her with him. "Yeah, fight me. Make the chase worth it. They all say no when they really mean yes. Do you know how I know? They all beg for more."

His grip tightened on her wrist to the point that Maggie flinched. "This girl is saying no and will never beg you for anything. Now, let go of me or I'll be forced to defend myself."

Maggie might be dressed in a frilly pink dress, but Hunter had underestimated her and now Charles had. She was tired of being underestimated.

Charles yanked her hard. Her shoulder protested as her body was pulled against his. Charles crashed his mouth against hers. His tongue demanded entrance, so Maggie gave it to him. Right before she snapped her mouth shut and bit his tongue, at the same time slamming her knee into his balls.

Charles yelped and fell back, cursing, while he grabbed

his balls. Maggie yanked her wrist free from his now limp grasp. She tightened her hand into a fist and punched Charles in the face as hard as she could. Charles went down. He didn't know what to hold—his mouth, his balls, or his cheek.

"Don't *ever* touch a woman without her permission again. When a woman says no, she means it." Maggie gave him one more swift kick to his torso before leaping into her car. "Freaking men."

Maggie drove straight to the police station. Sure, she could have let it go, but one thing she learned growing up in a small town was accountability. If she did something wrong, by the time she made it home, everyone had called her parents and told them what she'd done. At the time, she hated it, but now she realized what it was. It was a village raising the children to be well-mannered and accountable for their actions. Miss Winnie and Miss Ruby weren't here to dole out punishments to Charles, so Maggie did the next best thing.

"I'd like to file a report," Maggie told the officer sitting behind the desk at the local police station.

"Aw, crap," a man in a rumpled and ill-fitted suit cursed as he walked through the lobby. "You're one of them."

"One of who?" Maggie asked.

"Olivia Townsend's neighbors. I'm starting to think I know everyone in Shadows Landing. What happened now and do I have to deal with Olivia? Or can I go to bed?"

"I'm Magnum Bell and a date tried to force himself on me tonight. I don't want it happening to someone else."

The man frowned, his eyes going down to her wrist and then locking on her face. "Is that your blood?"

Maggie touched her face and shook her head. "I bit his tongue when he shoved it in my mouth."

"Yup, you're one of Olivia's. I'm Detective Chambers. I got this one," he told the desk officer.

Thirty minutes later, Charles Wicksmith was in jail. Detective Chambers picked him up at a bar as he was being thrown out for harassing a waitress.

"He'll spend the night in jail and I'll talk to the prosecutor. Someone will call you in the morning, but my guess is he'll plead out faster than a cat on a hot tin roof." He handed Maggie his card. "Call me if he bothers you again. And Miss Bell? Good job tonight. You did everything right."

"Can you tell Hunter Townsend that?" Maggie muttered, not intending for the exhausted looking detective to hear her.

"I guess I'm not the only one with a Townsend problem," Detective Chambers said with a grin that looked out of place on his normally glum face. "Maybe we should start a club?"

Maggie surprised the detective by suddenly hugging him. "Thank you, detective. You're a good one."

It took longer than Maggie wanted to finally climb into bed that night. She had to fill in her family and soothe their worries, and, to add insult to injury, freaking Hunter Townsend wouldn't get out of her mind.

10

Hunter faced a veritable firing squad comprised of all the people he loved and the entire town of Shadows Landing when he took his seat at Harper's Bar the next night. And he took it. He took every name they called him. Every insult to his intelligence. Every teasing joke about his complete FUBAR of a relationship with Maggie. Why? Because he deserved it.

So, he took it. He was man enough to own his mistakes and this was one of the biggest he'd ever made. He'd spent the last day researching Magnum Bell and all that she'd accomplished. She was freaking amazing. And he'd told her she was nothing but a ball of pink fluff. He had to be the biggest asshole to ever exist.

And what if she wasn't a good shot? It was still an asshole thing to do. The more he dug around, the more he discovered Maggie Bell was smart, charitable, and probably the kindest human in the world. She was known for her innate sportsmanship. Even her biggest rivals loved competing against her. Clients raved about all she did for them and their perfect days or conferences at Bell Landing.

The list went on and on, sinking him further and further into the hole he'd already dug for himself.

"Hunter."

Hunter looked up to find Ryker standing in front of him with Granger and Peter Castle. "Yes, I know. I'm a dumbass. I don't deserve Maggie. I'm thinking of a way to make it up to her."

"Good, but that's not why we're here," Ryker said, taking a seat at Hunter's table. Hunter looked around and noticed that most of the people had ventured off to other tables. Hunter was left with Damon and Forrest. "We got a hit on the man Maggie shot."

"Which terrorist group is he from?" Hunter asked.

"That's the thing. He's not a terrorist. He's a mercenary. His name is Alexey Kotov and he was part of the Borisenko Private Army out of Belarus," Ryker told him.

"That group broke up after Borisenko was killed four years ago," Hunter said, frowning. That didn't make sense.

"Could the people killed in Millevia also be Borisenko's men?" Peter asked.

"Sure. I don't know if they'd show up on a regular government search unless we had specific intel proving they were part of the private army. It's lucky you found that out with Alexey. Most of Borisenko's men wore ski masks as part of their uniforms. Identifying them was hard to do."

"We didn't use military or US government facial search for this," Peter said with a frown. "Well, we tried first, but they showed no results. We sent it off to a private company for identification."

"You broke the law? I'm so telling," Hunter teased. Peter shifted uncomfortably. He could probably lose his job over it if it were found out he shared details of an active case with a private citizen. "Tell me you already sent the other photos from Millevia."

"Tristan is asking their president for permission."

"Suck up," Hunter said, making Peter smile.

"Have you heard from Kane?" Ryker asked.

Hunter shook his head. His brother was scouring the underworld, and Hunter hoped Kane wasn't unknowingly walking into the hornet's nest. "No, but I'll text him this information. It might help him. Thanks for this. I'm still stuck on what they thought Landry had given me."

"I'm going to be added to these shifts of yours," Peter told him. "Dare has asked to help too. Paxton wants to as well. But with Tinsley so close to her due date, I told him we'd only call him in if necessary."

"I also called Blythe and let her know," Ryker informed him.

"I can help too," Damon added. "With more of us at the ready, we can take shorter shifts and stay better aware."

"I can help too," Forrest offered. "And I'm sure Wilder can too."

"I'd rather team you and Wilder up since you don't have law enforcement training, but I appreciate it. It will help a lot."

"I bet the Faulkners will help too," Damon added.

"We'll take some shifts, too," Gator said, turning on his stool at the bar to look at Hunter's table. He then pulled a giant knife out and began to clean his nails. "Would be right nice to meet that SOB who tried to hurt one of our own."

"Tank's grown stronger. I can knock someone out throwing him now," Turtle said, petting the juvenile snapping turtle, Tank, that he'd rescued from an alligator.

"The ghosts are mighty upset. The Langstons are

treasured. The kids leave presents for the ghosts every Halloween," Skeeter said, pulling out his own knife.

"Thank you all. I feel better having multiple people per shift. I'm sure Landry and Lydia will be thankful as well," Hunter said to the group.

The door opened and everyone sucked in a breath.

"You're in trouble now," Damon whispered.

Hunter turned toward the door and cursed. Yeah, he was in big trouble.

Hunter knew the hit was coming and did nothing to stop it. His instincts told him to fight, but Hunter tamped them down. The fist slammed into Hunter's face harder than Hunter thought it would, considering it was coming from a man in boat shoes wearing blue shorts with little pink palm trees on them.

"Outside. Now." Gage turned on his heel and strode out of the bar.

The entire bar was quiet, but several snickers echoed. Yeah, yeah. Hunter was an asshole. He got it.

Hunter pushed up from the table and headed outside to meet Maggie's older brother. Gage stood with his hands on his hips. He was only an inch or so shorter than Hunter. Unlike Maggie's strawberry blonde hair, Gage's was a light brown and currently shoved back from his face. His eyes flashed with anger and Hunter also noticed that Gage, for all he appeared to be a picture-perfect Southern Gentleman, wasn't shaking out the fist that was going to leave Hunter with a black eye. That meant Gage had used his fists before. It made Hunter like him more. He'd thought Gage was no more than a preppy frat boy who sailed a lot. Apparently, since he'd also made the Olympic shooting team, he was more than Hunter realized. A mistake Hunter realized he made with more than one member of the Bell family.

Gage stalked up to Hunter, stopping just inches from him, and glared right into Hunter's eyes. Damn, preppy boy wasn't backing down. Respect. "I've wanted to do that for so long."

"Good punch. I deserved it."

"I want a fight, but you're not going to give it to me, are you?" Gage asked, studying Hunter's face intently.

"Sorry. I won't fight you."

Gage cursed in a most ungentlemanly way. "After what happened tonight, I need a good fight. But, I guess since you're not giving me one, that means you actually do like her, don't you?"

Hunter didn't react. He'd trained for years not to react to interrogations.

"Of course he does. He just didn't give himself permission to until he looked her up and discovered he's been a big ol' cun—"

"Miss Mitzi!" Gage said, trying not to laugh at the old woman walking her cat on a leash down Main Street at night.

"Well, I won't insult Miss Priss here by calling Hunter a pussy," Miss Mitzi said with a shrug before walking by them. Miss Priss gave Hunter some serious side-eye, then sashayed her furry butt by him as if he were a piece of crap.

Gage snickered. "Even the cat hates you."

"Yeah, I'm getting the impression no one here likes me very much."

Gage glared at him again. "Don't you dare make this about you. Everyone loves you, even when you treated my sister like trash. And just like that asshole tonight."

"What asshole?" Hunter instantly focused on the way Gage was still fisting his fingers in anger.

"None of your business. I'm tired of men hurting my sister. You included."

"I never meant to treat her badly, Gage. I've been burned more than once by women who resemble your sister, so I was a jerk to her to protect myself. It's not right and I'm sorry. It also made me mad that I couldn't stop thinking of her and wanting her." Hunter ran his hand over his hair and took a deep breath. "Gage, I need your help."

"Unbelievable. I'm warning you off my sister and you want my help?"

"You'd only be here to warn me off her if she likes me. Give me a chance. I'll prove I'm not that jerk, but actually a good guy."

"Hunter, I know you're a good guy. You're great with the kids in town. You're great with the town elders too. You worked with Mr. Gann and Mr. Knoll, along with Damon to increase the speed of their scooters. You're nice to everyone and well respected. I just don't think you're a good guy for my sister, so back off or I'll shoot you myself."

Gage began to walk away, but Hunter stopped him. "Isn't that up to your sister?"

Gage turned around and looked him right in the eye. "Maggie is going to shoot at the Olympics in less than a month. Her focus needs to be on training, not on you. If you like her, you need to let her go so she can achieve something she's been working toward her whole life. Goodnight, Hunter."

"He's not wrong," Damon said from where he was leaning against the wall of the bar. "He's not right either."

"What does that mean?" Hunter asked, tired of everyone thinking they knew his relationship better than he did.

"It means you have one shot at making this right. Hit a bullseye or walk off the field."

Hunter groaned as Damon headed for his motorcycle. "Stop with the shooting analogies."

"Don't come out with your guns blazing, but make sure to take your best shot now that you've decided to pull the trigger," Damon called out with a little chuckle before throwing his leg over his motorcycle. "Make sure you are on target and your plan is bulletproof so you don't shoot blanks since it's a long shot she'll forgive you." He revved the engine and drove off, leaving Hunter staring after him with more pressure than he'd had last night with a gun to his head. He had to find a way to tell Maggie he was wrong and he was sorry. As Gage suggested, he could not screw up her chances at Olympic gold.

∼

Maggie spent the night in and out of sleep. Last night her parents had really made her think. What did she want? Did she want to give Hunter a chance or should she just move on? Yes, she liked him. Yes, she also was mad at him. Then she'd tried that horrible date to see if she could move on from Hunter. She knew one thing from the disaster of tonight—Hunter Townsend would never force himself on a woman.

Then there were the text messages and the videos she'd been sent of Gage punching Hunter right in the face in front of the whole town. Her initial reaction was to be mad at Gage and worried about Hunter. But then she really watched the videos. Hunter knew the punch was coming. He could have stopped it at any time. He could have easily killed her brother. He didn't even flinch when he was punched. He took it without a fight. Why?

Maggie had asked her brother when he'd come home, but he grumbled something about Miss Mitzi, respect, "that damn man," and went to bed.

As much as Maggie wanted to overthink it, she didn't have the time to do so. She needed Charles out of her mind. She needed Hunter out of her mind. She needed to practice. Her life's goal was a month away and no man was going to stop her from giving it her all.

Maggie showered, thinking of what Hunter's hands would look like on her body, and then dressed for practice. With an evil smile, Maggie picked her outfit.

Her father cleared his throat. Her mother smothered a smile. Gage cursed and stormed from the room. Perfect. She was ready for the day.

Maggie grabbed some of her mother's famous bacon, egg, and cheese biscuits she made for guests of the B&B and wrapped them up in a basket along with a thermos of freshly brewed coffee. She'd drop them off and check on Landry on the way to the shooting range in town she used when it was too windy outside for air rifle.

Maggie lowered the windows of her truck and sang country music at the top of her lungs on the drive to Charleston. Maggie pulled into downtown Charleston and noticed a car had been following her for several miles. Maybe it was a girl thing, but she instantly became suspicious. Was it Charles? Women were trained from a young age to be aware. It was sad that they had to be, but mothers always pulled their daughters aside and told them to be aware, follow their gut, and fight if you have to—be it words or fists. Just like last night.

Maggie followed her gut and turned before the hospital. The car with tinted windows turned with her. Maggie pulled over and parked. The car parked several spots behind her. Maggie's heart began to race as she opened the door and headed into the candy shop that she'd parked in front of. She pretended to look at the display but took a picture of the car that had been following her. She texted it to Granger and within ten seconds Granger had told her to stay put.

Maggie pretended to look around the shop and ended up getting some chocolate for Lydia and the children. Maggie was paying when she saw Peter Castle and Paxton Kendry approach the car with their guns drawn.

Maggie headed to the door, no longer caring that she was staring. Peter had a gun aimed at the driver's side door, the window of which slowly lowered.

"FBI. Hands up," Peter called out.

"Just give us the soldier and what he took and no one has to get hurt," the man said in stilted English.

"You're with Borisenko, aren't you?" Peter asked.

Before Maggie could comprehend what was happening, Peter shouted, "Gun!" Then he and Paxton were firing their guns. It happened so fast that there was no chance for the man to confirm or deny he was with Borisenko's private army.

The people in the candy shop screamed, but Maggie began to move. She went straight to her truck, unlocked the safe, and pulled out her shotgun even as an unnatural silence seemed to surround her in the middle of downtown Charleston.

Peter and Paxton nodded to each other and, as one,

opened both front doors. Maggie took up position by her truck, aiming her shotgun at the car to cover them. Peter and Paxton lowered their guns. Paxton pulled out his phone as people began to scream or record the aftermath of the shooting.

"Maggie, are you okay?" Peter called out after pulling a handgun from the dead man's hand.

"I'm good. Are you?" Maggie asked, finally lowering her weapon.

"Yeah, we have to call it in." Peter took a picture and then sent a text as the sound of sirens surrounded them. Peter hurried over to Maggie. "Get out of here. I don't want you involved," Peter whispered as he saw more cell phones recording. "Get to Landry. We need to move him. They're looking for him and we need to move him someplace they'll never find him."

~

Hunter took way too long at the shop, finding the exact perfect gift for Maggie. Well, the initial part was easy. It was the second part that was harder. Rows and rows of colorful fabrics to choose from. Then the thread color and the font he had to pick. He had to remember back to all the things he'd seen and pick the best one for Maggie.

"Are you sure you want to wait? This will take a while," the woman said, looking at the first part of the gift and then back to him.

"Do you have any questions? I'm sure this is new for you," Hunter asked the shop owner.

The grandmotherly woman looked as if she'd been insulted. "Honey, I do at least twenty of these a year."

"Really?" Hunter was surprised. He'd never known anyone with this. He thought he'd been original.

"Oh, sugar. Why do you think they gave you my name when you bought this?"

Hunter frowned. "I didn't think about that. Great. When can I pick it up?"

"For a rush fee, I can get it done by the end of the day."

"Done. Thanks so much." Hunter was walking out of the shop in Charleston when he got a text.

He pulled up his phone and saw it was from Peter. He didn't have time to frown when he finished reading what had happened to Maggie. He was already racing full speed to his truck parked down the street. He had to get to the hospital and fast.

Hunter put his phone on speaker as he navigated the old streets of downtown Charleston and called Maggie. "Hunter," she cried out desperately when she answered on the first ring.

The feeling Hunter got when he was about to be ambushed crawled up his spine. "What's the matter, Mags?"

"I think someone is at the hospital looking for Landry. I walked into the lobby and this man was talking to information. I heard him asking for his brother who had been injured overseas and flown in recently. He gave enough information that I don't know if the woman will give him the room number. I'm running up the stairs now to move him."

"I'm almost there, sweetheart. Are you armed?"

"No. I can't bring any weapons into a hospital. Everything's all locked up in my truck."

"Then move Landry and hide. Blythe will be there. She'll be armed. Find something to protect yourself with, just in case. I'm texting Peter now." Hunter floored his car, sent the text, and listened as Maggie sprinted up the stairwell of the hospital right as he tore into the parking garage.

"I'm on the floor," Maggie said, her voice slightly winded, but she was still very much in control. "Blythe! We need to move Landry. Someone is in the lobby looking for him. Hunter, I'm putting you in my pocket so I can help move him."

"I'm coming for you."

"I know you are. Hurry."

Hunter slammed on the brakes and slid to a stop by the parking garage stairwell. Hunter grabbed his gun and took the stairs two at a time, but then stopped when he reached Landry's floor. He tucked his sidearm into the back of his waistband, took a deep breath, and strode out of the door as if nothing was happening.

"I'm sorry, I can't help you, sir." Jen stood rigid behind the nurse's desk. A man who was clearly not from the area stood with his back to Hunter.

Jen's eyes moved toward Hunter's with relief. That is, until the man turned to look at Hunter. Recognition hit them both at the same time.

"Hunter Townsend," the man said with a South American accent.

"Pablo Soliz. You're a long way from Bolivia. Last time I saw you, you were personal security for the president."

"That was two coups ago." Pablo shrugged.

They were in a standoff, neither of them daring to break eye contact. Hunter knew the former soldier was probably armed like Hunter was. They were slowly inching closer together as they circled each other. Hunter moved to protect Jen, but then Jen screamed as Pablo launched himself at Hunter. They both realized they didn't have enough time and were too close together to grab their guns, so instead, they went hand to hand.

Hunter was ready for it. He met Pablo fist for fist. He heard Jen rush off screaming for security but was too focused on the fight in front of him to care about that.

Punch for punch, they dissolved into a fight that was so fast and furious it probably would have been hard to see the moves they were making. It took ten seconds or so, which felt like a lifetime, but Hunter felt the rhythm of the fight. All fights had rhythm—it was a dance. All fighters had it in their favorite combinations of hits. Jab, jab, cross. Cross, jab, hook, sweep. It didn't matter. Everyone had one. The best fighters knew when to change it up, which was exactly what Hunter did. When he would have gone for a kidney shot, he throat-punched Pablo, sending him to his knees, gasping for breath.

Knowing Hunter now had the advantage, Pablo did the only thing he could. He reached for his weapon. Hunter lifted his booted foot and slammed it into Pablo's chest, sending him flying backward as Hunter grabbed his own gun.

Although, he didn't have to use it. A vision of long legs in the shortest, pinkest shorts he'd ever seen smashed a stainless-steel bedpan over Pablo's head. The man's eyes rolled back and he was out cold.

"What are you doing, Mags? You could have been hurt!" Hunter tried not to scream as he grabbed Pablo's gun and stuffed it into his waistband.

Maggie shrugged one bare shoulder. The thin strap of her barely-there white camisole had slid down her arm during the head bashing. "You were losing. I made sure you won."

The sound of sirens and men rushing up the stairwell

could be heard as Hunter stared at Maggie. Her pearls were delicate looking, but the hand on her hip showed she was ready to give it as good as she got.

"I was not losing. I was learning his combinations so that I could make my move, which I did when you got here."

"He was pulling a gun, Hunter. You didn't have one. I couldn't let him hurt you." Hunter held up his left hand and wiggled it in the air. Her eyes went to the gun he had there. Her eyes widened in surprise and a cute blush stained her cheeks. "Oh. You're a lefty."

"That I am." Hunter put his gun away and felt bad when he saw the disappointment on Maggie's face. She'd wanted to save him. Again. "But thank you for having my back. I would have shot him. Thanks to your quick action, we can question him."

Maggie's face lit up. "Really?"

"Really. You did well. I was only upset because I was worried about you. I hate the thought of you in danger."

"You do?" Maggie asked with a shy smile.

"Yeah. I never want someone I care about in danger."

Maggie blushed further and Hunter loved it until his eyes narrowed in on the red angry mark on her wrist. "Maggie, who did that to you?" Hunter growled.

"Drop the bedpan!"

Hunter turned to see Charleston police filling the hall with their guns aimed at Maggie. Maggie dropped the bedpan with a rattling *clunk* on the industrial tile flooring.

Hunter raised his hand, showing them the gun before leaning over and setting it on the nurse's station. Handcuffs were pulled out, officers were shouting "hands," and a tired looking, rumpled man in a suit walked forward as if he were suffering daily from his job. "Dammit. Another one. Miss Bell, I see your problem is here."

"Another one, sir?" one of the officers asked.

"A Townsend. I don't even need to check his ID. Ladies and gentlemen, meet one of Olivia Townsend's brothers. I'm guessing Hunter. Do everything by the book so I don't have to put up with her in court. Unless Miss Bell wants him beaten. Then we can do that."

Hunter grinned at that. He loved how his sister could make grown men shake in their boots. He also liked that the man seemed to be protecting Maggie, but why was he protecting her from him?

"Wait, you can't arrest him!" Maggie cried out as Hunter held out his hands to be cuffed. "He's innocent."

The cops snickered, but then they raised their weapons again when Jen burst out of Landry's room with Blythe and Lydia. "Don't you dare put them in cuffs!" Lydia yelled as she charged forward.

"They saved us," Jen said. "Pull security cameras. While we wait, I'll call my best friend, Mrs. Faulkner. I believe Olivia Townsend is her husband Ryker's attorney. Maybe they need to be down here for this."

"Are you trying to intimidate me, ma'am?" the rumpled man asked.

"Is it working?" Jen barked.

The man didn't answer but let out a long, agonizing sigh. "Okay then. Let's start at the beginning. I'm Detective Chambers. What happened here?"

Hunter was quiet as Jen, Blythe, and Lydia filled them in. Maggie tried to speak, but Hunter gave her a small shake of the head and she closed her mouth. If there was anything Hunter had learned from his shark of a lawyer sister, it was to keep your mouth shut until your attorney arrived. Hunter glanced at the clock. Considering Olivia was in a meeting with Ryker in his Charleston office this morning, he bet she'd be here in less than five minutes.

It only took three minutes.

Police scattered and suddenly became very interested in their shoes when Olivia Townsend-Fox stepped from the elevator. The first spiked heel hadn't even hit the floor when Detective Chambers cursed under his breath.

"I'm honored. I feel the same, detective. I've missed you."

Hunter crossed his arms over his chest and moved to stand by Maggie. "Watch this," he whispered.

Olivia smiled and the detective might have shed a tear as Olivia informed him that Hunter Townsend and Maggie Bell had just saved a war hero from a terrorist. Then the elevator opened and Peter Castle hurried out. He further crushed poor Detective Chamber's day by announcing this was an FBI investigation in coordination with the US Military.

"I'm sorry it's taken me so long to tell you," Hunter said, smiling down at Maggie, "that you look beautiful today. And the force with which you knocked Pablo out was very sexy. But we need to talk about your wrist."

"Okay, you two. Go check on Landry. I'll be there shortly," Olivia announced as she and Peter helped wrap up the police investigation. Peter's team was surrounding Pablo, cuffing him, and administering first aid. They snapped an ampule of smelling salts under his nose and Pablo's eyes flew open. He cursed and then closed his eyes again as if that would make all his problems go away.

11

Hunter was flirting with her, right? She couldn't quite believe it when she heard it, but he told her she was beautiful. And he'd said he cared about her and wanted to protect her. Holy vapors. She suddenly understood why Southern women used to carry fans. She was practically panting with the desire to swoon right into his arms. His very buff, muscular arms.

No. Maggie stood up straight, giving herself a mental pep talk. A few pretty words weren't going to make her forget he'd been a jerk to her. Then there was heat on her lower back. Maggie glanced to her side to see that Hunter had put his hand on the small of her back and was walking slightly behind her toward Landry's room.

"Why are you touching me?"

Hunter glanced at her and she realized he'd been looking around the hall and not at her. "I'm sorry. I was protecting you in case Pablo wasn't alone. That way, I could get between you and the threat."

Hunter didn't drop his hand, but he removed the small

amount of pressure he'd been exerting. Maggie felt the loss of that pressure like a wrecking ball taking down a building.

"No, it's okay. Thank you for looking out for me. I never thought of a second attacker."

Hunter again let his hand rest on her back then, heavier than before. Heat raced up her spine and down her spine straight to her . . .

"Maggie? Are you okay?" Lydia asked. "Your face is all flushed."

Hunter's thumb began to stroke her skin at the top of her shorts, right below her camisole. Maggie shivered. It wasn't on purpose. It was because Hunter made her whole body hyper-aware of his touch.

"Oh dear. Your flush has moved to your chest." Lydia seemed concerned, but Blythe seemed to pick up on what was going on and was trying to hide her smile. "Should we call Jen?" Lydia asked.

Maggie refused to be embarrassed, and when Hunter chuckled under his breath at Lydia's words, Maggie decided two could play this game. She'd never backed down from their war of words. She wasn't going to now over this.

Instead, she turned toward Hunter, causing his hand to skim along her waist. "I'm okay, Lydia," she said as she met Hunter's eyes. She leaned forward, placing her hand on his chest, and used her nails to press into way more muscle than she'd ever felt on a man before. Hunter stopped breathing. He stopped laughing. His jaw tightened. His fingers flexed into her hip. "I was just so overwhelmed by having to save Hunter's ass, *again*, that I needed a moment to compose myself."

Then she looked up at Hunter, ran her tongue seductively over her lips, and leaned forward enough that her breasts brushed against his chest. "Poor guy. He's so shaken up he can't even talk," she said, noticing her voice had a breathlessness to it. This might be tormenting Hunter, but she was also tormenting herself.

"Yes," Hunter said, keeping his eyes locked with hers. "Magnum has once again proven herself to be bedpan-worthy."

Maggie snorted and Hunter smiled down at her. Then, neither was smiling because they realized their lips were a breath away from touching. Neither moved. She wasn't sure who was leaning closer, but they were leaning into each other. Her breasts were pushing against his chest. His hand was sliding around her waist.

"Okay, make room," Olivia said as she came to stand beside them. "Or I'll have to pay you for the show you're about to put on."

Maggie jumped back, but Hunter's hand didn't let her move too far away from him. Instead, he kept his hand on Maggie's hip as she turned to face the room. His hand on her felt nice—real nice.

Peter followed Olivia into the room and looked at Lydia. "I'm sorry. We need to move your husband again. I'm not sure where he's safe. I'm sure my friends in Keeneston, Kentucky would take great care of him."

Hunter nodded. "They would, Lydia. I spent some time there recently for a training exercise and they are definitely prepared to protect Landry."

"No. I'm not leaving him," Lydia said, gripping Landry's hand.

"Home."

The word croaked out and it took Maggie a moment to realize where it came from.

"Landry!" Lydia gasped.

Maggie rushed forward along with everyone else except Hunter, who ran into the hall and yelled for Jen to get the doctor. Then he was back and Maggie felt his steadying hand on her shoulder as he watched quietly from behind her.

Lydia was running her hands over Landry's face, fighting back tears. "Landry, open your eyes for me. Please. I'm here, honey. I'm here."

Jen and the doctor rushed in right as Landry's eyes fluttered open. They didn't try to move Lydia, but instead headed around to the other side of the bed to administer their exam.

"Water," Landry croaked out.

"I'll get it," Blythe said, moving quickly away.

"Where am I?" Landry asked, looking around before his eyes stopped and bore into Hunter's.

"You're in Charleston, honey," Lydia said as silent, happy tears ran down her cheeks. Maggie noticed how Landry hadn't looked away from Hunter.

"You," Landry croaked out, his voice rough and thready from the lack of use, "saved me. How's my team?"

Maggie's own emotions got a hold of her at the look of gratitude in Landry's eyes, combined with the way she felt Hunter stiffen behind her. His fingers tightened on her shoulder in a move he probably didn't realize he was doing. But Maggie noticed. It was the feeling of heartache from a man who would never admit it.

"I know I told you during the rescue, but I'm Olivia's brother, Hunter Townsend. You lost four teammates," Hunter said before listing their names. "Their families have been notified and I had them attach a letter of condolences from you. I hope you don't mind, but I gave permission for your name to be signed to it. I know I would want that if I were in your situation."

Blythe quietly walked to the bedside and put the straw to Landry's lips. He sipped and sighed as if it were the best thing he'd ever tasted.

"The rest of your team is on leave and with their families after debriefing," Hunter said, continuing what sounded like a very succinct military report. "We snuck you out of the country on a private jet. However, whoever was responsible for that ambush found me in Shadows Landing and just now tried to get to your hospital room. I don't know what they want because, so far, the men who are after us are from a mix of groups and countries. Which leads me to tell you we need to move you again for your safety."

"Move him to my guest house," Ryker's voice said from the doorway.

Maggie gasped in surprise, but Hunter hadn't reacted. He'd probably heard him while she'd been so engrossed in the report.

"No," Landry said, his voice sounding a little stronger. "Too dangerous."

"They won't look for you there, Landry. There's room for your whole family to stay and Blythe, who is private security. I won't change my mind. Move him now." Maggie was startled at the commanding tone Ryker used. She knew he was powerful, but he was always just Ryker back in Shadows Landing. This voice sent the doctor scrambling to order medicine and to get Landry prepared for the move.

"No . . ."

"We can put him in my car," Ryker said, ignoring Landry's protests. "My back windows are tinted."

Landry began to argue, but this time Lydia stopped him. "No, Landry. You're not in charge anymore. I am. You're going to Ryker's where your family and friends can look after you." Landry opened his mouth, but the glare from Lydia made him shut it. "Don't think for one moment that waking up is going to save you from the fact you lied to me about your job for our entire marriage."

"Not all of it. Just the past thirteen years or so," Landry grumbled. Maggie sucked in a breath along with all the women in the room as all the men cringed at the way Lydia's eyes narrowed.

"Let's get this straight," Lydia said, sounding as if she were scolding her children. "I love you with all my heart, but right now I'm so mad at you I could kill you myself. Don't. Push. It. You need to regain your strength so you can grovel like you've never groveled before."

Landry then smiled and winked at his wife. "You're so sexy when you're mad. I look forward to getting on my knees and begging your forgiveness. If I recall, that's how Levi was conceived."

Lydia blushed, but her glare never wavered. She was strong because Maggie would have melted into a puddle of goo if Hunter looked at her like that. The doctor came back in with a bag of medication and handed it to Lydia along with a printout of all the instructions.

"Kenzie is getting the house ready," Ryker said. "Let's move."

Maggie finally moved when Hunter's hand gently nudged her to the side. She stood back as Hunter moved forward to the bedside where Jen was pulling off cords left and right. "Ready?" he asked Jen who nodded as Blythe came back with a wheelchair.

"Sorry," Hunter said to Landry a moment before he

scooped him out of bed as if the man didn't weigh close to two hundred pounds.

"I could have done it myself," Landry protested after Hunter set him gently in the wheelchair. But Maggie didn't believe it. Landry's face had gone white from pain and sweat was covering his brow.

"I know you could have," Hunter said. "But we don't have time right now."

"Follow me," Ryker ordered.

Lydia grabbed the wheelchair and Hunter stepped back. "Blythe, take the lead. I'll take the rear," Hunter said to the bodyguard.

Then their troop hurried from the room.

"Maggie," Jen called out, rushing from the nurses' station with a white plastic bag. "These are his personal effects from Millevia. Nothing much left since they cut off his uniform, but it's all in there."

"Thanks, Jen."

Maggie took the bag and found Hunter watching her.

"What happened to your wrist?" Hunter asked quietly as they walked behind Landry.

"A bad date."

"Who hurt you, Magnum?" He wasn't asking. It was a clear order, but she didn't take orders from him.

"Don't worry. I took care of it with Detective Chamber's help. I'm okay but thank you for your concern. Let's just get Landry to safety."

Maggie got into her truck and looked in her rearview mirror to see Hunter watching her. She felt an intense gaze even thirty feet away with cars between them. The look in his eyes was different. No longer with disdain. They'd reached some kind of understanding. He'd come for her. Or maybe for Landry. Either way, he'd come to save them and she knew he would. Loyalty and bravery were never qualities Hunter lacked. The problem was that Maggie was starting to see a lot more good qualities in Hunter Townsend that were investing her heart in a man who had made it clear he wasn't interested in her.

12

Hunter turned back around and took the stairs two at a time. "Detective Chambers!" he called out as the detective was about to get on the elevator. The man looked annoyed but didn't get on when the doors opened. "What happened to Maggie last night?"

He would have sworn he saw a little smirk on the detective's face before his lips frowned. "Why do you care? From what I hear, you've been a jerk to her."

Why did he care? "Because I was an idiot. I do care about her, and I'll do anything to make it up to her. Something inside me broke, seeing that mark on her wrist. What happened?"

Hunter remained calm on the outside as Detective Chambers told him about Charles Wicksmith. Since his arrest, there had been five more women who came forward to report his assaults. They'd all thought since they'd never had intercourse with Wicksmith, no one would listen to them. Well, Chambers listened and Hunter was listening as well.

"He just bailed out. His first hearing is in two weeks,"

Chambers told him. "Now, don't do anything that will blow the case."

Hunter put his hand to his heart, the picture of innocence. "Me? Never."

Never his ass. Hunter had one stop to make before returning to Shadows Landing. Luckily, Charles's condo was on the way.

Hunter knocked on the door of the modern condo complex. It seemed out of place in a historic town like Charleston.

"Yeah?" Charles asked, sullenly as he opened the door, sounding as if he had marbles in his mouth.

Hunter was going to punch him, but he saw the swollen tongue and the black eye and smiled. "She got you good, huh?"

Charles went to slam the door, but Hunter reached out and held the door, shoving it back and hitting Charles in the face. "We need to have a little chat about how you treat women."

Hunter flexed his hand as he got back into his truck. Maggie had done a good job teaching Charles a lesson. However, Hunter made sure he drove the point home.

Damn. Hunter had never been so wrong about something in his life as he had been about Maggie Bell. The woman was a constant surprise. She shot a man to save him. Not just any shot, it had been a hell of a shot most snipers would have trouble making. Then she'd knocked a man out with a bedpan. She kept her head during a shootout all while looking as if she were in the middle of a garden party and beat up the guy who got handsy with her. The contradiction of that still boggled Hunter's mind as he drove back to Shadows Landing.

Maggie had gotten under his skin the first time they met. He was so mad at the attraction, thinking Maggie was like one of his exes. Now she was under his skin because she was everything he could ever want in a woman. Except for her love of pink. But if it meant he had Maggie in his life and heart, he'd deal with the pink.

Kenzie and Gavin were waiting for him at the guest house. They had worked together to get Landry set up in the first-floor bedroom. Blythe had turned the sitting room next to the bedroom into her room. The kids would need to share rooms upstairs, but Ryker told them he'd already ordered bunk beds that would be delivered within the next half hour. Kenzie told them she'd already stocked the kitchen. Everything was now in place.

The house quieted down as Kenzie called Georgie to have the kids brought over soon. Blythe worked with Ryker to go over the strengths and weaknesses in his security as Gavin finished his exam of Landry and called Lydia over to go over all the details.

Finally, Hunter had a moment alone with Landry. The man looked exhausted and in a lot of pain. "Can you talk for a moment?" Hunter asked.

"Yeah, I have some questions for you."

"And I have some for you," Hunter said, leaning against the door to the bedroom. "What do you remember?"

"I remember only flashes of the past week or so. I remember being shot. The pain of that. I remember fighting someone. I remember waking up to you donating blood to me. That's about it. Who were they and what did they want?"

"I was going to ask you the same questions," Hunter said

with a sigh before sitting down on the chair next to the bed. "Two people have been identified coming after me in order to get to you. Alexey Kotov, who was part of the Borisenko Private Army, found me in Shadows Landing and demanded to turn over what you had given me. He thought you had taken something from them."

Hunter saw the concentration on Landry's face. He was thinking hard and coming up empty. "I don't remember anything that sticks out. I don't even remember talking to anyone. I don't remember anything except fighting someone," Landry finally said.

Hunter had a feeling that's what he'd say, but disappointment hit hard anyway. They still needed to figure it all out. "The man at the hospital was Pablo Soliz. He was personal security to the former Bolivian president."

Landry frowned. "That doesn't make sense. They have nothing in common."

"Exactly. We need to figure out what they think you saw, know, or took to figure out what their move is."

Landry looked exhausted. Pain etched his face and Hunter knew their time was up. "Don't worry about it, Marine. I've got your six. You just focus on getting better."

Hunter heard a car park and then doors opening with lots of excited little voices. Landry heard it too. He smiled and looked over at Hunter. "Help me sit up better so the kids can't see how badly I'm hurt. I don't want to frighten them."

"I think you underestimate what would frighten your kids," Hunter said as he helped Landry sit up and wiped the sweat from his brow.

Landry had a smile on his face and his arms open when the Langston family swarmed the room en masse. The littlest kids leaped on the bed as Lydia scolded them to go easy on their father. Landry Jr., Lacy, Levi, and Leah stood back, giving the littles their time.

"Mr. Hunter," Landry Jr. said seriously.

"Yes?"

"I know you'll tell us the truth. How badly is our dad hurt?"

Hunter looked down at the older half of the Langston children. Their faces were set. Their eyes tense. They'd been fed the lies that Daddy was home and just needed to rest and didn't like the taste of it.

Hunter gave a little nod of his head to indicate that they should follow him out of the room. The four filed out and surrounded him. It was clear they needed to talk and Hunter would reassure them their father was going to be okay.

"No one will tell us the truth," Lacy said, sounding remarkably like her mother had in the hospital room when she'd been angry with Landry for lying to her.

"It's not my place. If your mother—"

Leah crossed her arms and Hunter suddenly felt out of his depth as the ten year old stared him down. "Miss Maggie used to babysit us. I bet she'd love to know what a meanie you are."

"I'm not mean. I can tell you stories and babysit you too," Hunter protested.

The four all wore matching expressions that gave Hunter the chills. He'd walked into an ambush. Leah pulled a cell phone from her pocket and held it up so Hunter could see the home screen as she opened her Contacts list.

"Miss Maggie," Lacy said with fake tears in her eyes, "Mr. Hunter called us stupid little brats." A tear rolled down her cheek as if on command.

Levi's lower lip wobbled. "Mr. Hunter said I was never going to make it in hockey and I should just give up now."

Hunter was being blackmailed.

"Miss Maggie," Leah said, big crocodile tears rolling down her cheeks. "Mr. Hunter said girls shouldn't play with weapons because we're not strong enough or smart enough to know how to use them."

Hunter actually sucked in a breath at that one. He turned to Landry Jr. "Are you part of this too?"

Landry Jr. shrugged. "I heard it all myself and I'll tell Miss Maggie that, too."

"Traitors," Hunter hissed at them. They only batted big, innocent, tear-filled eyes back at him. "Fine. Your father was shot in the line of duty and was unconscious for a week and underwent a long and complicated surgery to recover the bullets and patch him up. He woke up today after Maggie and I stopped two people trying to hurt him. Someone wants what he has, but he doesn't remember what that thing is. He's in danger, which is why he's hiding here. The good news is that it looks as if he'll make a full recovery if your mother doesn't kill him for lying about being a combat Marine for the past decade and not in communications."

Tears evaporated instantaneously as if they were never there. Leah tucked her cell phone with Maggie's name and number on the screen into her back pocket and smiled at him.

"Was that so hard?" Landry Jr. asked, one eyebrow lifted in a remarkably adult expression.

"You all could make the CIA break," Hunter muttered.

They all grinned in return as their mother poked her head out of the bedroom. "What's going on out here? Aren't you going to say hi to your dad?"

Lacy smiled so sweetly that Hunter had whiplash. "Yes,

Mom. We just wanted to thank Mr. Hunter for helping take care of Dad while we gave the littles some time with him." Lacy beamed up at him. "Thanks again, Mr. Hunter. You're the best."

Hunter was left standing in the hall feeling very unsure about himself and what, exactly, had just happened. That's when his phone rang.

"Hello?"

"Hello, Mr. Townsend. I got your rush order done. You can pick it up anytime."

His gift for Maggie was ready. It was time to make his mistake right. It was time to apologize properly and hope that Maggie would fully forgive him.

～

Hunter pulled into Bell Landing and drove the long tree-lined lane to the old brick plantation style house that sat near the river running along one side of Shadows Landing leading to Charleston and the Atlantic Ocean. The house was beautiful, but right now it was hostile territory. Especially when Gage opened the door and glared at him. It was considerably easier for Hunter to face combatants than the family of the woman he wanted to date. He was not on familiar ground here.

Hunter got out of the truck, reached into the truck bed, and grabbed the gift. He squared his shoulders and marched up the brick steps to where the Bell family had gathered, minus Maggie.

"Hello Mr. and Mrs. Bell. I'm here to see Maggie."

Mrs. Bell smiled. No one else did. "Come in, Hunter."

It sounded like an invitation, but it was an order.

Hunter followed them inside to a sitting room to the

right of the front door. It screamed modern antiques. The house had been modernized and updated to the latest interior design trends, but the woodwork in the house was original and several antiques sat on display or hung on the walls. There he found Revered Winston sitting with Melinda, the pastor in training. They were drinking iced tea and looked surprised to see Hunter joining them.

"Sir. Ma'am," Hunter said to them. They smiled back until they saw Gage's glare.

"What do you want?" Gage asked.

"Gage," his mother chided. "That is not how we treat a guest in our house. Even if he's been a dickhead to your sister."

It took a good ten seconds for Hunter to realize Mrs. Bell had just insulted him since she did so with such a sweet voice and kind smile.

"What's that?" Mr. Bell asked, nodding to what Hunter was carrying.

"It's a gift for Maggie, sir. To apologize for being such a . . . dickhead."

Mr. Bell and Gage didn't seem pleased. Mrs. Bell smiled sweetly.

"Is that what I think it is?" she asked as she reached down and turned it around. "Oh, Hunter." She put her hand to her chest and smiled. "You might actually get her to forgive you with a gift like this. It's very sweet and very Maggie. Isn't it, dear?"

Hunter had a feeling he might have won Maggie's mom over, and with the reluctant agreement from Mr. Bell, Hunter was feeling a little more optimistic.

"Why do you think Maggie should even forgive you? And why now? You finally saw she was an Olympic shooter and suddenly you're in love?" Gage crossed his arms and called him out without batting an eye. Pretty impressive for a man with tiny red sailboats embroidered on his shorts.

This is where Hunter would rather face enemy fire. He cleared his throat to buy him some time. He glanced at Reverend Winston and Melinda and saw them give him an encouraging nod. "I mistook Maggie for the type of woman I'd dated before, which hadn't ever ended well. I want to apologize for that because, as everyone has been telling me, she's nothing like that."

"And what kind of women were they?" Mrs. Bell asked.

Hunter cleared his throat again. "High maintenance, ma'am." She raised her brow but stayed silent. "The kind that liked the idea of being with a military man but not the military tours and the duties that came along with it. I thought a woman was beautiful, smart, kind, and into me, but the moment I had to skip a date because I was called up or when I couldn't tell her if I'd be back for the gala she wanted to go to, I was not supportive of her career or life. I was either cheated on or dumped by text."

"And you thought our Maggie was like that?" Mr. Bell asked with a bite to his voice.

"I'm sorry to say that I did, sir. She's beautiful, smart, and so bubbly that while I instantly wanted to get to know her, I put up a wall instead. I couldn't go through the disappointment and pain again."

"Hunter," Reverend Winston said, getting Hunter's attention, "did you know that every time you leave for a mission, Maggie comes to church and lights a candle for you? She comes and does it every day until you come home. That doesn't sound like someone who isn't supportive."

"She also wields a sword very well. I don't see her being the type to fear walking into a gala alone if you can't make it," Melinda added. "I'm new here, but that's the impression I've gotten of her."

"Hunter," Mr. Bell said, pulling his thoughts from that revelation that she thought of him while he was gone. "Walk with me."

Hunter got up, nodded to the room, and left, following Maggie's dad. "Yes, sir?"

"I see your knuckles are red."

"I had to see a man about how he treats women."

Mr. Bell's jaw tightened and then he gave a nod, dismissing it. "It occurred to me that you haven't seen our house before. You're new to Shadows Landing, so you might not know the history of it. See, there has been a Bell here since before the town's founding. This house started as a log cabin." They walked into an old library and there on the wall was a sketch of a log cabin and next to that a sketch of a woman. Mr. Clark stopped in front of it. "That's Mary Bell. She'd lived here in frontier days and knew how to defend herself. When the pirates settled Shadows Landing, Mary's husband, Josiah, joined them on their raids. Mary helped start the church's women's group with the first pirate reverend and retired pirates to teach them how to fight. When the wives of the pirates were left alone, Mary was one of the women who supported them being armed."

Mr. Clark stepped forward showing Hunter a portrait. "This is their son and his wife. She's the daughter of a pirate. They took the money from raiding and began to build this house. Here's how it progressed."

Hunter looked at paintings of each stage of the house. It was impressive for sure. "They further invested money in industries, which was smart. It led to long-term stability after the golden age of piracy was over. Then there was the Revolutionary War. These are the Bells who served." Oil paintings of three men hung on the wall along with an antique rifle in a display case on a table under the paintings. "While the men were away fighting, the women turned Bell Landing into a hospital. They tended wounded soldiers, defended their property, and spied for General Nathanael Greene, aiding in actions that led to the British being surrounded in Charles Town."

Hunter looked at letters that were framed giving information on the movements of the British. Military history was his passion and he could get lost in this room reading all the books and artifacts.

"Then came the Civil War, World War I, World War II, Korea, and Vietnam," Mr. Bell said, pointing to various paintings and then photographs of Bells through the centuries.

"Is that you?" Hunter asked at the last picture on the wall.

"It is. I was a pilot for the South Carolina Air National Guard."

Hunter turned to the last wall as Mr. Bell talked about his time in the National Guard. There was a side profile picture of a girl, around six years old, with her strawberry blonde hair up in pigtails, wearing a pink tutu, cowboy boots, and aiming a youth rifle. In the second half of the photo was Gage aiming a more advanced youth rifle. The photo brought a smile instantly to his face. Maggie's little face was so focused on the target and, like her, at complete odds with her outfit.

"Magnum wanted to try anything her brother did and do it better. She's all sugar and sweetness until there's competition involved. Then she's utterly merciless. Don't let the pink fool you. She'll take you down with a smile."

"I'm beginning to see that." Hunter looked over the wall

of family photographs. Family vacations, shooting competitions, and graduations.

"Gage graduated with honors, so Magnum had to as well. She worked her ass off and finished in the top ten of her class. While Gage went on to graduate school, Magnum decided to come home. Running events here at the bed and breakfast had always been her dream. Not just run it but take it to the next level. You should see the parties she plans and the companies she works with for events. She has a real talent. The CEO of a huge medical company pursued her strongly."

That got Hunter's attention. "What happened?"

Mr. Bell turned and looked him straight in the eye. "She met a soldier at a wedding."

It was like a punch to his heart. Maggie had waited for him to smarten up and thank goodness she had because the protective alpha instinct to grab Maggie and carry her to his house was surprisingly strong for someone who could control every emotion.

"Sir." Hunter stood straight with his hands clasped behind his back. "I know I don't deserve it, and I know it's all Maggie's choice, but I'd like to ask permission to date your daughter."

It was the longest thirty seconds of Hunter's life as Mr. Bell stared at him as if he could see clear through to Hunter's soul. "You'll find Magnum at the outdoor shooting range. It's at the back of the property. She's practicing for the Olympics. She leaves in two weeks. Good luck, son. You'll need it. Oh, and if you distract her from her goal of gold, I'll let Gage kill you like he wants. Mean Abe will snap up any body parts thrown to him."

"I'd never get in the way of her goals, sir." No way. There was nothing Hunter wanted to see more than Maggie standing on the podium at the Olympics as the national anthem played. Suddenly her goals became his and he'd do everything he could to make sure she achieved them.

In the back of his mind, Hunter heard Damon chuckling that he'd been right and Hunter didn't care. He finally understood what Granger and Stone had been talking about when they talked about falling in love. He was on a mission to win Maggie's heart and Hunter Townsend had never failed on a mission in his life.

13

It might not look like it, but Maggie was sweating. It took a lot of strength to hold a nine-pound shotgun for as long as she did. Landry was safe. He was reunited with his family and now it was a case for the FBI. No matter how much she wanted to stay and be near Hunter, she had goals of her own to pursue. No man, no matter how hot he was or how kind he was, was going to stand in her way of accomplishing it.

Maggie had learned a long time ago that men expected certain things from her. Yes, she liked to wear pearls and cute dresses and sip fruity drinks. No, that didn't mean she wanted to earn her Mrs. degree in college. She had plans. Goals. Dreams. The right man would support them, not dismiss them or tell her they were silly.

Maggie set the app on her phone that controlled the trap machine. She let all thoughts of men fall from her mind as she focused on her training.

The muted sound of clapping drew her from her focus after she completed a set of clays. Maggie pulled the earplugs from her ears and turned, expecting to see her father.

"Hunter," she said with surprise. Damn, he looked good. He was in thigh-hugging jeans and a tight black athletic T-shirt with ARMY written across the front in dark charcoal gray. "What are you doing here?"

"Let's talk later. How about we shoot now?"

Maggie smiled. Her heart began to race. "You mean, like a competition between us?"

Maggie was close to turning to goo when Hunter returned her smile. If this was what it was like to be the center of Hunter's attention, she might not survive.

"Yes, like a competition. Do you have an extra shotgun I can use?"

"Shotgun might not be fair. Want to use a rifle instead?"

"Minx. You'll kick my ass either way. At least let me pretend to blame it on my lack of experience with the shotgun."

Her breath came in fast and shallow. He complimented her and he didn't seem upset about it. She didn't know many men who could handle being beaten by her. This was a real test and for the first time, Maggie realized Hunter might actually pass it.

"Here you go. You can use mine." Maggie said, handing her pink shotgun to Hunter with a smirk. "I'll use my backup."

Maggie handed him her shotgun and then went to her truck and unlocked the gun safe, pulling out her backup.

"So, how do we do this?" Hunter asked, inspecting the weapon like a pro.

"That shotgun is a 12 gauge semi-automatic so we load three shells each round. I'll set a duel shot on the clays. We'll alternate three shots each. We'll do that for three cycles. Guests first." Maggie handed him the shotgun shells and pointed to the field. "Ready?"

She got a little nervous when Hunter loaded the gun easily. The nerves turned into pure lust at the sight of him lifting her gun to his shoulder and taking his stance. His jeans should be illegal. The way his ass filled them out and the way his package . . .

"Pull."

Oh, yeah. Competition. Maggie pressed the button in the app and then assumed her position. The first round was on the easy setting. The second round would be hard. The third would be elite. Hunter shot the clays down handily. Maggie barely looked and got her three.

In the second round, Hunter clipped the last clay. It counted, but barely. She got her three easily.

Hunter looked serious as he focused on the field. He got the first one, barely got the second, and missed the third. Maggie didn't have time to worry about his ego as her first clay went flying. She hit all three and prepared to see his reaction.

Maggie ejected her last shell, put the safety on her gun, and then set it on the table before looking at Hunter. Instead of the scowl she expected, he was grinning.

"You're going to win gold."

That was the sexiest thing Hunter could say to her. "I hope so. Trap is in my blood. Air rifle has been a little harder."

"Yet you're ranked number one."

"Still not as comfortably as I'd like."

She watched as Hunter secured his gun and set it on the table next to hers. "What happened to your hand?" His knuckles were red as he secured his weapon.

"Just a discussion with someone."

"Discussions involve words, not fists."

"This one didn't. So, do you want some help with the rifle?"

"Really?" Maggie asked.

"Yeah. I don't know how much I can really do, considering it's an air rifle and not a military rifle. But why don't you show me? I like to see you shoot anyway. You're beautiful when you do. Your focus is unlike anything I've ever seen."

The compliment actually made her feel shy. "Thank you. I'd like your opinion."

"Then you can give me some tips. My shotgun aiming could use some work."

Maggie smiled and rattled off all the tips she had. She'd already cataloged them. She didn't think Hunter would ask. Instead of playing the dumb female, Maggie told him how it was. To her surprise, he listened, asked questions, and then thanked her.

Thirty minutes later, Maggie's whole worldview had changed. Well, at least in terms of rifle shooting. She had to give Hunter credit. He was a damn good technical teacher. She might, well, she *did* outshoot him, but he saw things even her coach missed.

Maggie sat back and stared at the target. It looked as if two, maybe three, holes appeared on the paper. It certainly didn't match the thirty or more shots she'd fired. "I've never been so consistent. Thank you, Hunter. You just got me an Olympic medal."

Hunter smiled but shook his head. "Nah, that was all you. But I do want to give you something. To say I'm sorry for being such an ass."

"You don't have to do that. Well, okay, maybe you do,"

Maggie laughed as she watched Hunter stride off to his truck.

He reached into the back of his truck and paused. "Close your eyes, Mags. No peeking."

Maggie closed her eyes and heard Hunter walking toward her. She heard him move something in his hands. Most men would give her jewelry or flowers to say sorry. She didn't know why, but she'd be disappointed in Hunter if he went that route.

"Open your eyes." Maggie's heart sped up at the sound of nervousness in his voice. It was sweet and whatever he did it was clear he put thought into it.

Maggie opened her eyes and blinked. Her hand went to her mouth as she stared. "Oh, Hunter."

Hunter shifted nervously. "Do you like them? I'm sure you have something for the Olympics—"

"I do, but nothing as pretty as these," she said reaching out to trace her name on the quilt covered gun cases. The pink one was for her air rifle and the teal one was for her shotgun. They'd managed to put the bright, happy, cheery fabric over the hard gun carrying cases. The pink one was covered in pale white paisley with the Olympic rings right in the middle of the case and her name in purple script beneath it. The teal one also had the matching pale white paisley print, the Olympic rings, and her name in purple script.

They were perfect. "Oh my gosh, Hunter. These cases are top of the line. I've never seen them available to the public before."

"They're not available to the general public, but I pulled some military favors. The metal is thin and light but more durable than any plastic case and completely bulletproof."

Hunter looked so proud and he should be. This was the

most perfect gift any man had ever given her. "They're beautiful. I can't wait to use them. Thank you."

Maggie rose up and kissed his cheek. She loved the way he blushed slightly. She hadn't expected that from the rough and tough Hunter. "I thought about jewelry, but it didn't seem like you. I mean, you actually only wear a few family pieces all the time, so I figured you weren't one of those women who had to have stacks of jewelry."

Maggie smiled up at him. How was someone so masculine, so tall, so muscular, able to look so worried over a gift? "You're absolutely right. I love them, Hunter. Thank you."

Hunter returned her smile. "So, good enough for you to forgive me for being a jackass and to give me a chance to start over?"

"Hmm?" Maggie tapped her finger to her chin as if she were thinking about it. "I was really hoping for some groveling."

She could see the conflict race across his face. She was teasing him, but then Hunter set down the cases and dropped to his knees. "Magnum Bell, I was a complete ass and judged you before I got to know you. I'm so very sorry. If you forgive me, I'd love to take you out on a date tomorrow night."

Hunter Townsend on his knees before her was a sight to behold. Then he smirked and licked his lips as his eyes scanned her body and heat flooded her face . . . and elsewhere.

"Oh yeah, you look really sorry," she said with a laugh. "But yes, you're forgiven." Maggie held out her hand. "Hi. I'm Maggie Bell."

Hunter took her hand and placed his lips on her knuckles. Her breathing became erratic. How was it possible to be that turned on by a kiss on her hand? But she was. And Hunter knew it.

"Hunter Townsend. I'm looking forward to taking you," he said, then paused as she forgot to breathe at the heat in his eyes, "to dinner."

Maggie smacked his shoulder gently. "It's a good thing you're so good at apologizing or I wouldn't have said yes."

Hunter laughed and stood up, but didn't let go of her one hand. Instead, he ran his thumb over her hand and kept his eyes locked with hers. "I'll pick you up at seven. Should we eat at Kerri's?" he asked of the nice restaurant next to Harper's Bar.

"I would love to. Kerri said she has a new summer menu out and I can't wait to try it." Hunter dropped her hand and Maggie instantly missed it. "Thank you for the apology, Hunter," she said sincerely.

"I'm sorry you ever needed one. I'll make it up to you. I'll see you tomorrow, Mags."

Maggie watched as Hunter drove off. Her heart was doing flips and there was no way she'd be able to keep the smile off her face. A golf cart appeared not long after and Gage pulled up to her. He glanced down at the cases and frowned.

"You forgave him, didn't you?" Gage asked.

"Yes, I did. He asked me out on a date tomorrow night. Are you mad?" Maggie asked. She wouldn't say no based on her brother's opinion, but it would put a damper on it. After all, he'd dated some doozies before after she warned him off them.

Gage's lips thinned. "He's different from the others, you know?"

"I know," Maggie answered seriously.

"I only care if you're happy and so far, he's only made you mad. You're my little sister and I love you."

Maggie leaned into the golf cart and hugged her brother. "I love you too."

"Mom and Dad like him," Gage admitted. That made Maggie smile and Gage roll his eyes. "He better not break your heart."

"It's dinner, not marriage," Maggie said with a laugh. "Now, how about a little shooting? I can't wait to show you what Hunter helped me with."

14

Damon didn't knock when he walked into Hunter's house the following afternoon. Hunter looked up from the kitchen table where he was working to find Damon with his head in the fridge pulling out a sports drink.

"I thought I would find you primping," Damon said, twisting the cap off the bottle.

"Primping?" Hunter asked.

"For your date with Maggie."

"How did you know about that?"

Damon stared at him pityingly and shook his head. "Bro, small town. You make a reservation for two with Kerri, then the way Gage was grumbling about you not breaking his sister's heart when I saw him a little while ago. I put two and two together. I must admit. I'm shocked you didn't eff this up."

"Thanks for having my back, *bro*." Hunter scowled at him.

Damon took a sip and then stared at him. "I did. When I told you over and over again to stop being an ass and to look at what's right in front of you. Maggie's a better person than

I am. I would have punched you in the face and taken your gifts anyway."

Then it dawned on him what Damon had said about primping. Hunter looked at his watch and cursed. "I need to get ready. I was caught up watching the interrogation of Pablo Soliz and lost track of time."

That stopped any dry humor on Damon's part. "What did they find out?"

"Nothing so far," Hunter said, shutting down his computer. "Pablo refused to say anything except he was here visiting a sick friend at the hospital, but the blow to the head made him forget who."

"I'm sure you can find a way to get that information out of him," Damon said as Hunter walked to his bedroom with his brother trailing him.

"Not when he's in FBI custody. Washington, D.C. is freaking out over this. Every agency is demanding to take the lead, but I wouldn't be surprised if Pablo just disappears at the hands of some CIA SOGs or something." Hunter pulled off his shirt and headed to his closet. "Please tell me I don't have to wear dress slacks to Kerri's."

"You do know your date, right? She's going to be in a dress and you think to show up in jeans and an athletic shirt?"

"I was going to wear a polo," Hunter grumbled after being called out by his brother. He didn't wait for a response. He grabbed the black slacks and a dove gray polo that Olivia had gotten him since it matched his eyes.

Damon actually cracked a smile. "I love that she's nothing but bright colors and you have nothing but black, gray, navy blue, and camouflage."

Hunter shrugged. "It'll let her stand out even more."

Damon grinned and pushed off the door he was leaning

against. "I told you she was the one. When you marry her, I expect one hell of a thank-you gift."

"We are not talking about marriage. It's a first date!" Hunter yelled at Damon's retreating back.

～

"Are you excited?" Georgie asked from her seat on the couch in Maggie's bedroom.

Maggie was fighting her hair at her makeup table. She'd opted for very light makeup. Hunter didn't strike her as a man who cared if she had on fake eyelashes or the perfect cat eye.

"I'm more nervous than I've ever been. Excited, yes, but more nervous."

Georgie nodded understandingly. "Because he's different."

"Why does everyone say that?"

"Girl, you stayed single for him, even when he was a jerk. You knew you two were meant to be together just as Kord waited for me to see it. You waited for Hunter. Now the wait is over," Georgie grinned. "I bet he'll kiss you tonight and not just on your mouth."

"Georgie!" Maggie laughed, tossing a blush brush at her.

Georgie caught it and wagged it at her. "One, you've been waiting for this to happen. Two, Hunter doesn't strike me as someone who waits to go after what he wants and he's wanted you since that first night too. We all know it. We've all seen him staring at you. Now that the hurdles are gone, you better hang onto your panties. Or better yet, don't."

"I am not sleeping with Hunter on the first date. He has to earn it. However, he did get down on his knees to ask my forgiveness and his face was so close to *there* that I momentarily forgot how to talk."

"Told you so!" Georgie laughed before getting up and heading to Maggie's closet. "Now, if you really want him to suffer, wear this." Georgie pulled out a mini skirt that flipped and swung easily. It barely covered Maggie's bottom as long as there was no breeze. If there was a breeze . . .

"I'll flash half the town," Maggie said, staring at it.

"Good. Wear a thong and maybe drop something in front of Hunter."

"Georgie!" However, the idea made her very excited. What would he do if she did that?

"And these wedges that lace up your legs," Georgie said, pulling things from her closet and ignoring Maggie's wide eyes. "And this pale pink strappy top."

"What's wrong with this?" Maggie asked, looking down at the sundress she was wearing.

"It's cute, but it's not sexy. Tonight is all about sex. You don't have to have it, but you do have to get a little revenge by reminding Hunter about what he's been missing."

Okay, she couldn't fault Georgie for that logic. It would be a fun way to give him a little payback for all the times she drooled over him.

"I'll just try it on to show you why I can't wear it."

Maggie wore it. She even wore the thong. Her mother would throw a fit, or maybe not. Maggie was surprised by how encouraging her mom was of this date. However, because they had a full house at the B & B, her family was busy when it was time for Hunter to pick her up. Good, she was too old to have her parents meeting her dates at the door.

Instead, Maggie sat on the patio swing and waited for Hunter to arrive.

Hunter pulled up to the house five minutes early. He stepped out of the truck and Maggie's stomach flipped and warmed. He looked yummy. The slacks were tailored to show off all of his . . . assets. The polo, while casual, made his eyes pop while giving him a sexy, dangerous air.

But then he reached into his truck and came out with a bouquet of flowers. Not roses, thank goodness. Just like with jewelry, everyone expected roses as her favorite flowers, but they weren't. Hunter had a bouquet of ranunculus, sweet peas, and gardenias. It was perfect.

Maggie stood up to greet Hunter as he climbed the steps. His eyes ran over her body and he almost stumbled on the last step when a slight breeze made her skirt flutter and showed off even more leg. Okay, so Georgie was right about the outfit for tonight. It made Maggie feel powerful and sexy all at once.

"You look beautiful," Hunter said as he handed her the flowers. "I don't know how I got so lucky for you to say yes to a date."

Goo. She was going to turn into goo.

"Fam!" Timmons called out, walking around the house. "Whoa, Maggie. Your outfit slaps. No cap. Aww, the flowers are dank. Want me to put them in some water?"

"Bet," Hunter answered seamlessly leaving Maggie trying not to laugh. Hearing Gen Z slang from Hunter was so unnatural.

Maggie handed the flowers over to Timmons. "Thank you. I appreciate it."

Hunter held out his arm and Maggie hooked her hand through it as they walked down the steps. She was more nervous than she ever had been before. Everything about this date screamed that it was not just a first date. It was the beginning of something *more*.

"I can't thank you enough for helping me with the air rifle. I showed Gage what you taught me and he was impressed."

"Maybe he won't kill me then if I kiss you goodnight at the end of our date," Hunter said with a smile as he drove toward downtown. "Seriously though, you didn't need much help. You're one of the best shots I've ever seen. I went to Keeneston, where the Faulkners' cousins live, for this super strange and realistic training session. And damn, there were a couple of top-notch shooters there. It's enough to make a man feel inadequate."

The grin on his face told Maggie that Hunter didn't feel inadequate about anything, which was actually really sexy. He could be outshot, out-fought, outsmarted, and he didn't get mad. Instead, he learned from it. Blythe had told her about Hunter asking to be shown moves. He'd also asked for tips from Maggie. He constantly asked Olivia her thoughts on things and to explain anything he didn't know.

Yes, he was still groveling for being an egotistical jerk, but now she saw all sides of him. That ego was to protect his heart and that's the only reason she forgave him. That, and since she had, Hunter had done nothing but prove himself to be the man of her dreams. A kiss to end their date was now all she could think about because Maggie was sure he'd kiss like he walked through life—with complete confidence. No slobbering overeager kisses. No limp lips because they were unsure of themselves. Nope, she bet Hunter's kiss would wreck her for life and she couldn't wait.

15

Hunter pulled out Maggie's chair for her at Kerri's restaurant. Everyone was watching them. He could see looks of approval on women's faces who were judging how well he was trying to prove himself after being the biggest jackass in Shadows Landing.

He hoped he was doing a good job. Vulnerability didn't come naturally to him. In fact, he'd been trained to never be vulnerable. Maggie smiled up to him and he got a good look of cleavage when he looked down and smiled back. She was actively trying to kill him with her outfit tonight. If she wanted revenge, she was getting it in the form of a hard-on that wouldn't go away. He never thought he'd get blue balls over dinner, but there he was. The skirt swished when Maggie walked. He'd held the door open for her and a little breeze combined with the sexy sway of her hips gave the little skirt a flip and he almost died on the spot from the blood leaving his brain and rushing south. Maggie was wearing a thong and he knew because he got the perfect little peek of the roundest, sexiest butt cheek he'd ever seen. Now he was an addict. He wanted more. More of her butt cheek, more of her laugh, more of watching how crazy good she was at shooting . . . just more Maggie.

They placed their drink orders and Hunter leaned forward to hide his erection from the restaurant full of people watching them. "Tell me about how you got involved with shooting."

Maggie told him about growing up with her parents believing a woman could do anything a man could do and treating her like an equal when Gage started shooting. Then she asked about his life growing up with so many siblings and soon the food plates were cleared, the drinks were empty, and yet they still talked until Kerri cleared her throat.

"I'm sorry to interrupt, but we closed thirty minutes ago," Kerri said with a smile. A smile that told Hunter she'd be running straight over to her best friend, Harper, at the bar next door and telling everyone Hunter and Maggie hadn't noticed they were the only ones left in the entire restaurant.

Maggie's eyes widened as she looked around the room and then at the two empty bottles of wine sitting on the table. "Oh gosh. I didn't notice. I'm so sorry, Kerri."

"Don't apologize. It was worth it to see this," Kerri motioned between them, "finally happen."

"Mags, I'm so sorry," Hunter said, glancing at the table. "I didn't realize we finished two bottles of wine. I know my four glasses have been spread out over our time here, but I better not drive. Can I call Damon to pick us up? What a horrible impression. I'm so sorry."

"Don't be. I've never had a better date. Besides," Maggie said, reaching out to take his hand, "I'm not ready for the date to be over. Would you mind if we walked home? I know it's a couple of miles, but it's so nice out."

Hunter thought about holding her hand for their stroll.

Maybe stopping in the moonlight and kissing her. It would be so romantic and a perfect way to end the evening. "I'd love that, but what about your shoes? I can carry you if you want."

Kerri about swooned at that. And he could carry her. He was trained for carrying wounded soldiers long distances if need be. "I have an extra pair of tennis shoes. I'm a size eight. What are you, Maggie?"

"I'm close to an eight," Maggie said, looking excited, and not letting go of Hunter's hand. "Thanks so much, Kerri."

Hunter paid the bill as Maggie unlaced her shoes and put on the tennis shoes. What Hunter would give to be the one running his hand down her legs as he unwound those ribbons that tied up her calf.

"Shall we?" Hunter held out his hand and felt like he'd won the lottery when Maggie slipped her hand into his and looked up at him as if he were her hero. Damn. It hit him right in the heart.

Hunter opened the door and walked right into his sister.

"Oh," Olivia said with faux surprise and a not so innocent smile. "How funny to run into you. What are you two up to?"

"Hunter's walking me home," Maggie said sweetly. Poor girl didn't know what had just happened, but Hunter did. It was payback time for his sister and her evil, twisted, far too sweet smile told him just that.

"Oh good. I was going for a walk too and it would be so nice to have company. Shall we?"

Maggie's smile faltered. She got it now. "Olivia," she said quietly, "is this what you put Natalie through?"

Olivia smiled big. "Yup. I'm here to jam your clam."

Hunter groaned. "Come on, Liv. This is our first date."

"Do you remember my first date with Calvin, sophomore year of high school?" Olivia challenged.

"Not really, but if his name was Calvin, he probably deserved it."

Olivia poked him in the chest. "You met me at the end of the driveway and wouldn't even let him drop me off at the doorstep because, quote, 'I won't let a douche like you even think about dating my sister.'"

"Oh," Hunter said, grinning and turning to Maggie. "He was a douche. He wore two polos and popped both collars."

Olivia rolled her eyes as they turned to walk down Main Street. "Immaterial. What matters is it was *my* decision if he got a good night kiss, not yours." Olivia then squirmed her way between them, forcing Hunter to drop Maggie's hand as Olivia began walking between them. "Sorry, big shooter. You've been blocked. This penetration prevention is for her safety after all. I'd hate to see Maggie have regrets."

"I'm so getting you back," Hunter threatened, but his damn sister just laughed and held up her left hand, wiggling her fingers and showing off her wedding band.

"Good luck! Granger will shoot you. You can't muffin muzzle me anymore, bro."

Hunter made gagging noises. "I don't want to hear about your muffin."

Across from Olivia, Maggie snorted as she tried to hide her giggles. "I thought Gage was bad when he prevented his friends from asking me out. I am so sorry for all you went through, Olivia."

"Olivia?" Hunter said incredulously. "What about me? What about you? I was prepared for the most romantic and gentlemanly kiss goodnight. But now—"

"So not happening. You'll have to take a pass tonight." Olivia looked so freaking proud of herself as they turned left off Main Street and onto Palmetto. "So, how did my big bro do on his groveling tour? I think you should hold off on forgiving him a little longer. Really make him get creative."

"Olivia," Hunter warned, but his sister didn't care.

"Really make him crawl on his hands on knees, begging for your forgiveness while you make him confess all of his emotions and feelings," Olivia said, ignoring the death glares he was giving her.

"Oh, I'll crawl on my hands and knees and beg, but it won't be for forgiveness." Hunter leaned forward and let Maggie see all the pent-up heat he had for her.

Smack.

"Ow," Hunter grumbled at the swat to the back of his head.

"Not tonight, you aren't. That snatch is latched. The box is locked."

Olivia talked nonstop after that. To Maggie. About all the ways she should torture Hunter. It was a damn good thing he loved his sister, because he was strongly considering murdering her if she ruined this for him. To be fair, while she was talking about making him beg, it was always with the intention of forgiving him. She talked as if Maggie and Hunter were already a couple, or would be soon.

"Well, here we are. What a delightful evening," Olivia said as they approached the front door to Maggie's house.

The patio light flipped on and Gage walked out with his gun. He looked pissed, but when he saw Olivia standing between them, he grinned so broadly that Hunter wanted to groan. "Welcome back. I was just coming out here to clean my gun. Such a beautiful night, isn't it?"

"Exactly what I told Hunter and Maggie when I joined them for a walk home. Beautiful night," Olivia said, turning as a car drove down the lane. "And there's my ride. Now, Maggie, you better hurry inside. It's getting chilly out here. Don't want you catching a cold."

"I do feel a bit of a chill in the air," Gage agreed as he held open the front door. Wide.

"It's seventy-eight degrees outside," Hunter pointed out.

"Brrr. Downright chilly from the eighty-something that was the high today." Olivia rubbed her arms dramatically.

Maggie sighed and tried to walk around Olivia, but her brother hurried down the steps. "Here, sis. I'm sure you're tired. Let me help you up the steps."

Maggie rolled her eyes and, while it would be hard to kill Olivia, Hunter was pretty sure he could kill Gage in less than two seconds.

"Goodnight, Hunter," Maggie said, sounding resigned.

Gage smirked as he held his gun.

"Thank you for a wonderful evening, Magnum."

"It was perfect . . . almost." Maggie looked at Olivia and Gage who both smiled back triumphantly. "Goodnight."

"Goodnight."

Gage walked Maggie inside. When the door closed, Hunter heard the lock slide into place. He and Olivia walked to the side of the circular drive to get out of the way of the approaching car before Hunter realized it was Granger.

"Nice try, breaking the beaver dam but no luck for you. For what it's worth, I'm glad you're finally seeing what was right in front of you. There's hope for you yet." Olivia smirked at him and Hunter wanted to be mad, but he couldn't be. He might have done a lot of cockblocking and probably deserved one night of it in return.

"Ready, sweetheart?" Granger asked from where he'd pulled up to pick up Olivia.

"I sure am," she said, walking to his car.

"Hey, thanks for the brotherly support," Hunter called out as he began to walk toward the car.

Granger just laughed. "Yeah, just returning the favor . . . bro."

Hunter watched them drive off without offering him a ride. That's fine. He didn't need a ride. He turned and looked at the house. The back side window on the second floor came on. Maggie walked across the window and disappeared from sight.

Hunter glanced down the drive to where the taillights were getting smaller and then back to the house. Olivia forgot how resourceful Hunter was . . . how foolish of her.

Maggie changed into a silk cami and boxer set for bed. She'd cussed her brother up one side and down the other as they climbed the stairs of the private wing of the house. She'd waited so long for a kiss and the evening had been perfect.

Maggie crawled into bed and stared at the ceiling. She'd gotten to know so much about Hunter. What had started out as a simple crush was turning into so much more. It would have turned into even more if Olivia and Gage hadn't interrupted.

Okay, she could understand Olivia's need for payback, but Gage? She wasn't a teenager anymore and Hunter wasn't one of his friends. It was ridiculous and she was going to get him back for this somehow.

Maggie reached over and turned off the main lights to her room then turned on the reading lamp beside her bed. It had been thirty minutes. Hunter was probably home by now. Would it be wrong to text him? Would she scare him off? She wasn't ready for the night to end. That connection had formed and all she wanted to do was keep on feeling it.

Tap, tap, tap.

Maggie didn't notice the noise at first as she stared at her phone, starting a text to Hunter at least three different ways.

Tap, tap, tap.

Maggie set down her phone and looked around. The house was haunted, as were all Charleston area historic houses were. But the ghost seemed much more corporeal when she saw a face hovering in her second story window. Only . . . "Hunter?" she scrambled out of bed. His face slid out of view as she unlocked the window and lifted it up. "What on earth?" Maggie looked out and saw Hunter hanging by his fingertips on the brick windowsill.

Hunter pulled himself up and adjusted his hands so his arms were locked straight and his face was now even with hers, even as his legs perched precariously on the brick below. "Thank you for tonight, Maggie. It was the best date of my life. I wanted to ask, in person, if you'd like to go out with me again?"

Maggie placed her hands around his biceps, which were bulging with use. "I'd love to. Now get in here before you fall."

"I won't fall, Mags. Well, I'll fall for you, but not out of the window. There is one more thing before I leave."

"What's that?" Maggie asked, still very worried about the fact that he was dangling off the side of her house.

Hunter pushed forward and kissed her. It wasn't a tongue down your throat, take command, make you submit type of kiss. It was confident as hell, inviting you to join, and making you wish he was kissing you while naked type of kiss.

When Hunter pulled away, she gave a little whimper of protest. "Goodnight, Magnum."

Then he dropped from view.

Maggie gasped and leaned out over the window to see Hunter using a drainage pipe to quickly rappel down the side of her house.

His feet hit the ground and he looked up at her, gave her a wink, and strode off whistling a happy tune. Maggie watched as he disappeared into the shadows before collapsing back onto her bed. That was so much better than *Romeo and Juliet*. No poison necessary. Only thoughts of an actual future with someone who scaled a brick wall for her.

16

Hunter fell asleep that night with a smile on his face. It quickly vanished in the morning when Kane called him.

"I'm going deep and still coming up with only whispers with no substance. I finally got a name. Had to pay a million for it and you're not going to like it," Kane told him.

"Who?"

"Hamid Saeed," Kane said, dropping a bomb. Literally.

"The Yemen bomber? I thought he was in jail."

"He was," Kane told him. "In Iran. But with the military taking control of the country, Saeed appeared to have paid his way out of jail four years ago."

"Where is he now?" Hunter asked.

"Don't know. I got some leads on the names you gave me. Both Soliz and Kotov have been in Millevia within the past six months. David, Tristan's friend, has helped me. Alexey Kotov left for the U.S. about five hours after you did. I'm assuming when he didn't check in, it triggered something and that's when Pablo Soliz left Millevia. The question is: what are three soldiers from three different countries, which have no agreements in place, doing in Millevia in the first place?"

"I wish I knew. Any word on what's missing? Whatever they think Landry has?"

"Not a peep. I'll keep digging."

"Thanks, Kane. Let me know if you need backup."

"I have people I can call if I do. You need to stay in Shadows Landing with Landry. See if you can find out what's going on. That will help the most. I'll call again soon. Oh, and I heard you got cockblocked last night. Ouch, bro."

"Screw you."

Kane laughed. "We both know you weren't the one doing any screwing."

"Laugh all you want. Olivia will come after you when you find someone."

"Not going to happen. My life doesn't allow for personal relationships. For the record though, we all love Maggie. I'm glad you got your head out of your ass."

"Thanks," Hunter said dryly. "Be safe, Kane. I have contacts too. Let me know if I need to use them."

"I will."

Hunter hung up the phone. It was time to check in on Landry.

Hunter was met with a gun to the head. "It's me, Blythe."

"I know. I'm waiting to hear how the date went before I decide if I should shoot you or not."

"You too?"

"Girls gotta stick together," Blythe replied, keeping the gun aimed at him. Hunter smiled a little as he thought about the date and Blythe lowered the gun. "That tells me all I need to know. Glad you got that stick out of your ass."

"What is it about my ass today?" Hunter grumbled as he walked inside.

"You have a good ass. Even if you're not my type, I can respect a nice ass."

"Watch out, Veronica," Hunter teased about Blythe's long-term girlfriend who was frighteningly efficient.

"It's not *that* nice an ass. Landry is in here. There have been no attempts. The family is bonding nicely and Landry's been working with Stone's wife, Natalie, to get some strength back. He's even been upgraded to a wheelchair this morning," Blythe told him as they walked into Landry's room where Natalie, an expert in sports rehabilitation, was working with him.

"Hey, Hunter. Congrats on pulling your head out of your ass and taking Maggie on a date. How did it go?"

Landry smiled, the traitor. Lydia at least turned away to smirk.

"It went well. I'm so glad so many people are so concerned with my ass. I've been told it's a very nice one."

"Doesn't matter how nice of an ass it is, it's still an ass," Natalie pointed out.

"Hey, I thought you were supposed to be my favorite sister-in-law."

"I'm your only sister-in-law," Natalie said with a twinkle in her eye. "Therefore, I'm your favorite and least favorite all rolled into one."

Hunter made a face at her, but then winked. He loved how Natalie fit seamlessly into his crazy family. It was just how Maggie did. Yeah, he really had had his head up his ass not to see that. "How's our patient?"

"It feels so good to be out of bed," Landry said as he used a band to work his arms.

"I talked to Kane," Hunter started before filling Landry in. "Has any more of your memory come back?"

The obvious look of frustration on Landry's face answered that question for Hunter. "I'm trying. Natalie has Lydia doing these memory games with me to see if waking up my brain will help. I'm sorry."

"Don't be sorry. I'm just glad you're here with us. We'll figure it out. Besides, I'm going to meet my team and my commander at the end of the week. We'll see if any progress has been made. You just focus on your recovery."

Hunter was walking to his car when Lydia quietly slipped from the house and caught up with him. "Hunter," she whispered, glancing back to the house. "Gavin said not to push Landry's memory. It'll come back as he heals. But, at night, when he's asleep, he has nightmares. He talks in his sleep. He keeps saying, 'all this death for control.'"

"Control?" Hunter repeated, making sure he heard her right. Lydia nodded. Hunter's mind raced over all the facts he knew. "I wonder if Landry took something that will gain someone control over something?" It still didn't make sense. How could he do that?

"I don't know, but that's all he yells at night. It's about control."

"One of the men is a bomber. They could be building bombs to try to hijack something. I'll text Kane and see if that helps him. Thanks, Lydia. Let me know if he says anything else in his sleep."

"I will. Thanks, Hunter."

Hunter glanced at his watch. Was it too soon to call Maggie? He knew she was putting on a corporate event today and decided against it. He would work out and then shoot her a text to see if she had time to have dinner tonight. He was determined to prove to Maggie that he was worth the second chance she'd given him.

~

Hunter's lips pulled back from hers. His hand slid free from where it cupped her cheek as he smiled down at her. "Thank you for another excellent dinner date. Goodnight, Magnum."

Maggie plastered on a smile. It had been a wonderful date until the kiss ended. Just like every date over the past week had been. "Goodnight, Hunter."

She watched as he walked down the steps, the same as she had done the past seven nights, and got into his truck. He waved and drove down the drive leaving Maggie feeling, well, confused.

"What the hell?" Maggie muttered, pulling out her phone and sending a quick text to Georgie. One week of dates. One week of great conversations. One week of sharing their hopes and dreams. One week of practicing shooting together. One week of knee buckling kisses goodnight. And one week of being left standing alone on her porch.

She was still standing there when the old truck sped down the drive. It parked, the door flew open, and Georgie jumped out, holding a bottle of wine. "What happened? Tell me everything."

"Nothing happened."

"Again?" Georgie's mouth dropped open. "I thought for sure after the third date you two would be having wild sex every chance you got."

"Me too," Maggie said, grabbing the bottle and stomping inside. She snagged a bottle opener and two glasses from the public living room before heading to the private side of the bed and breakfast and up to her room.

"Give me a rundown on tonight's date," Georgie said as Maggie opened the bottle of wine and poured two glasses.

"We talked about me leaving for the Olympics next week. He told me how proud he was of me and how I was going to win gold for sure. He's been working with me every day. Sometimes just shooting with me. Other times, he's actually being very helpful with some coaching. My coach taught Hunter in the Army and said he's one of the best. Hunter even called him and asked permission to help me before doing so. We talked about growing up, about our friends and family—all good things, I promise," Maggie said, smiling at her bestie. "Then we walked home in the moonlight. He kissed me and it was so hot I was clinging to him. I mean, my knees just melted! And then he said goodnight and left. Again."

The door opened and Gage walked in without knocking. "Hey, Mags. Do you . . . oh, sorry. Didn't know you had company. Hi Georgie."

"Gage. Did you seriously walk into your sister's room without knocking after she had a date? You do know she could have Hunter in here, right?"

Gage fake gagged. "Gross. Do you know where my Olympic bag is?"

"It's in the attic with mine. Can you grab mine too when you go up there?"

"Sure. Night, you two."

Georgie frowned. "So, one. That's a problem," Georgie said, pointing to the now closed door. "And two, it sounds as if Hunter's being a respectful gentleman."

"I know and it sucks," Maggie groaned.

"Then maybe you should get out of your house filled with people and stop being the perfect Southern lady."

Maggie paused in sipping her wine. "I couldn't—"

"Think of Hunter naked and how long you've been waiting."

That was the best thing about best friends. They know you better than you know yourself.

17

Hunter was livid. Beyond livid. He was raging. Hunter and his team were at the base being updated by their commander. They were on forced vacation leave while the government went full FUBAR.

"They've taken the case away from FBI Agent Castle, away from Sheriff Fox, and away from South Carolina completely?" Hunter asked with disbelief as his team cursed under their breaths.

"That's right. They said they have intel that all activity was taking place in Millevia and therefore the CIA is in charge of the case overseas with the help of Millevia."

"And the attacks right here in Charleston and Shadows Landing mean nothing?" Freaking government pissing contest.

"It's been quiet for over a week. There's no indication there's any terrorist event planned on American soil. But they did say they are tracking a former terrorist bomber whose last known location was Iran. Plus, all the attacks on American soil were people coming over from Millevia. Your team has a month of R and R coming your way since you've been working overtime. Enjoy it," his commander told them.

That made his team happy, but it didn't make Hunter happy. He'd talked to his brother Kane just that morning and he was trying to hunt down Hamid Saeed. He and every CIA agent in Europe and the Middle East. If Saeed was involved, it was clear whatever was planned would involve bombs, and that was never a good thing.

Hunter pulled into his driveway still fuming over the fact they believed Landry knew nothing and needed no protection. He'd talked to Ryker who had agreed that the threat to Landry wasn't over yet. Blythe had flown home for three days as another bodyguard replaced her. He was a serious man who didn't chat. But he was good at what he did. Blythe was back today and she would start four days on, three off until Ryker was satisfied a threat no longer remained.

Damon leaning against his bike in his driveway was the last thing Hunter needed right now. Hunter loved his big brother, who was more of a father to them since their parents had been so busy working and having kids to give any one kid a lot of attention. Not that they didn't love and respect their parents. They did. Hunter just knew Damon was the one who made ballet classes possible for Penelope and helped pay for college textbooks for Olivia. Then when Stone was drafted and Hunter was finally getting a small paycheck in the Army, they both stepped up and sent money home. It helped the younger kids go to camp, get new sneakers, and so on while their father worked multiple jobs to pay for their house, utilities, and Christmas presents.

"Damon, whatever it is. Not now. I have a date to get ready for."

"Hunter. This isn't hard and won't take long." Damn. Damon's lip twitched just a bit, indicating he was amused about something.

"What's going on? I'm having a shitty day, so just spill it."

"I had an interesting conversation with your girlfriend this morning."

"Maggie and I aren't official yet. I'm taking my time. I'm showing her I can be patient, respectful, and supportive, and I want to get to know all of her. What did Maggie want with you?"

Damon was struggling to keep his face neutral. "Apparently, you've been a little too respectful."

Hunter frowned. "What the hell does that mean? She has to know I'm interested in her. I take her out every night."

Damon bit his lip and Hunter knew he was screwed. "Yes, she knows you're interested. In fact, she's the one who called herself your girlfriend when she was talking to me. However, she wanted to talk to me privately to see if you had any"—Damon paused and tried to regain his composure—"sexual dysfunction she should be considerate of."

Damon almost snorted as it dawned on Hunter what Maggie had asked. "She thinks I have erectile dysfunction?" Hunter yelled in shock. "Why the hell would she think that? It was Forrest, wasn't it? No, it was Olivia getting back at me for her prom date."

Damon shook his head. "It was all you, bro. She said you've only kissed her and never tried anything else, so she worried that maybe you were embarrassed about ED. As your girlfriend, she wanted to help you with it."

Hunter's mouth opened and then closed. His brother was enjoying this way too much. Finally, Hunter took a deep breath and stormed past his brother and into his house. "Try to be a freaking gentleman . . ." Hunter muttered.

"Even gentlemen please their women, Hunter!" Damon called out with a chuckle.

Hunter pulled off his sand-colored athletic top and reached down to untie his combat boots. "Do I even want to know what you told her?"

"Just be thankful she came to me and not to Stone or Olivia. I told Maggie you were trying to show her how much she meant to you by taking things slow and that you had no such problems, down there."

"Have I ever told you that you're my favorite sibling?" Hunter kicked off his pants and headed for the bathroom to turn on the shower while Damon smirked. Damon was quiet, but Hunter knew that he was proud of them all. Plus, Damon liked being the go-to when someone needed help.

"I'll let you get ready for your date with your *girlfriend*." Damon chuckled again on his way out of Hunter's house.

Hunter wasn't laughing though. Come hell or high water, he was going to be a proper boyfriend tonight and show Maggie why he was worth the wait.

~

Maggie was nervous. She'd poked the bear. Technically, she'd poked the bear's penis. Did she need to do that? No. Did it give her a little bit of pleasure in the form of a little bit of revenge for the things Hunter had teased her about? Yes. Did she want to give Hunter a little push to see how he hunted her down to prove his manhood? Hell yes.

The thought of his control snapping had been the focus of her very hot dreams these past couple of days. The idea of it made her smile. Could she, sweet, petite Maggie Bell, make a man so strong and controlled as Hunter Townsend lose control? She certainly hoped so. She dreamt about it every night, yet every night ended with only a kiss. A very hot kiss, but a kiss and not the hot, sweaty, heart-pounding sex she wanted.

Maggie checked herself out in the mirror and nodded. She was dressed for a reaction. She wore a skintight, mid-thigh length dress with no underwear. It was practically a red flag for a bull.

Maggie pulled her hair back into a slick low ponytail and headed down the stairs in her high heels. She heard Hunter arrive the second she hit the first floor. Maggie opened the door, stepped out onto the porch, closed the door, and gasped.

The look in Hunter's eyes answered every question she had. He devoured her as he stalked up the steps.

"If you had a question on whether you make me hard, you could have felt for yourself instead of asking my brother." The way Hunter growled that between clenched teeth would have made her panties wet if she'd been wearing any.

"I wanted to be respectful in case you had an issue," Maggie said, holding on to the front door handle behind her for support as Hunter stopped inches from her and towered over her.

"No, you didn't. You wanted to find out what happened if you pushed me." Busted. "Well, hang on sweetheart, because you're about to find out."

Hunter's mouth devoured hers. It didn't start off slow and sweet like his other kisses had. This one smeared her lipstick, stole her breath, and set her afire. His mouth demanded her submission, and as Maggie clung to him, she was happy to submit to anything Hunter wanted.

Maggie let go of the door and flung her arms around him, holding on to his neck for dear life as he shoved her against the door. Hunter definitely did not have ED. She felt him, large, hard, and eagerly pressing against her.

His hands were no longer stationary, as they'd been during prior kisses. Hunter's hands moved confidently over her body as if knowing he could bring her to her knees with his touch and he was right. Her knees were slowly turning to goo.

"*Ack!*" Maggie's world tilted. Literally. The door behind her that had been holding her up was suddenly opened and she was falling.

Maggie prepared to hit the hard ground, but it never came. When she landed, she landed on Hunter who had somehow twisted as they fell so that he took the brunt of the hit and she landed safely on him.

"Eww, were you two making out?"

Maggie turned and looked up at her brother. "What the hell, Gage?"

"I thought someone was knocking on the door."

Hunter rolled to the side, stood up, and in one quick motion, had Maggie on her feet. Maggie caught sight of herself in the mirror. Her lipstick was gone. Her face was flushed. Her eyes were so bright she hardly recognized herself. Now that was how a man should kiss.

"What time will you be home?" Gage asked as Hunter began to pull her from the house.

"She won't," was all Hunter growled as he almost dragged her down the steps.

"Aww man, that's my sister!"

"And she's my girlfriend. See you tomorrow."

Maggie couldn't have hidden her smile if somebody offered her a million dollars.

. . .

Hunter was barely in control of himself as they ate dinner at Harper's. The plan had been dinner, some drinks, some pool or darts, and then he'd respectfully take her home, kiss her goodnight, and spend the night talking to her on the phone.

Hunter had been so proud of himself for his self-control until Maggie had talked to Damon. Now, knowing she wanted him as much as he wanted her, the self-control was gone. She'd pushed and now she was going to find out how Hunter responded.

Instead of taking the seat across from her, Hunter slid onto the bench beside her. Their table was in the back. It was the most private one you could get in the bar. He waited until she had a sip of her drink in her mouth and leaned over, placing his lips against her ear, making her shiver. "I see you forgot to get dressed all the way. Did your panties not have a monogram reminding you to put them on?"

He smirked when she coughed on her drink, but because their sides were plastered against each other, he felt her shiver of excitement.

"You seemed to be having trouble finding your way there, so I thought it better to leave them off so you wouldn't get lost. Should I draw you a diagram?"

"I'd love to see a picture instead. Or better yet, why don't you show me."

Hunter placed his hand on her thigh and began to move it upward as he turned his body to shield her from the rest of the bar. He slid his hand under her dress and then paused the second her eyes began to glaze over and her legs widened in invitation. "Let's skip dessert. I know what I want to feast on."

"What's that? Because Kerri makes the best desserts that we can also serve here."

Hunter didn't move. He saw Maggie's eyes go wide, but he ignored the intruder. "Go away, Harper. Or better yet, bring us the check."

"So bossy," Harper said with a little mischievousness in her voice. "Lucky Maggie."

"I'm going to freshen up," Maggie said in a whisper as Harper slowly took her time clearing the table.

"Here," Hunter said, handing Harper more than enough cash to cover dinner.

"I'll get your change."

"No need," Hunter said, standing up and following Maggie to the back.

He waited for her in the dark hallway. The second she came out of the bathroom, he had her in his arms, his mouth to hers, their bodies struggling to get closer to each other.

"I want you so bad," Hunter told her as he kissed his way down her neck. "Ready to get out of here?"

"Where are you going?"

"Dammit, Olivia. Get lost," Hunter snapped.

"It looks as if you're the one who is lost. This is a hallway in a bar, not your bedroom."

"Hurry up and take me to your bedroom," Maggie whispered in his ear. Holy hell, that was hot. They were both panting with need and his sister was standing in the freaking way.

"Excuse us, Liv."

Hunter tried to move past his sister who smiled and he knew it wasn't going to be easy. "Actually, I'm so glad you're here. I've been meaning to talk to you about this interesting legal history I read on civilian versus military courts. See, the Supreme Court was established in the Judiciary Act of 1789 in the Constitution—"

Hunter could feel Maggie's arousal dying, so he did the only thing he could. He reached out, picked his sister up, spun around and set her down behind them. He grabbed Maggie's hand and rushed off as Olivia began spouting something about the court-martial being established by the Continental Congress and the first hearing was in 1775.

Hunter looked up and cursed under his breath. There were cockblocking mines in the form of supposedly loving family members between him and the door. "Don't make eye contact. Think of how many times I'm going to make you orgasm," Hunter told Maggie as he put his head down and plowed forward.

"Hey, Hunter. Maggie, how is training going?" Rowan asked.

"Good," Maggie called out as Hunter darted around his brother.

"You all should come to WET," Wilder said of his nightclub in Charleston. Wilder had some of the best nightclubs all over the world.

"What do you think I'm trying to do here?" Hunter grumbled, causing Maggie to smack him as she giggled.

"Bro!" Stone called out. "Thought we could get a workout in. How's tomorrow morning at five?"

"Show up at my house in the next twenty-four hours and I'll shoot you," Hunter called out, taking a sharp right to try to find his way around the bar toward the front door only to be stopped by Forrest.

"You can't go out there," Forrest warned.

Hunter pushed past his brother, opened the door, and stopped in his tracks.

"Told you so. We're waiting for Gator to get here because

Mean Abe is pissed about something. Oh, and he took a bite out of your tire and you now have a flat," Forrest told him as Mean Abe, the town's problem alligator, opened his mouth wide and hissed.

"Back door," Hunter said, turning around, only to be blocked by a grinning Harper.

"I heard the back door is jammed," Damon told him.

"It's okay," Maggie whispered. "We can wait. We've waited this long. We can wait until tomorrow."

"You're not wearing underwear. You questioned my manhood. We've waited long enough."

"Hunter, it's Mean Abe," Maggie warned.

"Yeah, well, I'm Sexually Frustrated Hunter. Hold on and think of me eating my dessert." Hunter grabbed someone's shot glass from the nearest table, tossed it back, and flung open the door.

Mean Abe hissed at Hunter as he spat the alcohol onto the sidewalk, held his lighter to it, and watched it flare up. Mean Abe hissed, but backed up. However, not enough for Hunter and Maggie to safely leave.

"Dammit," Hunter muttered before jumping to the side, grabbing Mean Abe's tail, and giving him a hard yank. Mean Abe turned around to snap, but Hunter jumped behind a light pole. He pulled as Mean Abe fought him, but eventually Mean Abe was facing away from the door to the bar.

"What in tarnation are you doin'?" Gator asked as he hooked his thumbs in his overalls.

"Getting Mean Abe out of the way," Hunter grunted. Alligators were crazy strong.

"Looks like he took a bite out of your tire. That would make me right ornery too, if I were you."

"I'm not ornery," Hunter said. "I'm hor—"

"Gonna hurt yourself. Here, let me handle this." In a quick move, Gator had a bag over Mean Abe's eyes and the alligator instantly calmed down.

Maggie clapped. "Good job, Gator!"

Hunter was too busy looking for a ride to do anything other than quickly thank Gator. "Let's take Forrest's car."

Hunter went to open the door, but found it locked. Was the world against him tonight? No, just interfering family members and alligators. Hunter stuck his arm down the partially opened window to unlock the car—he'd hotwire the damn thing just to piss off Forrest for cockblocking him tonight.

Suddenly a bright flashlight showed in his face. "Step away from the vehicle and put your hands up."

"Granger, what the hell?" Hunter groaned. "I'm just borrowing Forrest's car since Mean Abe ate my tire."

"Borrowing involves a key, not hotwiring. Now, hands up."

"Granger," Hunter said, his voice low. "What are you doing?"

Maggie was watching from the sidewalk, so she didn't see Granger's face. Only his back. His face split into a grin as he leaned forward and whispered to Hunter. "I told you I'd pay you back for trying to stop me from dating Olivia." Then Granger leaned back, and pulled out his cuffs. "Do I need to arrest you?"

"Granger Fox," Maggie said, her voice annoyed. "So, help me, if you mess up my night, I will tell everyone about *that* night."

"What night?" Hunter asked.

Granger put the cuffs away. "Have a good night."

"I'm guessing you won't give us a ride?" Hunter asked.

"Don't you have a spare tire?"

"He ate two tires," Hunter said through clenched teeth. "I'm sure you can see that."

"Huh. Will you look at that? Sorry, I'm too busy taking a police report on a suspected car thief to drive you home."

Hunter turned, glanced at the sexy as hell high heels Maggie was wearing and made up his mind. He walked over to her, tossed her over his shoulder, and ran away before any other family member, supposed friend, or feisty alligator made an appearance.

18

Maggie gasped as suddenly her feet were off the ground, her ass was in the air, and her head was hanging over Hunter's side. "Hunter! Put me down!"

"Nope," he said as he jogged down Main Street with her draped across his back in a fireman's carry. "You can't run in those heels and I'm not about to let Olivia beaver dam me, or Bubba gator block me, or one of my brothers cockblock me."

Maggie laughed. This was not how she imagined their first time, but it was actually incredibly sexy. He carried her as if she weighed nothing while he jogged with her over his shoulders. Cars honked. People whistled and somehow Hunter wasn't even breathing hard.

"It's a mile, Hunter. Put me down. I'll take off my shoes and walk."

"No way, Mags. This is faster. A mile is nothing. You should see what I have to carry on missions. I've been training for years just for this romantic gesture. Let me have it."

Maggie heard the humor in his voice and laughed along

with him. It was a sight, she was sure. But she appreciated that instead of ruining their night, it seemed to only bring them closer.

"When I get you home, we are dead bolting the doors. Checking the window locks, drawing the curtains, and disconnecting the garage door."

"Why?" Maggie asked flirtatiously.

"Because, then I'm going strip you naked, kiss your body in the kitchen, make you come in the living room, and then scream in the bedroom. And I don't want anyone interrupting us."

"What will we do in the dining room?"

"Feast," Hunter answered immediately. "You did promise me dessert."

"Then hurry because I can't wait to show you what I can do in the pantry."

Hunter slammed the door shut, set Maggie on his countertop, locked every window and door, and returned to find Maggie with her dress hiked up, barely concealing what was underneath, as she leaned against the cabinets holding a glass of water.

"You're not even breathing heavily and you ran for over a mile carrying me."

Hunter tossed back the glass of water and set the glass down. "Imagine what I can do and for how long when I'm not running."

"Oh, trust me. I've been thinking about it since I first met you."

Hunter stepped between her legs, which she automatically wrapped around his waist. He leaned down, stopping a breath away from her lips. He loved how Maggie closed her eyes and tilted her lips up, offering them to him. However, he didn't take them. He kissed her jaw, just under her ear before skimming his lips down her neck.

Maggie arched her back, but Hunter didn't take her up on the invitation. She pulled him close with her legs, but Hunter didn't budge. Instead, he picked up her hand and placed a kiss in the palm of her hand, on the inside of her wrist where he felt her pulse flutter under his lips.

It was torturous to go slow. Painful to kiss up the smooth skin on the inside of her forearm as Maggie made these cute panting noises mixed with frustration. He moved back to her neck, up and over her jaw, but refused to meet her lips. He taunted. He teased. He tasted.

Until she fisted her hand in his hair and yanked his mouth to hers. There was no more teasing then. Except that every touch of hers, every sound Maggie made, every rock of her hips were the biggest turn-ons Hunter had ever experienced.

Hunter slid his hands until they gripped her under her upper thighs, lifted her up with one hand, and shoved her dress up to her waist with the other. He had a promise to fulfill and that started with stripping her in the kitchen.

Hunter broke his kiss only long enough to pull Maggie's dress over her head. He tossed it behind him, not bothering to look where it landed. "You're so freaking beautiful," he told her before kissing her shoulder, using his teeth to pull the straps of her bra down her arm before feathering kisses along the swell of her breasts still covered by the bra's cups.

Maggie's hand was in his hair, her legs were clasped around his waist, and her head was tossed back as he kissed his way down each arm, over her hip, behind her knee, and only stopping to slip off her shoes.

Hunter kissed his way back up her body before

capturing her mouth in his as his fingers flicked the bra's hooks open. He peeled the bra from her body and tossed it in the vicinity of the discarded dress.

Maggie's smell, her taste, and the velvet softness of her tongue were unlike anything he'd ever experienced. It was warm and welcoming yet had him so on edge he could barely control himself. Sweet, yet fierce. That summed up Maggie perfectly. She was all goodness, yet all backbone. She took, and she gave. She pushed, and she pulled. She was his perfect balance.

Hunter slid his arms around her back, holding her close to him, and picked her up from the counter. She tightened her legs around him and he thought twice about holding true to his promise. It would be so easy to make love to her right here and now.

"I believe the living room was next."

Hunter laid her down on the couch and grinned. She was splayed out just for him and it was the sexiest thing he'd ever seen.

Maggie's body tightened, her eyes squeezed shut, and the wave of pleasure rushed through her body. She was still catching her breath when Hunter, still fully clothed, picked her up from the couch.

Eventually she'd tell him how great that was, but right now she was trying to catch her breath as he carried her up the stairs.

"Sorry, I combined the living room and dining room."

Maggie smiled, and placed a kiss on his shoulder. "I can walk, you know. Well, maybe. That was . . . wow."

Hunter nudged the bedroom door open and then used his foot to close it. His room was how she imagined it. Clean, organized, and smelled just like him. The bed was large for a bachelor, but the pillows were soft and fluffed. Hunter set her down on the dark gray bedspread and smiled down at her as he pulled his shirt free of his jeans.

"Finally," she teased. She'd been dying to see Hunter naked and it was worth the wait.

He dropped his shirt on the floor, but Maggie didn't notice. She saw the muscles, a couple of scars, and then the washboard abs that ended in a V by his pants, which were quickly being pushed down.

Maggie licked her lips and Hunter groaned. "Not tonight, sweetheart, but soon. You're all mine now."

"I think that goes both ways. You're mine now too."

"Always."

Maggie rolled over onto her hands and knees to scamper up the bed, but suddenly she felt Hunter's hands on her hips. "You have a tattoo?"

"So do you," Maggie pointed out, looking over her shoulder as he ran his finger over the Olympic ring tattoo she, and the whole team, had gotten four years ago.

"Yeah," Hunter said of the tattoo on his bicep and the one on his chest. "But mine aren't hidden so adorably on my ass. It's sexy as hell. You're the last person I would expect to have a tattoo."

"I guess there's still a lot for you to learn about me."

"There's one thing I'm going to learn right now. How you feel when I make love to you."

The second the condom was on, Hunter was behind her. He held her hip the entire time, not letting her move up the bed. Instead, he bent down and kissed the tattoo. That was the last coherent thought Maggie had before he fulfilled his promise. He made her scream in the bedroom all night long. However, Hunter forgot one thing. She was very competitive, which led to him cursing in the middle of the night when she woke him up in the best possible way.

Maggie fell asleep in Hunter's arms, naked, sated, and completely besotted. By the way Hunter wouldn't let her go, the way he kissed her, and the way he made love to her, Maggie knew she wasn't the only one feeling that way. It was just one more reason to go to bed that night, well, early morning, with a smile on her face.

19

Hunter had woken that morning with Maggie in his arms. Last night his whole world had changed with each kiss. With each touch. With each thrust. Between times they'd lain in bed, touching each other, and talking. Hunter had pulled her against him as Maggie rested her head on his chest and they bared their souls, their dreams, their hearts.

Then Maggie had thrown her leg over his hips and taken control. He was only too happy to let her. Seeing Maggie completely uninhibited was something he wished he saw every day. Maybe he could if he married her.

Hunter shook his head. Who was talking about marriage? Not them. It was one night. A night he wished to repeat every day of his life.

"Swing!" Leo Langston pulled him from his thoughts. However, they only shifted to wondering if Maggie would want a big family.

Hunter and Damon each had a kid in their arms in the late afternoon sun. Damon was feeding baby Lennie as Hunter lifted Leo up and set him on the swing. Granger and Landry Jr were off surfing and would be back after dinner.

Maggie was with Landry Sr., waiting to pick up Lacy and Leah for weapons training. Stone had Levi at the ice rink. And Forrest and Rowan were playing hide and seek with Lindsey and Lyle even though there weren't a lot of places to hide in the park.

"I take it last night went well. You have a stupid little smile on your face and everyone is talking about the full moon over Shadows Landing."

"No thanks to you all," Hunter grumbled.

"It's sweeter if you work for it." Damon didn't seem bothered by Hunter's annoyance at their interference last night.

"There will be payback," Hunter promised, and he never broke a promise.

Damon shrugged as if he wasn't scared. And knowing Damon, he wasn't.

"Wait, full moon? There wasn't a full moon last night," Hunter said, thinking back to last night.

"Oh yeah there was. A full Maggie Moon. It's the rarest of full moons."

Hunter closed his eyes and inwardly groaned. He'd tossed Maggie over his shoulder in that short little skirt of hers. Hopefully not too many people saw it. Only, he'd been interrupted by half the town. Great. Just great.

Hunter pushed Leo in the swing as the kids raced around the playground with Rowan and Forrest in full pursuit.

"There's something else I want to talk to you about. I'm worried that Kane hasn't found Hamid Saeed or found a connection between Alexey and Pablo," Damon told him. "Do you think the threat to Landry is over?"

Hunter frowned. Kane was bribing people left and right and coming up empty. It was frustrating for everyone.

However, Kane was still positive he'd find out the truth. "These things take time," Kane had told him that morning when they'd talked.

"I don't like it, that's for sure." Hunter pushed Leo, who giggled, and then there was a loud bang.

"Was that a backfire?" Damon asked, but Hunter was already grabbing Leo off the swing.

"Gunfire," he said, shoving Leo at Damon. "Get the kids to safety!" Hunter yelled as his brothers jumped into action.

Maggie sat with Landry, Mr. Gann, and Mr. Knoll as Lacy and Leah got ready for weapons class. Lydia had gone grocery shopping and would meet them there. They were going to be five minutes late, but Maggie didn't rush them. The girls had been having fun playing a game with Landry and she hadn't wanted to interrupt that.

Mr. Gann and Mr. Knoll arrived just minutes ago. The two old men had her and Landry in stitches as they told old racing stories. Mr. Gann had built cars for dirt track racing and Mr. Knoll had been both a competitor and a neighbor. They had a very close friendship built on intense competition, including which one of their motorized handicap scooters could go faster. They'd both been altered, and listening to them now, could go almost forty-five miles per hour.

Landry shook his head as they got into a tiff over who had the better engine on their scooters. Blythe sat in the corner of the room. When Maggie's and her eyes met, they both struggled not to laugh.

BANG!

Blythe was moving before Maggie even registered the sound of a gun. She knew it was a gun, but it didn't cross her mind it was a threat until she saw Blythe pull her own gun and aim it at the door.

"What was that?" Lacy asked as she and Leah raced down the stairs right as the window exploded from another shot.

"Girls!" Landry was trying to jump out of his wheelchair to get to his daughters, but Blythe wasn't letting that happen, so Maggie went on instinct. She ducked down and ran as bullets peppered the front of the house.

"Get down!" Maggie reached out, grabbed their arms, and yanked them down. They half fell down the last few stairs, but then Maggie was covering them with her body. Her gun was in the truck outside. She was useless here.

"Blythe? Do you have another gun?"

"Over the refrigerator. 1-7-3-0."

"Under the mattress," Landry called out too.

"Stay here," Maggie ordered the girls. The bedroom was closest so she grabbed the gun and handed it to Landry as she ran bent over for the kitchen.

Maggie pulled out a chair, reached up, and entered the lock combination. A rifle was there waiting. Maggie grabbed it and the ammo. As she jumped off the chair, movement behind her caught her eye. "They're two men coming up the back from the river!"

"We need to get Landry out of here," Blythe called out.

"Where to?" Maggie asked. She aimed the rifle, placed the crosshairs on her target, and pulled the trigger. The second man took cover behind a tree. "One man down in the back."

There was a blast of gunfire, but no bullets hit the house. "They just shot up the cars. We don't have transportation," Blythe called out.

"Sure you do. I have my all-terrain tires on. This thing

can climb a mountain or drive through a swamp if you need," Mr. Gann said.

"Only after mine made a path for it," Mr. Knoll challenged.

"Daddy!" Leah screamed as the gunfire started up again.

Maggie rushed toward the girls. She'd kill anyone coming in through that door to protect them. "Stay down," Maggie ordered, wrapping her arms around them, prepared to shield them with her body.

"Landry, we need to evacuate as we discussed," Blythe told him as she took a tactical position and asked for the rifle. "Maggie, how are you with a handgun?"

"Not as good. I only have a 99% accuracy rate within two inches of the target at twenty-five yards when standing still and a 96% rate when running."

"You're a damn wonder, Maggie. That's better than anyone I know. We need to take out the man in the back. Then, wheel Landry and take the girls to Skye and Trent's house. The gate between the properties is unlocked. Then, get him to the church. I'll lay cover out front until the sheriff's department gets here."

"Landry, take my wheels," Mr. Gann ordered as he climbed off his scooter. "It'll get you there faster than any car, and you can cut through the backyards to remain unseen."

"Lacy, take mine," Mr. Knoll instructed. "Put your sister in the basket."

"What about you both?' Landry asked. "We can't leave you here."

"Bah! I've been in more fights than you can imagine, sonny. We got this," Mr. Gann said with a twinkle in his eyes.

"We can't leave Maggie," Lacy said as she got onto Mr. Knoll's scooter.

"Landry," Maggie said as she looked at the scooters, "we're about to get to know each other a lot better. Give me the gun and get on the scooter. Lacy you're always to be on the far side of your dad. Never between him and the danger. Can you do that?"

"Yes, Miss Maggie," Lacy said seriously.

Maggie bent and used all her strength to help Landry get on the scooter. Thank goodness she was dressed for weapons class in athletic leggings as she faced Landry and tossed her leg over his lap, effectively straddling him as she sat in his lap on the motorized scooter. "Does this hurt you?"

"A little, but I'm more worried about explaining this to Lydia."

"Yeah, let's not mention this to Hunter either. Now, give me your gun."

Maggie checked the gun, and leaned to the side. "The man in the back?"

Blythe turned to the two old men. "Who is comfortable shooting a gun? You don't have to hit anything. Just keep them busy while I take out the man in the back."

Mr. Knoll cursed so creatively that Lacy and Leah giggled. "You have to give it to Gann. My cataracts will mess up my aim."

Mr. Gann looked victorious as he took the gun and hobbled to the window. With a nod to Blythe, he got in position.

"Let's go," Blythe ordered as she ran to the back, kicked the door open, and aimed her rifle. "Hey, asshole!" The idiot stuck his head out from behind the tree. He shouldn't have done that. "Now, Gann!" Gunfire erupted out front as Blythe held the door open and out they flew on the most powerful scooters Maggie had ever seen.

. . .

Hunter wasn't armed. Why the hell didn't he have a gun on him? Because he was playing with kids, that's why. It also meant they didn't have a car. They'd all walked to Ryker's, picked up the kids, and walked to the park to help them burn off some energy.

His brothers had the kids in their arms and were racing toward Granger's boat. They would get the kids onto the boat and drive it behind the church after Damon hotwired it. They'd be safe. Hunter's concern was now for Landry and Blythe. Hopefully Maggie and the girls were already safe at the church.

All Hunter could do was run. He sprinted as fast as he could up to the street, then ran full speed down the road. All his years of training kicked in. He saw and heard everything. The sirens from the sheriff's station as they got in their cruisers. The sounds of doors opening and people shouting. The sound of two rumbling engines to his right and the revving of a car engine ahead of him.

Hunter was approaching Oliva and Granger's cottage when the source of the rumbling engines showed itself. Hunter skidded to a stop as Lacy, with Leah standing on the back of Mr. Knoll's scooter and clinging to her sister, burst from the hedge, slid on the concrete like a dirt track racer, and took off toward downtown. Right behind her was Mr. Gann's scooter. Landry was driving and Maggie was straddling him. One hand was clutching Landry's waist as she leaned to the side so that he could see over her shoulder. They took the same slide onto the road as Lacy had, but now he could see the gun in Maggie's hand.

Hunter looked down the road, and coming up fast behind them was an SUV. The passenger window was down and a man was leaning out with a gun. "Look out!" Hunter yelled, but he didn't need to. Maggie was already firing.

"This isn't what it looks like, Hunter! Don't tell my wife!" Landry yelled as they took off down the street.

Hunter grabbed the first thing he could. A decent sized rock Olivia used to line the flowers around her mailbox. He waited for the SUV to draw closer. Maggie fired once more. The driver suddenly jerked. It was a direct hit. The wheel spun and the SUV headed straight for Hunter.

Hunter jumped out of the way as the SUV careened toward him and straight into a tree. Hunter made his move then. He was racing toward the passenger door even as it opened. Hunter grabbed it, and slammed it, catching the shooter's arm in the process. There was a howl of pain as a second SUV went flying by him and heading for downtown.

Hunter glanced behind him and saw a third SUV tearing down the street toward him and toward Maggie and Landry who had now turned onto Main Street.

There was no time for interrogation. He could only diffuse the situation as fast as he could and hope he wasn't too late. He yanked the door open, grabbed the man by the shirt, and pulled him to the ground. One whack with the rock in his hand and the threat was eliminated.

Hunter picked up the gun the man had been firing and took off running back in the direction of downtown. Suddenly Gavin's car raced by, heading to Ryker's as a sheriff's cruiser pulled a U-turn and slid to a stop.

"Get in!" Tristan yelled.

Hunter raced across the front of the cruiser and into the passenger's seat. "Status?"

"Injuries at Ryker's. Gavin's on it. Threats at the church. Kord is trying to contain it, but he needs backup."

"Maggie? Landry?" Hunter's heart was pounding. Please let them be safe.

"Drove the scooters straight into the church. The

women's group is in there. It's the safest place they could be. Now, let's go get 'em."

Tristan gunned the cruiser as cold anger seeped into Hunter's bones. They attacked the woman he loved. They attacked children. Whoever these assholes were, they would pay for it with their lives.

Landry skidded the scooter to a stop as Reverend Winston bolted the church doors closed behind them. The entire women's weapons class was waiting for them.

"Blythe sent out an SOS text," Miss Ruby said as she tossed a sword to Maggie.

"Here you go, dearies," Miss Winnie said, handing a dagger to Leah and a rapier to Lacy.

"Thank you for protecting my babies," Lydia said, sword in hand. "Now, open the doors, Rev."

"I don't think that's a good idea. Let the sheriff's department handle this," Reverend Winston said as bullets crashed through the front window.

"They came after my family. *I'll* handle it," Lydia said in a manner that brooked no argument and sent shivers down Maggie's spine.

Maggie nodded as she came shoulder to shoulder with Lydia, Lacy, and Leah.

"*We'll* handle it," Edie corrected, stepping forward to join them.

"Maggie, give me the gun. I'll protect you all," Landry said, holding out his hand.

"Honey, I love you, but get your ass back out of our way. Let the women handle this," Lydia snapped just as the first man tried to breach the window.

Lydia leaped forward and swung. Three fingers fell to the floor as the man screamed.

"Yes, ma'am," Landry said, backing up the scooter.

"Don't worry, Daddy. I'll protect you," Lacy said, placing herself between the front of the church and her father.

"I'll help," Kord said, appearing from the hidden tunnels. "Tristan and Hunter are on their way."

Maggie nodded, but her eye was on the window. There was a deep *thump* sound and then a canister flew into the church. "Smoke!"

"I got it!" Leah grabbed it and tossed it out of the window before anyone could move.

"Good throw, baby girl," Landry cheered.

"Two by two at the window," Maggie said as the women broke off into formation.

"Let them in," Lydia whispered.

"What do I do?" Melinda asked.

"Stay behind me. You're not trained yet," Reverend Winston said. He pushed open his clerical robe and pulled out a double-bladed spear. Melinda gasped but tightened her grip on her dagger. "Ladies. Defend the innocent. Protect the weak. Destroy those who wish us harm."

Maggie should be scared. Instead, she was furious. The calm, tight focus she got when she was shooting settled over her. She had her sword in one hand and handed her gun to Landry who looked a little wide-eyed. Not at the terrorists trying to kill him, but at his wife who had just lopped off some fingers and his young daughters, armed to the teeth and ready to protect him.

The ladies moved into position silently. A second smoke grenade was tossed into the window. Maggie kicked it to the side, but let it explode. The women were prepared. Their ears were covered so when the sound went off no one was startled. Smoke began to fill the church, but that's what they wanted.

Maggie ducked behind a pillar. Leah rolled under a pew. Edie, Lydia, Miss Winnie, Miss Mitzi, and Miss Ruby, were all in positions. Tamara, the waitress from the Pink Pig, seemed to melt into the smoke. No one made a sound as the men climbed through the window.

"Just hand it over, Langston, and no one needs to be killed. Except you. You've been a pain in our ass." The accent was unknown to Maggie, but it was an accent. Possibly Middle Eastern? Northern African? It was too hard to tell.

"What do you think I have?" Landry asked as Maggie watched the men walk through the smoke and up the aisle toward Landry.

"You know what you have. Have you told anyone about it? It won't matter. Nothing will stop us now."

The man raised his gun. The sound of tapping began. Miss Ruby was tapping her pike against the stone floor and the sound was echoing through the church. Miss Winnie started hers up across the church from Miss Ruby. They began to speed it up. Maggie knew what was happening, but it still gave her chills. The cold breeze through the church told her the pirate ghosts weren't happy with these uninvited guests either.

Maggie only saw the smoke blur and then the man screamed. A dagger was sticking out of his foot and Leah rolled back under the pew.

The sound of a sword slicing through the air and into a body, blood splattering on the stone, and the scream of a man, filled the church as Maggie crept forward in the smoke. They were all closing in on them the invaders who didn't even realize their time was up.

The man with the dagger in the foot chuckled as he leaned down and yanked it free with a grunt. Then suddenly he lunged at Landry. Landry's gun fired and then Maggie heard it drop to the ground and skid on the stone a moment before there was another scream and the sound of a second body hitting the ground.

"Step away from my husband or I'll let my daughter have at you. You have no idea how much rage a teenage girl has with all those hormones."

"Mrs. Langston. Tell your husband to hand it over and I won't gut your children like the brats they are. Nice dagger though. Can you see it as I cut your husband's throat?" he asked as he stood to Landry's side, his feet wide, and holding the dagger to Landry's throat.

Maggie finally got a clear view as the smoke began to clear. Lacy rose silently from the smoke behind the man.

"Can you see my rapier as I cut your balls off?" Lacy asked, but she didn't wait for a response. She held the two foot long blade up close to her body as she dove between the man's legs, rolled onto her back, and sliced upwards.

The door to the church crashed open at the same time. The women turned, ready for battle, but it wasn't a threat. It was Hunter and Tristan. Maggie moved then. They didn't need the backup, but it was nice to have it. Shots were fired. Swords, pikes, and daggers were swung.

"Behind you," she heard Hunter yell as she felt the air shift behind her. Maggie dropped to the ground as a shot rang out.

Instead of a bullet to her head, she got a kick to the stomach. She tightened her grip on her sword, rolling and bringing it up, but she was too late. Hunter had the man by the throat, his feet dangling off the ground, and then he slammed him against the stone pillar. The man went limp, and Hunter dropped him without a second thought.

"Are you hurt?" Hunter asked as he picked her up and ran his hands over her.

"I'm good. Protect the Langstons."

Hunter gave her a quick kiss and waded back into the fight. Maggie looked over and saw the Langston family didn't need help. Lydia, Lacy, and Leah were fierce in their defense of Landry. The man who had held Landry at knifepoint was rolling on the floor, clutching what was left of his balls as Miss Mitzy clucked at him.

"I'd be crying too, if I was you. That's one ugly pecker. And it's so *small*. No wonder you're an angry man, bless your heart."

It felt as if the fight went on forever, but it was over in a few short minutes. Some men were tied up. Others were dead. But Shadows Landing was still standing.

The smoke cleared and Landry grabbed Lydia, pulled her onto his lap of the scooter and kissed her so passionately that Lacy gagged.

"Is that how Lennie was made?" Leah asked with a grossed-out look on her face as Lydia deepened the kiss.

"Hey," Maggie overheard Tristian say to Hunter. "Blythe's been shot. Gavin got her stabilized and is racing her to the hospital."

Hunter's jaw tightened. He turned to Maggie, grabbed the sword from her hand, and walked to the nearest live terrorist. The tip of the blade was pressed to his stomach, slowly cutting into the skin. "Who sent you and what is your objective?"

The man laughed even though he was in pain. "You'll all find out soon enough. It's clear he doesn't know and our mission is safe. You'll all know soon. You can't stop it."

20

The entire town of Shadows Landing seemed to be crammed into the Faulkner Suite at the hospital. Gavin had driven Blythe to the hospital while Kenzie worked on her wound. Blythe had suffered substantial blood loss and now Kenzie was standing in the room wearing scrubs instead of the blood-soaked clothes she'd been wearing.

Kord and Tristan had secured Landry and his family in the church where they both stayed, guarding them. Granger and Stone had brought the kids back and Granger was with them at the hospital, waiting for news.

Mr. Gann and Mr. Knoll were back on their scooters after they'd been gassed up and were also waiting for Blythe to come out of surgery. They'd told the room how Blythe had jumped in front of bullets meant for them. Even after being shot, she'd been able to hold off the attack until help arrived.

The sound of staccato high heels pinging the floor in a rushed walk echoed down the hall as Reverend Winston finished up a prayer for Blythe.

"Holy Mother of God," the nurse gasped as the woman

strode into the room. The nurse ducked behind the reverend and might have been shaking in fear.

"Update." The stunning woman was no nonsense, even if her mascara was slightly smudged from tears.

"Veronica," Olivia said, standing up to hug the woman. "Blythe is in surgery."

"I need to talk to a doctor. Now."

Kenzie cleared her throat and stepped forward. "Veronica, I'm sorry we have to see you under these circumstances. I was with Dr. Faulkner, you know Gavin, as we got Blythe to the hospital. She was shot in the stomach, just below her vest. She's lost quite a bit of blood and there will most likely be intestinal damage. We'll know more soon. Gavin is in the operating room with her along with the best the hospital has."

Veronica took a shuddering breath as if to control herself. "Who did this to my girlfriend? Who did this to the woman I love? I will end them."

Maggie shivered. She'd thought Hunter was scary when he was fighting and she'd thought Olivia was scary in court. Veronica, the executive assistant to the Rahmi royal family who lived in the small town of Keeneston, was next level.

Hunter stepped forward and gave her a brief rundown of what had been happening. Classified information be damned.

"What does Landry have?" Veronica asked when Hunter finished his report.

"We don't know and Landry doesn't remember," Hunter told her as a very nervous looking nurse walked in holding a clear plastic bag.

"Ma'am," she said, her voice wobbling in fear. Veronica turned on one spiked heel and stared at her. "I brought you Blythe's personal effects from the operating room. I didn't want them to get left behind. Dr. Faulkner is right behind me with an update."

Maggie looked at the bag, her mind whirling, and then it hit her like a freight train. "Oh crap. I got it. Is Ryker at home?" Maggie asked Kenzie.

"Yes, he's getting the house put back together and reinforcing his security down at the river. That's how they got in."

Maggie pulled out her phone and called Ryker. "Ryker, go into Landry's bedroom. On the floor of his closet is a clear plastic bag from the hospital in Millevia. Bring it and Landry to your hospital suite now." Ryker tried to ask questions but Gavin walked into the room. "Just do it."

Maggie hung up as Hunter came to offer silent support to Veronica on one side while his sister took Veronica's other hand and held her tight.

"How's Blythe?"

Gavin gave a tight smile. "She's alive."

Veronica swayed on her heels, but Hunter and Olivia steadied her.

"They had to remove some of her intestines, but she'll make it. We have to monitor her closely for infection. She'll be staying at the hospital for a while as she recovers."

"But she will recover?" Veronica asked.

"She will," Gavin confirmed.

Veronica took a deep, steadying breath. "Thank you, Gavin. When can I see her?"

"In about an hour. I'll come back to get you when it's time."

Gavin left with the nervous looking nurse as Veronica clutched the clear bag. "What are you thinking?" Hunter asked.

"It might be nothing, but I was handed Landry's effects.

His clothes had been cut off in Millevia and stuffed into a bag. While Landry doesn't remember taking anything, maybe he did and hid it in his uniform."

Kenzie looked down at her phone. "We'll find out in ten minutes. Ryker is flying the helicopter in with Landry."

"How are you doing? This was a lot for civilians," Hunter asked Maggie as they stood on the roof of the hospital waiting for Ryker and Landry to arrive. He was worried about Maggie. She looked about ready to fall over from exhaustion as the adrenaline drained from her body.

"I'm just relieved no one died. Well, none of us died."

"I'm always amazed by the women of Shadows Landing. You're very formidable with a sword, Mags." All the women had been. It was impressive that women from ten to eighty years old didn't hesitate to defend their loved ones. He about died when he saw Lacy slice her rapier into the man's balls. Landry was just as shocked, but extremely proud. Sure, the guys knew that the women trained, but seeing them in action was completely different. They were a more cohesive team than Hunter's Special Forces team.

Hunter put his arm around Maggie and pulled her to his side. He had to reassure himself that she was still there and not hurt. Seeing her straddling an injured Landry and shooting at the cars chasing them was not something he'd ever forget. It had twisted his heart in a way that he'd never be the same again.

Maggie leaned against him as he watched the sky for Ryker's helicopter. "I wish I never had to use my sword or my gun, but I will always defend the people I love."

Hunter bent his head and kissed her. His whole world, his whole being had changed in the past weeks. It was no longer about him. It was about her. Everything was about her. "That's just one of the things I love about you."

Maggie almost jerked with surprise and it made him smile. "Did you just—"

"Tell you I love you? Yes. I did. Because I do love you, Magnum Bell. I would like to say it was love at first sight, but we know that's not true. But it was love as soon as I pulled my head out of my ass. I know it's not a romantic gesture, but my heart stopped today when I saw you under fire. I couldn't go another day without you knowing I love you, that I'm in awe of you, and I'm so damned proud of you. You're amazing and I don't know how I'm lucky enough to be with you. I love you, Magnum."

Hunter could practically hear Damon rubbing it in that he'd been right. But if that meant Hunter had Maggie in his life, he'd take all the crap Damon would tease him with. Maggie was worth it.

"Hunter, really?"

Hunter brushed back her loose hair falling in her face and cupped her cheeks with his hands. He angled her face up so he could place a kiss on her lips. "Really. I love you."

His stomach actually got a little loopy as he waited to hear if she loved him. She smirked and he knew he was in trouble. "Hmm," she said as she tapped her finger to her chin. "How do I feel about Hunter Townsend?"

She loved him. Hunter knew it. She wouldn't tease him if she didn't.

"That's easy. I love you too," Maggie smiled up at him, placing her hand over his heart. "I mean it, Hunter. It's never been like this before. For me, it's you."

"And for me, it's you and only you."

Hunter kissed her again. It was strange how a few words could change everything. How a kiss could feel completely different from how their last kiss had been. It was a huge shift in their relationship and Hunter wasn't nervous about it. Instead, it felt right. But he also knew, his future had changed forever.

Hunter looked around the nurses' break room as he, Tristan, Veronica, Ryker, and Landry all stared at Maggie as she upended the plastic hospital bag. Out came Landry's uniform, socks, boots, and military knife. His gun has been kept out of the hospital.

"I'm telling you. I don't remember taking anything," Landry said as he separated his clothes.

Nothing fell out as Landry shook out the pockets and patted down the uniform.

"If you knew you were going to be searched, where would you hide something?" Maggie asked, as she picked up his pants and began examining them.

Landry froze. Hunter saw it. He could see the gears in Landry's mind spinning to remember something. Then he reached for his boots. He reached inside and yanked out the sole of the first one. Nothing. He reached into the second boot and pulled out the sole. "I don't believe it," he muttered, pulling a folded piece of paper from the boot. "You were right. But I don't remember this." Landry unfolded the paper and everyone leaned forward.

"It's a map," Ryker said, stating the obvious.

"Of Italy," Tristan added. "I know several of those towns."

"What would be special about Italy?" Veronica wondered.

Hunter looked at the map. Three towns were circled. Next to him, Maggie gasped suddenly. "What is it?"

"These locations. They're all associated with the Olympics. Either hosting athletes, fans, or events," Maggie explained pointing to one of the circles on the map. "That area is where the track and field stadium is. Shooting is over here, which is at the edge of that circled area. Then this is where gymnastics will be held. Swimming, here. Then this is where the athlete dorms are. These are hotels for the families. They all fall within these circled areas."

"If a bomb or bombs go off in any of these areas, there would be mass casualties," Hunter said slowly, taking it all in. "But what is their reasoning?"

"Big international events have always been a target for illegal activity. Human trafficking, drugs, cyberattacks, and terrorist attacks," Tristan told them.

Maggie nodded. "Remember the bombing in Atlanta in 1996? There was also the Munich massacre in 1972 when the Israeli team was attacked. In recent years though, we've been warned more about cyberattacks than actual physical attacks."

"We know the where, although it's a large area. We kind of know the when, but the big questions that remain—who and why?" Hunter asked. "I'll call Kane and fill him in."

"I'll call President Gastaud and see if she can talk to Italy's leaders. She'll hold more sway than us," Tristan said, stepping out of the room.

"I leave on Wednesday. I'll let you know what I hear on the ground," Maggie told him.

"The hell you are," Hunter snapped, mid-dial. "There's no way the woman I love is walking into a known planned terrorist attack."

Hunter saw the mulish way Maggie's mouth turned, but he'd just gotten her into his life. He wasn't going to have her walk into a bombing. Not until they stopped it.

"I've worked my whole life for this, Hunter. I'm going."

"All your work won't matter if you're dead," Hunter replied as the rest of the room watched them.

He stared at her, trying to get Maggie to see how much he cared. This wasn't about her skill. This was about her safety.

Veronica cleared her throat. "Hunter, what would it take to make you feel better about Maggie going?"

"These people caught and the bombs found."

"We don't know for sure this is a bombing," Maggie pointed out.

"You're not dumb, Magnum. You know what this is," Hunter said, knowing it was going to make her mad. "Stolen fertilizer. A missing bomber. Mercenaries and former military working together. The map. They're not picking out a guy's trip, Mags, and you know it."

Her lips thinned because she did know it. Then she crossed her arms and he knew he was in trouble. "Then you better catch them because I'm going. I'll hire personal security when I'm over there."

"If you're going, I'm going." Hunter crossed his arms and dared her to deny him.

"Hunter, I can't get you the access you need. I can have someone with me though, if I hire someone through the games. Plus, spectator tickets are completely sold out. You can't even go as a spectator." Maggie explained it, but Hunter didn't care. He knew this was her dream, but his protective instincts were telling him to whisk her away to a bunker and not let her come out until this was over.

"I have a solution," Veronica said, interrupting them. "Hunter, if I get you all access passes *and* full security clearance, will you feel better about Maggie being there?"

Hunter noticed Veronica didn't say *if* Maggie went but

when Maggie went. Maggie looked at him expectantly. He saw the eagerness and hope in her eyes. "Fine. But if this isn't settled by then, you do whatever I say to keep you safe."

"As long as I can compete," Maggie agreed.

"I don't like it, but I'll agree only if I can get those passes."

Veronica looked insulted. She picked up her phone and made a call. Thirty seconds later Hunter was Maggie's personal coach with security clearance, permission to carry, and an all-access pass.

"Who are you?" Hunter asked seriously as Tristan came back into the room.

"I'm the person who organized the multinational, joint military and law enforcement training session in Keeneston that you participated in recently. If I can do that, I can get in touch with anyone," Veronica said casually. Good point. That was an incredibly well-planned and organized training session.

"Well, you might need to work your magic with the Italian government. Millevia's president reached out, but they're not returning her call," Tristan said with anger in his eyes. Emily Gastaud was young and a woman. She got a lot of pushback from bigger countries. Plus, she was dating Tristan's best friend, David. They were more friends of Tristian's than leaders.

"President Serro can be stubborn, but at his heart is a good guy," Veronica said, scrolling through her phone. "I'll take care of it. Plus, I'll bring in some help on the tech front."

"No need," Ryker interjected. "I have the tech side covered."

Veronica didn't question him, she just nodded and headed out of the room with her phone to her ear and speaking in rapid-fire Italian. Whatever she said had Tristan's eyebrows rising. "That woman scares the crap out of me. I almost feel sorry for whoever is behind this. They've unleashed a power so strong it can't be stopped."

"Hunter," Maggie said, dropping her voice as everyone left the room. "Just because you love me doesn't mean you control me. I don't tell you not to go on missions. Instead, I'll be here supporting you. I know you're worried, but this is my whole life's work. I know we've disagreed in the past, but this is different. We're a couple now and as a couple, we talk things through and come up with a plan so there's not a breakdown of communication."

Hunter ran his hand through his hair in frustration. "I know. Olivia would have hurt me for telling her what to do. You support me when I leave for missions. I'll support you. I'm so damn proud of what you've accomplished and want to see you win gold, but I want you safe more. We'll communicate our plans and work together to find a course of action. But, I'm serious, Magnum. If something is off, I love you too much to let you die for it. No gold medal is worth your life."

Maggie nodded. "Okay. We'll talk about it though. Make the decisions together unless I'm in imminent danger."

"Deal. Now I need to call my contacts in Italian Special Forces and see if I can get some security details," Hunter said as they walked out of the room.

"I'm sending them to you now," Ryker answered from where he was leaning against the wall. "I'm also sending you a burner phone number. Don't ask who owns it. It'll be tossed as soon as this is over. But you can use it for tech support. Run facials, ask for schematics, whatever you need, ask them. If they can't help you, they'll know someone who can."

"Is this illegal?" Hunter asked, looking at the number.

"Let's not ask. Got it?"

Hunter pulled up the text and stared at such detailed maps that it was as if he'd been in on the planning of the setup and security of the games. "Thanks. This helps a lot."

"Blythe is awake," Kenzie said, joining her husband. "Veronica just left to see her, but she's asking for you, Hunter."

21

Maggie watched as Hunter rushed off to be by Blythe's side. She took a deep breath and let it out slowly. There was noise all around her, but in the hallway she was alone. Nurses and doctors walked by, but they weren't stopping to talk to her or tell her bad news. She just needed a moment to gather herself because it had been a lot.

Maggie's phone rang. There went her moment.

"Hello, Coach Weisz," Maggie said, knowing her Olympic shooting coach was probably calling to see why he suddenly had another coach on the team.

"Maggie, why did the President of the United States just call to inform me that you have a new private coach? One Hunter Townsend, who will be part of the Olympic team. I assume this is the same First Sergeant Hunter Townsend that I have coached myself?" Coach Weisz was in his sixties and had taught at the Army Marksman School until his retirement. In fact, he'd taught one Hunter Townsend when Hunter had gone through the school.

"Wait, the *president* called you?" Maggie stuttered out in

surprise. *That* was who Veronica had called? Who was this woman?

"Yes. Are you dissatisfied with me as your coach? I got the impression you and Hunter didn't get along."

Maggie blushed even though she was on the phone. "We get along well now. We worked it out. This has nothing to do with your coaching and has everything to do with things going on at the Olympics and Hunter being worried about my safety."

Coach Weisz was quiet for a moment. He was military. He knew what she was saying even if she didn't have to spell it out. "I'll call my new coach and come up with a training plan for you and the team."

"Hunter is with someone who was injured. Give him a little bit. I'm sorry, Coach. We're trying to get this resolved by the time I leave on Wednesday, but so far we haven't had any luck. I won't let it distract us though."

"There should be no we, or even any I, Maggie. You may outshoot my troops, but you aren't one of them. Let Hunter take care of this. It's his job and he's damn good at it. I'll see if we can get read into it and if we can help," he said of himself and Allison Mullins, who was on her team but was also in the military. All in all, about a third of the team were either active or retired military.

"Or you could ask me since I know exactly what's going on." Discounted. Dismissed. That's what Maggie felt. First Hunter when he'd first met her, now her coach. "I know I'm not military but you don't know what I'm capable of. I've already killed one man who was holding Hunter hostage and knocked another out. I might look sweet. I might look cute. But you know damn well I'm so much more than that. Use me to help. Use my abilities. Use the fact that I don't look like a soldier to get things done that someone like Hunter couldn't."

"I'll talk to Hunter, Maggie. I'm sorry you had to kill someone. How are you holding up?"

"Do you ask all your soldiers that?" Maggie asked.

"I do. It's something that is discussed at length during marksmanship. We have psychologists and everything come in to talk about the mental ramifications of taking a life. So, how are you doing, Maggie?"

Dang. Her coach got her. She took a shuddering breath. "I'm okay. I saw it as a target. I still think about it at night, but it's getting better. I know it needed to be done and I didn't hesitate."

"You always take the tough shots, Maggie. Allison and I are here if you ever want to talk about it. I'll wait and then call Hunter. I might change up our team's arrival on Wednesday. I'll be in touch. And Maggie," Coach Weisz said, "share the burden with your team, be it your friends, Hunter, or us. You're not alone here."

"Thanks, Coach." Maggie took a deep breath after hanging up. She wasn't alone. She had Hunter now. She had her family. She had her whole town backing her.

Hunter hated to interrupt Veronica and Blythe. Veronica was sitting by the bed, holding Blythe's hand. She placed a kiss on Blythe's knuckles and smiled. Blythe's gaze turned to see Hunter hiding by the door.

"Hey, Hunter. V tells me everyone is okay, but didn't have specifics," Blythe said as if it pained her to speak.

"Mr. Gann and Mr. Knoll are uninjured but furious about what happened to you. Landry and Maggie zoomed by me on a scooter with Maggie shooting at the SUV chasing them. Leah stabbed a man before Lacy practically sliced his balls off. I think Lydia got to work out a lot of rage. Chopped off three fingers and took down two men. No one from Shadows Landing is hurt, thanks to you," Hunter reported.

Blythe smiled. "I love this town. You know, our priest is trying to start up a weapons class because of your church here. But V was telling me you all found a map."

Hunter wouldn't insult her by telling her not to worry or to rest. "Maggie figured it out. It's the three locations of the games in Italy. Veronica got me in as a coach and armed security for the games. But that's all I have."

"President Serro didn't like President Gastaud, a young president of a small country, trying to tell him he had a problem he didn't know about. These games are his crowning glory to a less than stellar presidency. He's refusing to admit there is an issue, of course in the nicest way possible. He's sending me cannoli," Veronica told them and rolled her eyes. "Don't worry. I have ways around him. He may be the host country, but I know the committee will think differently and will help us out."

"V," Blythe said with a weak smile, "can you get me some water? I'm so thirsty."

Veronica nodded and got up, even if she was reluctant to do so.

"I only have a moment," Blythe said to Hunter. "Veronica will take down a country and not think twice about it. You think, because she's just an assistant to a prince, she can't do it. She can and she will. Don't let her do something she'll regret later. Call your contacts, get to Italy, and take down this group before Veronica does. Because, the second I'm stable, she'll go scorched earth without giving a damn that it'll make her a target." Hunter heard Veronica coming, and so did Blythe. "Promise me."

"I promise."

"Oh, and could you get engaged two Saturdays from now? I might have a bet going with your brothers. And Gator. And Skeeter. And Turtle. And the Faulkners. And the Rev."

"Engaged," Hunter said, blinking. They'd just started dating.

"Yes, now go. You have work to do."

Hunter stood up and numbly said goodbye to the women. Engaged? He'd never given much thought to getting married. Only, he had thought about having Maggie in his life forever. Hunter paused out in the hall to see how he felt about that. Hmm, it didn't send him running for the hills. Instead, it had him turning to go see Maggie.

Hunter's wish to see Maggie was on hold. First, he called Damon. Second, he called the mystery number that Ryker had given him. A man answered. He seemed to already know about Veronica and Blythe and understood the urgency. Hunter talked and sent pictures of the men they'd killed. The man promised to get back to him ASAP. Then Hunter had to call Kane and fill him in that he'd be in Italy on Wednesday.

"Can't you get Maggie to stay home?" Kane asked.

"Would you stay home?"

Kane cursed. "No. Whatever this is, it is locked down tight. The people who know aren't talking no matter how much money I promise them."

"Send me the names of the people who are in the know.

Maybe combined with the men we've identified we can find a connection."

"Good idea. Send me your flight information and I'll meet you when you land."

Hunter looked up and saw Maggie walking toward him. "Thanks, Kane. See you soon."

"Has Kane learned anything yet?" Maggie asked.

"He's sending me some information, but no one is talking. He's going to meet us at the airport when the team lands to offer some added protection," Hunter explained.

"Coach Weisz wants a word, too," Maggie said, seeming annoyed.

"What's the matter?" Hunter asked, taking Maggie by the hand and leading her from the hospital.

"I'm not a soldier."

Hunter was confused. "I know."

"Coach won't let me in on what's going on because I'm not a soldier. He wants me to sit back and let you all handle this."

Ah. He saw the problem. Maggie was a smart, competent woman and liked to be useful.

"I won't tell Coach if you won't. I'll keep you in the loop. We promised never to lie or hide anything from each other. I won't if you promise to listen to me."

"I can shoot, Hunter. Better than you."

"I know, but this is no longer about who can shoot better. It's about strategy, military intelligence, boots on the ground, and knowing how to enter a combat situation." Hunter pulled her close and looked down into her face. She needed to hear this and understand it. "There is no one I trust more to take the hard shot than you. You've proven yourself, Magnum, over and over again. Let me prove to you what I can do now. Together, we'll catch them. Okay?"

"You'll let me help?" Maggie asked, hopefully.

"I don't think I could stop you. That's beside the point, though. I trust you, Maggie. You don't act impulsively. You're focused. You know how to limit collateral damage and you have nerves of steel. Plus, no one will see the hot girl in pink and purple coming. I sure as hell didn't." Hunter kissed her then. It wasn't passionate, but it was supportive. It told her he loved her and trusted her.

"We'll do it together, then. I want to be an asset to you."

"I know, sweetheart. You already are in more ways than one." Hunter's phone rang. It was the unknown blocked number. Hunter pulled Maggie into the nearest empty room and closed the door. "Townsend," Hunter said as he answered it on speaker.

"And Bell," the voice said. "Hello, Maggie."

Hunter looked around the room and zeroed in on the security camera. "How do you know Maggie?"

"Do you want to know what I found out or do you want to chit-chat?" the male voice on the phone asked.

Maggie cocked her head. Her brow was creased and it was clear she was trying to figure out who it was.

"You found something?" Hunter asked, his heart rate picking up as he kept his breathing calm. He was excited but if you let that excitement take over you missed details.

"I identified the men killed or injured at the church. It's a very interesting mix of nationalities. Then I inputted the information you sent from your brother, Kane. Dude, he's cool." The man cursed and Hunter heard a female voice giggle over the phone.

"It's contagious," the female voice whispered.

"Sorry, I normally don't say 'dude.' Anyway, I inputted their information and found some connections."

"What are they?" Hunter asked, keeping his eyes on

Maggie. She looked so desperate to speak, but she didn't. She was letting him take the lead.

"They're not direct, they're circumstantial. The fighters come from seven countries: Belarus, Bolivia, Crusina, South Sudan, Syria, Iran, and Yemen."

Hunter nodded. Maggie didn't see it. "They're all countries with power struggles. Crusina is more stable now, but Deming Nikan took power after his father was deposed and he turned the country into a democracy. Belarus is famous for its mercenaries who answer to no one. Bolivia has coups more often than not. The rest are in a continual battle for power between fractions. Except Iran, which is run with an iron fist. The leaders have power and have no one to answer to. Because of that, it amounts to one of the most corrupt governments in the world."

"Yes," the man said. "The men we identified from the countries, except Iran, are all from sections that failed in coups or were kicked out of power. The man Lydia Langston killed was with the Iranian military. So, whatever the plan is, the Iranian government is supporting it along with these disenfranchised former militaries."

"Which is why an international event the size of the Olympics would be the perfect place to hit," Maggie said.

"Exactly. The question is: what is their common goal? It could be political. It could be monetary. It could be revenge. Or it could be all three. Also, the people Kane had identified are known black market weapons dealers and owners of shady corporations that masquerade as construction companies but are really fronts for the government or friends of the leaders of those corrupt countries. We are sending someone over to have a word with them. I'll let you know what they find out."

"Wait," Hunter said, stopping him. "We? And who are you sending?"

"I can't tell you," the man replied. "But if someone asks you if your watch is waterproof, you'll know they're with us and might need help."

"What organization are you with?" Hunter asked.

"I'm sending a care package to you, Maggie. Do what the note says. It'll arrive tomorrow. Good luck at the games. Know you've got people working on this and hopefully you'll have no distractions when it's time for you to compete. I'll call if I have any other news."

The line went dead and Hunter looked back up at the camera in the room. "He hacked into the hospital security to watch us."

Maggie didn't seem to care. She looked lost in thought. "So, you have a bunch of power-hungry men who got pushed out of power or who want more power, right?" Maggie didn't wait for him to reply. He could see the gears in her head spinning. "I know what this is about."

"You do?"

Maggie nodded. "I saw it in sororities all the time. Sadly, mine included."

Hunter struggled not to groan. "You are equating a world terrorist threat to your sorority?"

"Tara May was chapter president of my sorority sophomore year. Normally, the president is a senior, but Emma-Lou, the senior running for president, had nudes released and that left Tara May, a junior, as the only viable candidate. Well, she let the power go to her head. She and her little group took control of everything and relegated those who had opposed them to the worst roles in the sorority. That wasn't enough. They wanted more. Our chapter GPA began to slide. We started to get a bad reputation. We saw that our recruitment was going down and we saw our sisterhood was threatened," Maggie explained. "So, we had a coup. We organized over the summer and before the election could take place, because we didn't trust Tara May and her group to count the votes accurately, we challenged her on the grounds listed in our by-laws. We tossed her out and I was installed as the new president. *Then* we held an election, where I was confirmed as president. Tara May ran against me, but only received the votes from her minions. However, after that things began to go wrong—things broke in the house, money went missing, rumors were started."

"Tara May?" Hunter guessed.

"That's right. We ended up stripping her of her letters and kicking her out of the sorority, both our chapter *and* National. For her last year, she did nothing but try to ruin us. Tell me this doesn't look like that."

Hunter wanted to say it wasn't the same, but on a basic level, it was. "They were all stripped of power and now they want it back."

"I was Tara May's biggest target since, as the new president, I was the symbol of what she'd lost. Next were those who supported me. That could be the target. Whoever doesn't support these fighters."

Hunter nodded. "It's the best we have to go on. I'll send it to the number and have him pass it along. Maybe we'll know more soon. In the meantime, have any friends on any of those teams?"

Maggie smiled. "As a matter of fact, I do. And they all tend to be current or former military. I'll meet with them on Thursday. It will be less obvious if we meet in the athlete's village or talk at the range, plus some of their phones might not be secure."

"Make it a place where I can be in the background watching out for you."

Maggie slipped her hand into his as they made their way to his truck. "We do make a good team."

"In more ways than one," Hunter said as the elevator doors closed. He pulled her tight, slid his hand to her ass for a squeeze, and kissed her.

His phone vibrated and he groaned when it vibrated again. He pulled it out and then raised his middle finger to the camera in the elevator.

Unknown Number: She's smart. I'll pass along the information. Also, an engagement during opening ceremonies would be romantic.

22

Rome, Italy . . .

"Hey, Kane." Hunter hugged his brother as they got off the plane in Italy.

Kane shoved him aside and hugged Maggie. "There's my girl."

Hunter rolled his eyes and Maggie laughed. "Thanks for helping," she told his brother.

"Guess who else has been named a coach for the shooting team?" Kane asked, spinning around to show off a Team USA windbreaker. A windbreaker that looked identical to the ones Maggie received in the mail, complete with matching pants. The package included team uniforms, team outfits, all designated with a smiley face label inside and a note that said, *wear only me in Italy*.

"We're overrun by Townsends," Coach Weisz grumbled as he joined them along with Gage and Allison. "We need to check in and get situated in the village. Allison and Maggie will be rooming together. I'm putting you two brothers together on one floor below. The women's team is on the fourth floor, and the men's team is on the third," Coach explained as they all got their bags and moved to the large bus reserved for them.

"I've seen the security," Hunter told Kane. "Eighty-five thousand security personnel. Double fences around the village, and X-ray security to even get into the place."

Maggie cleared her throat and looked a little nervous. "What is it?" Hunter asked.

"So, you need to understand that what happens in the village, stays in the village. There's going to be a lot of coming and going, and in more ways than one."

Allison smiled. "And you better not get in my way. Four years ago, I caught four water polo players. This year, it's all about rugby. We have a bingo card," Allison said, nodding to one of the other women shooters on the bus, who grinned. "First one to fill it wins."

Maggie blushed a little. "The Italians do have a reputation. Don't be surprised to see their doors open, music blaring, and clothing very optional."

"The rumors are true? It's like one big party?" Kane asked.

Maggie nodded and didn't meet Hunter's eyes. "Who was on your bingo card last time?" he asked her.

Allison laughed. "I took water polo. She took swimmers. Although, she did have a couple of track and field stars thrown in."

"Alli," Maggie hissed, but Hunter just smiled.

"Prim and proper Magnum Bell went wild? I have to hear more," Hunter said to Allison, ignoring how freaked out Maggie looked.

"The village is its own paradise. No overbearing parents, all this training, and then bam, you're in a confined, safe space where everyone has something in common," Allison explained. "Although, we did hold off until we were done with our events. Then we went wild."

"Hunter, I can explain," Maggie whispered miserably.

"Babe, you don't have to explain. I like that you're comfortable in your sexuality. I am with mine. I'm not going to pretend I've never had crazy hookups before. You don't have to pretend either. The past is the past. I'm glad you have experience so you can know the difference between a hookup and forever."

"Our sex is as hot as hookup sex with the longevity of forever," Maggie whispered in his ear.

"Best of both worlds." Hunter kissed her and Alli groaned.

"There goes my wingwoman."

"Well, this doesn't sound bad to me," Kane grinned. "I'll happily question the other teams over sex."

"I'll make you a bingo card since I'm pretty sure these two will be occupied," Allison said with a wink.

Hunter held on to Maggie as the bus made its way to the Olympic Village. It took some effort, but with the right passes, he and Kane were able to get their guns through security.

"I'll be downstairs. Are you okay?" Hunter asked as he and Kane got off on the fourth floor. The other coaches were staying in a different building. Instead, he had Gage and the rest of the men following to their rooms.

"I'm good. We're safe here. I'll see you at dinner." Maggie kissed him and then waved. "Ameera!" Maggie dropped her voice. "She's from Iran. I'll see what I can learn."

Kane shoved him down the hall. "Come on. I have a list of people to, um, talk to."

Hunter opened the door to their room. Before it was

even all the way open, he had his gun drawn. "Hands up," Hunter ordered the two men standing by the window.

The men raised their arms. "Nice watch. Is it waterproof?" one of them asked in a clear American accent.

"Aye, let's hope Kane's is too since he has a handful of condoms," the second man said with a slight Scottish accent. He was massive. It would take Hunter a minute to disarm him.

"Who are you two?"

"I'm Dalton and this is my friend Grant. We thought you might want in on an interrogation."

Hunter looked at Kane who was clearly assessing the two men standing in their room.

"Can I go say hi to the Swedish volleyball team first?" Kane asked.

"No," Dalton said simply.

"Spoilsport."

"My lass doesn't like to be kept waiting and we're already making her wait by coming to ask you to join us." Grant shrugged his shoulders.

"Are you military?" Hunter asked. They both had the military look but also seemed more relaxed in who they were, which meant they weren't bound by the confines of the military.

"They're not military, not anymore," Kane said, all the teasing about his bingo card gone. "I'd guess private. I think off-books is more likely, right boys?"

"Let's not ask questions you're not allowed to know the answers to. Are you in or not?" Dalton asked, getting right to the point.

"In. Who do you have?" Hunter asked even as he silently agreed with his brother.

"Kane's contact led us to a farmer in Millevia. The

farmer was paid by the man we have in custody to rat out the other farmers with large storages of fertilizer ripe for stealing," Dalton explained as he headed out of the room.

Hunter fell in line next to Dalton and Kane next to Grant as they walked out of the building. "Does he know where the fertilizer went?" Hunter asked.

"That's what we're going to find out," Grant answered.

"And your wife is with him now?" Kane said, clearly trying to get more information from the two men.

"Aye. Both of our wives."

"You're not worried about their safety?" Kane asked as they approached a black SUV with tinted windows.

Grant chuckled. Dalton grinned. Neither answered.

"Interesting," Kane muttered.

"Are you done working up your profile, Agent Townsend?" Dalton asked after they got into the SUV.

"I'm no longer with the FBI." Hunter noticed Kane didn't answer about the profile.

"What do you make of us?" Grant asked, noticing Kane's lack of an answer.

"I'll tell you after I meet your wives. I can tell a lot about a person based on their spouse."

Grant turned in his seat and grinned at them. "You'll love Val. Watch your balls, boys."

Hunter thought Grant might be joking about watching their balls. He wasn't. They entered the abandoned warehouse outside of the village to find a beautiful and pregnant Latina woman with a knife to the balls of the man tied to the chair.

"Took you long enough," the blonde who was supervising said, barely casting a glance at them. "Did you have to drag them away from the volleyball team? Or was it the equestrian team?"

"Who is he?" Hunter asked taking in the man in his late twenties who was tied to the chair.

"Yusuf Assad. Former bankroller for a Syrian terror group that was defeated and scattered about five years ago," she answered.

"What have you found out?" Dalton asked the woman with the knife.

"He thinks he won't lose his balls. He's wrong," she answered.

Hunter stepped forward and pulled out his phone. He selected a picture and turned it so the man could see it. "The guy in this picture didn't think he'd have his balls cut off by a teenager. He was also wrong," Hunter said in Arabic.

"You think teen hormones are bad? Wait until you see pregnancy hormones," the woman said, also in Arabic, as she sliced through the man's pants with her knife. "Three seconds to tell me what you have planned for that fertilizer or I cut off one of your balls. Which do you prefer? Your right or left?"

The man clearly didn't think she would do it. Hunter didn't know if she would either. She did. Or she would have. She got through the delicate layer of what appeared to be bikini briefs before Kane stopped her.

"Back down, now," Kane snapped, coming to stand between the woman the Yusuf. Hunter saw that the woman looked ready to cut Kane's balls off, but she backed down. "Yusuf, let me help you. We don't need some stupid woman cutting off your balls when she doesn't understand that you were just following orders. Who gave you those orders?"

Yusuf stayed quiet.

"Get out of my way or I'll cut yours off," she ground out.

Kane looked to Dalton and Grant. "Someone control her." Kane dismissed the woman with the knife and turned back to Yusuf. "I can only keep her contained if you talk. We know this isn't about religion. Your group is from too many countries of differing religious and cultural customs. However, all your countries are highly unstable and you were all once in power but now have none, or are currently in power by the skin of your balls. I bet it feels as if your country cut off your balls like she wants to do to you, doesn't it?"

Hunter saw what Kane was doing now. He was trained in psychology and he was using it against Yusuf. He was the good cop to the woman's bad cop.

"Look, Yusuf," Kane said, keeping Yusuf's attention on him. "I'm the one chance you have of getting out of here not only alive but with both balls attached. Let me help you. Don't pay attention to her. Pay attention to me. Who do you report to?"

Out came everything the young man knew. Including who he reported to.

Hunter watched as the big Scot dragged the man into a van that pulled up. Yusuf was turned over to two men in all black wearing bulletproof vests and was shoved into the back of the van.

"Sorry about that, but I knew he wouldn't talk to a woman. His profile read that he'd refuse out of sheer spite. But he was also afraid, so he needed an excuse to break." Kane held out his hand to the woman who had put away her knife. "Kane Townsend."

"I know," she grinned before turning to Grant, ignoring Kane's hand. "Honey, the baby is so hungry and pissed that Mommy didn't get to make a fried snack from Yusuf's balls. Do you have anything to eat?"

Grant kissed the woman and pulled out a backpack. "Of course, babe. Good job, you two. You worked well together."

"I'm glad you could join us," the blonde said, holding out her hand. "I'm Elizabeth, the team leader. You met Dalton and Grant. The angry pregnant woman stuffing her face with a bacon-wrapped pickle is Val. Our mutual friend said you needed help."

Hunter looked at the group. Val and Grant weren't the only married couple. Even he could see the love between Elizabeth and Dalton. "Who are you all?"

"Absolutely no one," Elizabeth responded. "Now, we found out his boss. We found out there are four bombs, each around three thousand pounds. You search for the bombs while we work on tracking the boss down. We will let you know when we have him in custody."

"I'm going to interrogate the shooting teams from the countries involved," Kane told them. "We have a woman who is also helping us. She's military and is going to interview men from the shooting, boxing, and wrestling teams. They typically have the highest rate of military men competing in them."

Val snorted. "Sure. You're 'interviewing' them. You're just going to sleep with them." Kane smirked and Val laughed. "I like you," she said before biting off more pickle.

"Good. I like my balls. Let them work for you, not against you," Kane replied.

"Anything for the good old U.S. of A.," Val said. Kane smirked and Val cursed.

"What?" Elizabeth asked.

"I said too much and now he's figured us out, haven't you?"

"Our secret." Kane winked.

"What have you figured out?" Hunter asked.

"They're government funded but off-books. They're military," Kane said, pointing to Dalton and Grant. "They're government agents. I'd bet FBI," he said pointing to Elizabeth, "But not you, Val. You're too much of a loose cannon for the FBI. I'll think on it. But you're an agent of one of the alphabet groups. Or were. I'm guessing you all gave it all up and now will never be acknowledged for the work you do. The only person powerful enough to make that happen is the president."

"They're an off the books group for the president?" Hunter asked. They all just stared blankly back at him, neither confirming nor denying his question. Ah, so Kane was right. "Damn, bro. You're good at this."

"Yet, you don't do it anymore," Elizabeth pointed out. "Maybe we're more alike than you realize. But now, I want a gelato. We'll be in touch."

The group turned and left, leaving Hunter and Kane in the warehouse without a car. It was only three miles back to the village.

"Interesting group," Kane said as they began to walk.

"Very. Now, if you had four bombs, where would you put them?"

23

Days passed by and yet they seemed to last forever. Maggie had either Kane or Hunter with her or near her at all times. When one was with her, the other would disappear for hours, if not the entire day. Kane and Hunter searched for the bombs and always came up empty. But the nights were hers and Hunter's. At night, the troubles of the world were blocked out and there was only the love they shared.

Maggie had also had more coffee in the last four days than she'd probably ever had. She'd had to switch to decaf or she wouldn't be able to even hold her gun for practice. However, in her coffee dates with her fellow friends on opposing shooting teams, she'd learned several things.

Maggie had learned that several countries were so politically unstable that there were grassroots movements to overthrow the current leaders. Bolivia, Syria, and Crusina were the main ones. Iran was helping several of these groups since some of the leaders, or want-to-be new leaders, favored working with other nations to establish peace and prosperity. Iran did not approve and saw it as a threat to their power, so they were leading a group to destroy the

Syrian rebels and keep their puppet government in place. Similarly, Russia and China were funneling money and weapons to overthrow President Deming Nikan in favor of a dictatorship like the one Crusina had just gotten out of. Since Crusina had turned democratic, their Russian and Chinese neighbors' influence on them had dwindled, and they wanted control back. So did the former political and military members who had been in charge before Deming's presidency. Similarly, the same thing was happening in Bolivia. Belarus's dictator, who was technically a president but in name only, was assisting in the Bolivian coup in exchange for a deal on Bolivian natural resources, most specifically, lithium.

Hunter had taken the information gathered by her, Kane, and Allison and had turned it over to his mystery caller just this morning. They'd all been given a phone number to call if they found anything else out. They weren't told who it belonged to, but it was crucial to call with new information.

"Are you ready to go?" Hunter asked as Maggie pulled on the Team USA jacket.

She was going to be just an Olympian for the next couple of hours. Tonight was something special. It was the opening ceremony.

"I am," she said, checking herself out in the outfit the mystery caller had sent. "I heard from my parents. They're here and so are a bunch of people from Shadows Landing. Ryker chartered a plane for everyone."

She liked how Hunter smiled and for the first time since they arrived looked happy. "I'm glad they're here." His phone buzzed and the smile turned into a frown. "President Serro won't pause the games. President Stratton called him to tell him there was a credible threat. Serro said his men will handle it and they don't have any intelligence showing such a threat. However, Stratton then called the committee heads and they will do anything we need. They're bringing in extra security for high-risk areas and made sure to give us all access passes that let us bypass security."

"Do you think Serro is in on it?" Maggie asked as she grabbed her phone so she could record walking in the opening ceremony.

"No. He just believes they're prepared for anything and that nothing will happen. It's Italy, the country of love, art, music, good wine, and good food. He believes no one would attack them. Be alert tonight. This would be a good target to hit."

There went the joy of the evening. Back to being on constant guard.

Hunter hung back from Maggie under the stadium. He was in sight, but he was letting Maggie have her own time. Athletes from around the world took pictures, met, exchanged numbers, and talked excitedly. The "famous" athletes were well in demand, but Maggie loved meeting those in lesser-known sports. They worked hard all their life for very little fanfare. There were no television spots, no ad campaigns, no ticker tape parades . . . they just ground it out and competed for the love of the sport.

Maggie talked to badminton players, handball players, fencers, sport climbers, synchronized swimmers, and trampoline jumpers. The excitement was electric. Many people didn't speak the same language, but they all loved sports and they all loved competing.

Maggie was talking to a handball player from Hungary when she felt someone shove her from behind. It was packed in the holding area, so pushing wasn't uncommon. However, the person leaned in and whispered, "You should have backed off," in very heavily accented English.

Maggie turned to see someone with an Iranian outfit on, but his accent wasn't quite right. It was more Eastern European than Middle Eastern. She opened her mouth to ask him who he was when a flash of a knife caught her eye.

"Hunter!" she screamed as the knife stabbed her in the abdomen.

She fell backward from the impact, the handballer caught her, yelling something she didn't understand as his teammates came running forward, ready to defend her. The man who stabbed her looked surprised, but then took off in the crowds. Team Iran had over sixty athletes and he was easily lost to Maggie, but not to Hunter. Maggie saw Hunter take off into the crowd, shoving athletes out of the way, as he chased after the man.

"Okay, yes?" the handballer asked her. Maggie realized he was still holding her, but the pain and blood she was expecting wasn't there.

She looked down to find the knife at her feet and not in her stomach. The uniform. It had stopped the knife attack. She lifted her shirt and looked at her stomach. There was a red mark as if something had poked into her abdomen, but there was no cut.

"I'm okay. Thank you."

"Police?" the handballer asked as his teammates formed a circle around her, protecting her from any other threats.

"No. There's my security now." Maggie saw Kane pushing through the crowd, although the fierce look on his face made many people jump out of his way before he even got to them. "Kane, these nice men from the Hungarian handball team helped me."

Kane nodded at them, "Thank you, gentleman. Good luck." Kane casually bent down and picked up the knife before slipping his arm around Maggie. "Let's stick with your team for a bit. They're starting to call out the countries."

"Where is Hunter?" Maggie asked, trying to look around and find him. However, he was lost in the swarm of athletes getting in place and starting to walk out of the holding area.

"I'm sure he's fine. Let's go." Kane didn't give her a choice. He could have made her leave the ceremony, but at least he was letting her stay, as long as she was surrounded by her team.

Hunter shoved his way through the Iranian team's athletes. He had eyes on the man who had attacked Maggie and he wasn't going to lose him. Hunter tried not to draw attention to himself, but it was hard not to. He ducked behind a cement block pillar and observed the man slip through a door. Hunter followed casually, pushing open the door and finding a long hallway with the man running down it.

Hunter didn't yell. He pulled his gun and ran. If anyone saw him, they'd mistake him for a sprinter. He pushed himself hard, especially when the man turned and saw him. He picked up speed, so Hunter picked up speed. The only sound was of their breathing and the echo of the footfalls.

The hallway curved, following the outline of the stadium, and once they sped around it, Hunter saw an exit ahead. The man was sprinting toward it. Hunter wouldn't make it in time to stop him before he lost him outside the stadium.

Hunter abruptly stopped, aimed his gun, and fired.

The man didn't have time to yell. The shot hit him in the back. He was flung forward with his momentum and the impact of the hit. Hunter resumed the sprint as the man tried to crawl his way toward the door, now just yards away from him.

Hunter slowed to a stop and aimed the gun down at the man. "It's over," Hunter said, his tone deadly.

The man stopped crawling and rolled over onto his back. His breathing was shallow. He wouldn't make it and the man knew it. "I might be, but we will live on forever. It's all set. You're too late." The man closed his eyes and took his last breath.

"Dammit," Hunter cursed. He wanted to question him further, but now there was still one thing he could do. Hunter pulled out his phone, took a picture, and sent a text before patting the man down looking for clues.

A text came in five minutes later from Hunter's mystery contact. *Open the door.*

Hunter stepped over the man and opened the door to find Elizabeth, Dalton, Grant, and Val. Grant was wearing an outfit identical to athletes from Great Britain. Dalton was in a US outfit. Val and Elizabeth were dressed in generic Olympic merchandise.

"I'm going to hang out with your lass and send your brother back here," Grant told Hunter before kissing his wife, telling her to behave, smacking her on the bottom, and then sauntering off whistling a jaunty drinking song.

"We have an ID on him," Elizabeth told Hunter. "We'll wait for your brother and then come up with a plan because we also have news that came from the information submitted by Maggie, Kane, and Allison."

"He had a cell phone. I'm worried it was the trigger for the bomb," Hunter said, pointing to the phone.

Elizabeth nodded and picked it up. "Call our team," Elizabeth ordered Val.

The phone rang and Hunter heard someone pick up. "Dude?"

"We have a phone we need to get into. It's locked, no facial unlock, only a six number code," Val said before stepping away to talk to whoever was on the other end of the phone.

Waiting was not Hunter's strong suit. It seemed to take forever for Val to finish her call and for Kane to reach them. Before Elizabeth could give the update, her phone rang.

"What's up?" Elizabeth asked before her face turned to stone. A frown tugged at her lips as she turned away from them. "That doesn't fit the profile," she said into the phone.

Hunter shared a look with Dalton. They were both on the same page. This didn't fit.

"It doesn't fit. It has to be a distraction," Elizabeth said again into the phone. "Help Val with the phone we recovered. I have to go."

Elizabeth spun around and Hunter knew it was bad.

"What is it?" Hunter asked.

"First," Elizabeth said as if she were in a briefing, "that man you just killed is from Crusina, not Iran. His best friend was an international hacker and blackmailer who was recently killed. Both of their fathers were higher ups in the Crusina government. Both fathers were executed for crimes against their citizens after President Deming Nikan took office. Maggie told us about the political issues. The people who lost power now want it back. Allison has said the same. Men had been telling her tonight was a big night. Then Allison called us an hour ago and said the men she'd talked to—the ones who seemed angry about the current state of politics on various teams and who did have contacts with the military or were former military—were not at the opening ceremonies."

Hunter opened his mouth, but Elizabeth held up her hand to stop him. "The call I just got . . . a bomb threat was called into the city. They said there was a bomb across town on Embassy Row. They wanted a hundred million dollars or they'd blow it up."

"Who are *they*?" Hunter asked, thinking back to the map. Embassy Row was part of the area circled as it was near the gymnastics arena.

"The caller didn't say. They just sent an account number for a Swiss bank. Police have been pulled from this area of town and are searching for the bomb on the other side of town," Elizabeth told them.

"They're going to blow up the stadium. Now. Tonight." Hunter felt the ripple of goosebumps run up his arms to freeze his heart. He couldn't think of the tens of thousands of people in the stadium. He couldn't think about Maggie. All he could do was figure out how to stop it. "The map had the embassies circled, not the gymnastics arena. The second place circled was out of town, near the shooting range. We searched for it, but all we found was commercial storage. The last place circled was here. The stadium. The place has been searched from top to bottom. There's not a single bomb here," Hunter said. "But there has to be. It has to be here."

Elizabeth nodded and typed something out. Her frown deepened. "There's a reported fire at a commercial storage location located in the middle of the second circled part of the map. All fire and rescue are there. Everyone has been pulled away from this location, but where could the bombs be?"

"What about under us?" Dalton asked suddenly.

"Historically, Julius Ceasar became *dictator perpetuo* of the Roman Empire, granting him the full power of the state for life, basically a dictatorship like these who were overthrown want back. Archeologists have uncovered where Julius Caesar was stabbed. It's *beneath* the current city. Ancient Rome is still here," Dalton tapped his foot on the floor, "just below us. It's open to the public and no more than three blocks from here," Dalton explained. "It was well known during WWII and used as bomb shelters and even for growing mushrooms. After the war, people stopped using them so most of the current generation seems to have forgotten about them. Geoscientists have started to map them because they are a danger to infrastructure. I bet those tunnels are under us. Would that work for the bombs?"

24

Maggie couldn't stop looking around. Kane was acting as if everything was normal, but she saw him scanning the crowds too. With her nerves on edge, Maggie put her hand in her pocket and rubbed her lucky bullet. It might be a strange thing to carry, but it was a bullet given to her after the last Olympics by her hero, the best military sharpshooter in modern day history. He'd told her it would shoot straight to gold. She'd kept it with her at every competition since.

"What's going on, Mags?" Gage asked her as soon as he saw the new addition to her side. The shooting team had closed ranks fast when they saw Kane rush her over to them and hadn't let up since.

"Someone tried to stab me. Hunter is chasing after them. I must have talked to someone who ratted me out," Maggie whispered as her brother quickly began looking for blood. "I'm okay. Whatever this material is, it stopped the blade. Also, remind me to send a gift to Hungary's handball team."

"That's it. You're leaving," Gage grabbed her hand, but Maggie pulled it back. "No. Just wait. Hunter told me he'd tell me if I needed to leave and I promised to do so if that time came. Until then, I want to soak this up. We've worked so hard for this. I won't let anyone take it from me."

Gage looked to Kane for backup, but Kane just shrugged. "I'll let you know when I know more," was all he said as Angola was called out to parade in front of the crowd. The ceremony was starting, but now even Allison was looking nervous.

"Did you notice half of Crusina's team isn't here? Same with Iran and the "neutral" athletes from Russia and Belarus," Allison pointed out. "I sent the information to the number they gave us when I noticed it. But I don't like it."

Kane frowned. Gage frowned. Allison frowned. And suddenly Maggie had a very bad feeling.

A huge man strode forward wearing the outfit belonging to the team from Great Britain. "Lass! I'm excited to finally meet you. I'm Hunter's friend, Grant," he said in an absolutely charming Scottish accent.

"What happened?" Kane asked instantly, not giving Maggie or Gage time to ask any questions. Kane apparently knew this giant of a man with a cocky grin and confident air about him.

"You're needed down that hallway. Third door down. Hurry. I got Miss Bell." Kane took off, but Gage wasn't happy.

"No, I have her. Who are you?" Gage asked.

"Grant. And you're the big brother. I got a gift for you two. Both of you turn and look out over there. Don't move until I tell you."

Maggie turned, but Gage was being stubborn. "Gage, just do it."

Maggie felt Grant move close behind them after her brother turned around. He slung one arm over her shoulder as if they were all looking at something. She felt her jacket being lifted and then the familiar feel of a gun being put in her waistband.

"What the hell?" Gage hissed. "How did you get that in here?"

"Came in a different door. You want to protect her? Now you can. Although, I have a feeling she'll do just fine on her own." Grant gave her a wink and began chatting up everyone around them.

"Did he just give us guns?" Gage whispered to her.

"Yup. I just hope we don't have to use them."

~

Dalton had found maps of the tunnels under Rome and handed them to Hunter. Hunter was looking at them as Kane stared over his shoulder. They both wore matching frowns.

"Roman emperor Augustus declared the Curia of Pompey cursed after Caesar's murder," Dalton, clearly a history buff, explained. "Many think it's newly discovered, but it was actually rediscovered in the 1920s. It was taken over by cats after the second world war. Fashion and history go hand in hand in Rome. The fashion house, Bulgari, funded the restoration. Actually, Bulgari also funded the restoration of the Spanish Steps."

"Fendi funded the refresh of the Trevi fountain and Tod's helped pay for half of the renovations of the Colosseum," Elizabeth added, clearly having heard about this before. "Which is why I didn't feel too bad spending that money when I bought some new purses here."

"I hate to interrupt the history lesson," Hunter said, turning the phone with the map on it around to the group. "But the bombs can't be in the tunnels."

"Why not?" Dalton asked, luckily with no hint of defensiveness but with curiosity. He wasn't going to waste time arguing with Hunter.

"The tunnels are too deep. Even driving a four-thousand-pound ANFO bomb down there wouldn't take down the stadium. It would feel like a small earthquake. That's it. Just a little shake," he explained about the ammonium nitrate fuel oil bombs they were assuming the terrorists were using based on the stolen fertilizer. "Think back to the World Trade Center bombing of 1993. That VBIED," Hunter said of the *vehicle-born improvised explosive device*, "was in a parking garage and nothing. That garage was a lot closer to the building than these tunnels are. Add in thick stone, tons of dirt, and earthquake-proof new build of the stadium, and it won't touch it."

"Then what would?" Elizabeth asked.

Hunter turned to his brother because his take on this would depend on the direction Hunter would turn his attention. "In your profile of this group, would you say they've been planning this for a long time or they're new and taking advantage of the first international event they can?"

Kane didn't hesitate. "No, this isn't a new group flying by the seat of their pants. This is an organized, multinational group that has figured out a way to work together and utilize all its resources. That takes time and planning. They got their bomb maker out of jail four years ago. They hijacked the bulk of their fertilizer three years ago. They took a year to quietly steal the rest of the fertilizer in small, rural areas across Europe, but never in Italy. Right now, we think their goal is revenge, and what other target would be bigger than this? Tonight, it's not just about the athletes. Almost every country with athletes also has a diplomat in attendance from presidents, to vice presidents, to royalty, to ambassadors. This is a well-thought-out plan with contingencies."

"I know he's the profiler, but that's what our intel says, too," Elizabeth added. "Why?"

"Because that will tell us where the bombs are." Hunter thought about everything he saw in the stadium. He ran through the ticket takers, the security, the merchandise, the bathrooms, the food . . . "The stadium was built specifically for the games," Hunter told them. "If they have been planning this, they could put it all in place during construction when security is lax. No one was doing bomb sweeps then."

"But some of the fertilizer was stolen over the past year," Val pointed out.

"Right, but it would be really obvious to mix up and transport it in during construction, even with lax security. First, you need all of the ammonium nitrate, about two to four thousand pounds per bomb. Then you need diesel fuel to mix it with. That stuff not only smells, but it would weigh down a truck to the point anyone walking by would do a double take. However, if you break it up, say just move some of the fertilizer in a storage container filled with stuff, so it could pass inspection. Then you could bring in the rest mixed in with supplies over the years and then add the fuel later."

"Like when making sure all the emergency generators are filled," Kane said, nodding. "A false wall in the storage containers with a generator located right behind it and no one will think twice about the scheduled fuel delivery."

"Exactly. You could move in more fertilizer that way too. Large containers of onions, T-shirts, or coffee on the top, with fertilizer under it. There will be a storage container with a nearby generator. As the generators were filling up, it would be easy to carry the fuel into the nearest storage container without drawing attention. Only six percent of an ANFO bomb is fuel. That's maybe twenty-five gallons, max."

"I'm kind of annoyed they're that easy to make," Val said with a roll of her eyes. "How do we find them?"

"There are four bombs upstairs. I would bet equally spread out. Look for storage containers and generators. Most importantly, smell. Ask around to see if anyone remembers someone with a strong diesel smell. That stuff doesn't wash out after you mix a bomb. It's in your shoelaces, in your hair, it's memorable," Hunter explained as they rushed down the hallway.

"How about a trigger?" Val asked.

"It'll be a phone or an alarm clock that's on a countdown. We'll know which when we find the bombs, but I'm guessing it's a cell phone that will spark the blasting cap. It essentially strikes the match to light the cast boosters, which is a type of explosive that will then detonate the bomb," Hunter explained.

"We're looking for someone with a cell phone? Gee, that won't be hard," Val said sarcastically.

"Focus on the containers and generators. Then look around them. Whoever is behind this will have eyes on their bombs. Nothing, especially a wandering worker or a random security guard, will get in their way to pull this off. Divide up and start encircling the stadium. Text in your location the second you see something," Hunter ordered.

"What about evacuating?" Elizabeth asked.

Kane shook his head. "The second we try, they'll blow

the place. I can guarantee it. But I can get some people out. Want me to find Maggie?"

"I'll fill her and Grant in," Val told them. "I'll see if I can get her to leave. I know Grant will make me go. I don't want to, but he'll make me since I'm pregnant."

"Thanks, Val. Be safe everyone." Hunter reached the door to the holding area and quietly opened it. He and his team slipped out, breaking off in different directions.

25

Maggie was getting nervous as the athletes of each country began to walk into the stadium in turn. There was so much excitement around her, but at the same time, she was acutely aware Hunter hadn't returned.

"Stop staring at the door, lass," Grant whispered.

Maggie was about to look away when the door opened. "There he is," she whispered back as she saw several people exit, including Hunter and Kane. However, they didn't come her way. They slipped away into the crowd headed in different directions. Except for one woman. "Who is that?" Maggie asked Grant.

Grant glanced casually and then smiled. "That's my wife, Val, and she looks pissed. It's either because she knows I'm going to make her leave if there's credible danger or she's hungry. The wee bairn has been giving her quite the cravings and you haven't seen *hangry* yet until you see a pregnant woman who can't get her peanut butter-smeared bacon."

"I'm Maggie. What's going on?" Maggie asked the second the woman stopped by them.

Maggie listened as Val told them about their idea of the bombs' locations. Maggie frowned and cursed. "It'll take them thirty minutes just to walk the length of the stadium with these crowds. How are they going to search everywhere?"

"We need help searching," Gage said almost absently.

"Yes, we do," Maggie said, pulling out her phone and shooting off a long text message.

Val frowned. "What did you just do?"

"We have friends and family here. I've asked them to help."

"I don't like it," Val grumbled. "But what I would like is some gelato. Come on, before you make me leave, let's grab one. You too, blondie."

"If she's going, I'm going. I'm her brother, Gage."

The woman smiled then. "Like a shotgun gauge?"

Gage nodded. "And Maggie's real name is Magnum."

"Great baby names. Put them on the list, babe. Much more original than Remington. Now, baby weapon needs ice cream."

There was a gelato cart in the staging area. The poor worker looked ready to pass out as Maggie and her group approached them. Suddenly, Val's nose twitched. She lifted her nose in the air and inhaled deeply before spinning on her heel. She sniffed the air as the rest of them shared a confused look.

"Do you smell that?" Val asked, looking around.

"What?" Grant asked.

"Diesel fuel."

Maggie sniffed the air but didn't smell anything until someone walked by and caused the air to stir. Then she smelled the faint traces of it. "Yeah. So?"

"Could be the bomb maker. Hunter told us that the

smell doesn't wash off well." Val sniffed the air, walked four feet in one direction, turned around and faced the other direction. "This way." Grant chuckled but kept his mouth shut as they all followed Val. Her nose twitched, and suddenly she stopped. "That man, right there. I can't believe I've turned into a pregnant bomb detection sniffer, just like a freaking Labrador."

"If you capture the bad guy, I'll get you a treat." Grant couldn't resist and Val elbowed him in the stomach for it. Grant didn't seem to mind. Instead, he pulled out his phone. "Group photo," he said as he held up the camera.

There was zero percent chance of them being in the photo. Grant sent the photo off and a second later he received a text back. "It's Hamid Saeed, the bomb maker," Grant said, all joking aside. "Val, time to go. Now."

"But I didn't get my gelato," Val grumbled, but she listened, surprisingly. "After you kill them all and dismantle the bombs, I want two scoops of chocolate."

"You got it, babe." Grant kissed her and watched her walk off quickly.

"This can't be easy, putting your life on the line like this," Maggie said quietly.

"You could leave too, lass. I know your man would appreciate it."

"If I leave, who has his back?" Maggie asked, watching the international criminal scope out the area. "Plus, if he's here, one of the bombs must be close. He's probably checking them one last time, right? He's moving up to the main level," Maggie said as she took a selfie of her and Gage so that she could watch him with her camera.

Maggie snapped the shot and texted it out. She instantly got replies. Her friends and family were on it.

~

Hunter and Kane split up the second they were out of the hallway. Hunter caught sight of Maggie, but he couldn't stop. The faster he found these bombs, the faster she'd be safe.

Hunter strode through the main floor where all the vendors were selling things ranging from stuffed animals to flags to merchandise. T-shirts, jackets, posters . . . everything you could think of was lined up along the main walkway circling the stadium.

Stuffed animals didn't require generators though, so he discounted the storage containers for stuffies of the mascot. But, keeping gelato cold did require a generator and storage. So did the food stands. There was no built-in storage behind the vendors. Instead, they were packed in as tight as they could be in more of a street festival feel. Behind them were storage containers of various sizes that they shared. Generators sat between some of the storage containers.

His phone buzzed and he glanced down at the text from Maggie. It wasn't just to him though. It was to a list of people from Shadows Landing—all the people who happened to be at the ceremony tonight. It was a text asking for help and telling them what to look for.

Hunter stopped in his tracks. Now he'd have to protect the people of Shadows Landing while hunting down terrorists and bombs. Just great. Before he could put away his phone, Hunter got a text from Grant. They'd found Hamid Saeed. Then a text came through of a photo with a location in the upper right of the photo. He was on the move and heading right for Hunter.

Hunter sent a text to tell everyone to back off of Hamid. Just to keep Hunter notified if they see him. Hunter grabbed a baseball cap from a stand and walked with his head down toward the location where he thought Hamid would pop up.

Found the first bomb. I want an apple pie for it. Waiting for orders.

The text came from Kane with an exact location.

Hunter looked around and saw Mr. and Mrs. Bell rushing toward him. Hunter looked at the location again and then looked at where he was standing. It was almost the exact same spot, just on the opposite side of the stadium.

Hunter scanned the crowd and saw a food truck. A worker was going into the open storage container behind them and pulling out food supplies. The distance the worker walked to the back of the storage container to get those supplies was not the full distance of the container.

"Hunter, what's going on?" Clark asked as they joined him.

"See that shipping container? I think there's a bomb behind a false wall. Pretend to order food and look around for anyone else watching the area."

Mr. and Mrs. Bell looked nervous, but they did what he said. Hunter scanned the area from a distance and caught sight of a man watching the food stall. Hunter slid through the crowd until he was able to come up behind the man.

The man sensed him, but Hunter stopped him from turning around by putting his hand on the man's shoulder and squeezing it tightly. "Keeping an eye on your bomb?"

"I don't know what you're talking about," the man answered, but he also didn't try to turn around. That wasn't the standard reaction to hearing about a bomb. Most civilians would instinctually shout, "Bomb?" and freak out. This man didn't and that told Hunter everything he needed to know.

Hunter knew it was coming. He could have used a gun,

but he didn't want any bystanders hurt. The man spun, trying to break Hunter's hold. Hunter pushed when the man thought he was going to pull. It knocked the man off balance. Hunter dropped a shoulder and plowed the man into the ten foot tall costumed mascot—Augie the Holy Cannoli. Augie for Caesar Augustus. Holy representing the Vatican, so the mascot was an honorary bishop complete with an oversized bishop's mitre, the headdress bishops wear, perched on top of the cream-filled cannoli, representing one of Italy's most beloved culinary creations.

The three of them crashed into the merchandise table, breaking it and causing them to all fall a second time to the ground. Augie lost his bishop's hat as the man and Hunter landed on top of him. The man in the giant cannoli cursed in rapid fire Italian and flailed around like an upended tortoise, unable to get up as Hunter slammed his fist into the terrorist's face.

The fight was on. Punches were exchanged, people were filming, and Clark and Suze were doing all they could to prevent other people from interfering, including security who was shouting at everyone in the area.

Hunter had to finish this and finish it now. Hunter pulled a knife from his waistband and holding the blade flat, shoved it between the man's ribs and into his lungs. The man didn't scream, but the cannoli did. Augie cursed, wiggled, and screamed for help. Hunter got off of the man and security swarmed him. He didn't have time for this. He had a bomb to disarm and two more bombs to find.

Hunter unzipped his jacket and around his neck was the all-access security pass Veronica had gotten for him. "Don't call this in. Say it was a drunk and disorderly fight and the men have been escorted from the premises," Hunter said quietly as the guards ran his name and security clearance.

"Yes, sir," the lead guard finally said, leaning down to scoot the dead man off the Holy Cannoli.

"Bless your heart," Suze said, holding out her hand to help the mascot up. "What a shame that man tripped and fell right into you, knocking himself unconscious. Too much vino," she said, shaking her head as she stepped in front of the knife still sticking out of the man's chest as Clark tossed his jacket over him, hiding the evidence.

Third bomb found. Man watching from three o'clock. Elizabeth texted.

Fourth bomb found. Timmons says some guy giving off bad vibes is about twenty feet catty corner from the bomb. Hunter smiled at Gator's text.

Hunter pulled up the locations as Suze sweet-talked everyone around them, spinning a story that the man had harassed her after having too much wine and security had come to her rescue.

"You don't have much time," Clark told Hunter. "Everyone has their phones out."

Hunter cursed and pulled his phone back out. *Get into position behind the sentries. We need to take them out simultaneously before they can warn whoever is setting them off.*

Dalton and Kane responded with knife emojis.

Gator responded by asking if the pretty woman was with them or if she needed to be fed to the gators and then he asked if Italy had alligators.

She's with us, Hunter responded.

She's too pretty to get messy. That was all Gator said and Hunter had to assume he'd take care of business.

Make your moves in two minutes. Hunter scanned the area, keeping his eyes open for Hamid Saeed as Hunter approached the container. "Clark, search the man's pockets for ID and also any phones."

The cannoli mascot was now up and his oversized white stuffed hands were trying to give Hunter the middle finger, but he only had four fingers, so it was a little difficult. He settled on the traditional Italian F-U sign with his arms. Suze gasped and shoved him backward, sending the cannoli stumbling into a woman holding two cups of gelato. Augie's big hands landed right on the woman's breasts. The woman in turn, shoved the frozen treats into the very small eye holes and screamed.

The "drunk" fight between the two men was forgotten as everyone turned to see the woman pull back her leg and kick the cream right out of that cannoli.

"I got a phone and a badge. It says he's working concessions," Clark said. "I saw a crime show where they used the dead guy's face to open the phone and look, it worked."

Hunter took the phone and went straight to the open tabs. Nothing. Next, he went to the contacts list. There was only one phone number listed. He was about to send the number to his contact to see if they could identify the owner of the number when a text message popped up from that number.

Ten minutes until the American delegation walks and then we leave. Is everything clear? Hunter read the text that was written in Arabic before responding that everything was clear.

"We have ten minutes," Hunter said, sending out a text to the others telling them to go on the takedown, to reply to any text from the unknown number, and then to evacuate.

Kane responded with a middle finger emoji.

Dalton sent a GIF from the movie *Armageddon*, where the astronaut was riding a nuclear weapon.

"Mr. and Mrs. Bell, you need to leave now," Hunter pleaded.

"We're not leaving without our children," Suze said in a tone that left no room for argument. Hunter thought she sounded remarkably similar to how Lydia had back at the church.

"Then go get them and get the hell out of here so I can focus on dismantling four bombs."

Clark cocked his head and looked around as if he were thinking. "'Then we leave.' That's what you said was in the text, right?" Hunter nodded. "Then the person who can set off those bombs is here. We just have to find him."

"I'll give you five minutes to get Maggie and Gage. But then I want you to leave. Deal?"

Suze patted his cheek. "Such a nice boy. Now, go take a look at that bomb. We'll see you soon."

They walked off hand in hand and it wasn't until Kane called his phone that Hunter realized the Bells hadn't agreed to anything.

"What?" Hunter asked as he answered.

"I have eyes on the bomb. It's an ANFO with a cell phone acting as the blasting cap attached to cast boosters by wires. There are enough cast boosters here to light the ANFO into the next century."

"Hold on. Let me see." Hunter walked around the table and into the storage container. "How did you get into the container?"

"Hidden lever top left corner."

Hunter felt around and then pushed the small metal piece he felt. The door unlocked and Hunter was able to pry it open and slip inside. He paused and took a deep breath. This was a lot of ANFO. Just one of these would be detrimental, but four? Four was a statement. There would be nothing left of the stadium. Everyone and everything would burn.

"Disarm or evacuate?" Kane asked right as Hunter got a call from Gator.

Hunter merged the calls.

"This pretty lady looks madder than a wet hen. What do you need me to do?" Gator asked.

"Have everyone call on video. I'm going to walk you through disarming the bombs." Hunter hung up and began an examination of the bomb. Bombs didn't need to be complex to be deadly. This was fuel and fertilizer with a cell phone. Yet, it could kill everyone here.

"What do we do?" Dalton asked once Hunter had everyone on video.

"You need something to cut the wires. A very sharp knife will do."

Suddenly a huge hunting knife was on the screen as Skeeter handed it to Elizabeth. "I never leave home without it."

"How did you get a knife in here?" she asked.

"I put it under my hat. They never wave those wands over your head."

Skeeter had a point.

Kane and Dalton were soon ready and Hunter held the camera to the device. "There are two ways to detonate this kind of bomb. A timer, which we don't have here, or a command detonation. That means someone has to call this cell phone to detonate the bomb. There are two ways to disarm it too. Get the people who will call the bombs or cut the wires. We're going to cut the wires."

"There's several wires," Dalton pointed out. "Which do we cut?"

"We're doing this down and dirty. Cut them all at the same time," Hunter instructed.

"That doesn't seem very safe. Shouldn't it be a specific wire?" Elizabeth asked.

"Not in this case. If it were a timer, it would be different. Here, the only thing that will set it off is if this cell phone rings so cut the wires."

Hunter slid the knife he'd gotten from the vendor under the wires and took hold.

"Well, that was easy. I'm kind of disappointed," Gator muttered.

"Take the cell phones with you. Now, let's find the person holding the switch."

26

Maggie wanted to follow Hamid Saeed, but Grant refused to let her. Instead, Grant moved her into position with her team. The holding area was starting to empty out as country after country was called to join the opening ceremony.

Waiting made it worse. The texts were coming through and Maggie was forced to sit back and wait as her friends, her family, and the man she loved put their lives on the line.

That's right disappointing, Skeeter texted. *There was no countdown or dramatic music. Just cut the wires and be done.*

Maggie smiled at that. The bombs were disarmed and her friends and family were walking from all over the stadium back to their seats together.

"You can relax now, lass," Grant said. "Here's your man."

Maggie looked over her shoulder to see Hunter and Kane walking toward them. Maggie wanted to fling herself into his arms, but this wasn't over yet. Instead, she squeezed his hand as soon as he reached her and looked between her team of protectors. "This isn't over yet. Hamid still hasn't been caught. Did you see him after he left the holding area? Could he be the person behind all of this?"

"Hamid could be behind it," Grant suggested but didn't look happy about it.

"You don't think so, though?" Maggie asked Hunter when she saw his expression of doubt.

Hunter shook his head. "No, I don't. Someone had to get him out of jail. That someone has to be pretty powerful."

"We have people, mercenaries, and former soldiers from multiple countries. Maybe instead of asking who, we should be asking why," Maggie told them.

"We thought we knew. For them to regain power," Grant said.

"But, that's a lot of power spread out. For real power, it would need to be consolidated, right?" Maggie asked.

"It's like a business conglomerate," Gage added. He'd been mostly quiet, but he was the one with the MBA. "There's one company that owns all the subsidiaries. Even as they operate independently, the parent company is the one with all the power, yet all the subsidiaries get something out of it."

"Iran, Crusina, Russia, and China have all been mentioned," Maggie said, thinking out loud.

"I don't think Crusina is running this. I think they're trying to benefit from it. They're too small and not powerful enough globally to pull this off," Kane told them.

"Not Russia," Grant said instantly. "They're more concerned with Ukraine and recreating the old Soviet bloc."

"Except they need weapons and allies," Hunter pointed out.

"Just like Crusina needs someone to help overthrow Deming Nikan," Grant said, nodding as if he were putting pieces together.

"Iran has been making moves to become more international instead of regional," Gage told them.

"Most crimes come down to two things: money and power," Maggie said, more to herself, but Hunter responded instantly by hugging her.

"I'm so stupid. I was focusing on power and forgot about money. Which country is slowly buying up land, ports, and transportation facilities all under the guise of helping the poorer country's economy when in reality these overblown loans can never be paid back and instead, the country comes in and seizes control?"

"China," Gage said instantly. "They want to start The New Silk Road or the Belt and Road Initiative. It's two-fold. They either make bad loans or build poor infrastructures that break down and can never be paid off, then seize control when payment can't be made. They've done it to Pakistan, Sri Lanka, Angola, and Ecuador to name just a few, leaving them billions of dollars in debt to China, who now has leverage to exert control over them. It started in neighboring countries and then spread to Africa. Or they make allies with the leaders. In Djibouti, they've built a port on the Gulf of Aden which is the gateway of the Suez Canal. About twenty percent of the world's trade goes through there. Then they established a military base that they refused to call a military base but a *support facility*, bribed officials to kick previous terminal operators out, and brought in a state-controlled firm from China to run it. Then they expanded to South America and Cuba. In return, China will help the rulers of those countries stay in power. The list goes on and on."

"But we have caught people from other countries, not China," Maggie said, pointing out the countries of the men they'd either captured or killed.

"Follow the money," Hunter said. "Or in this case, the favors. How much do you want to bet China is running this from the shadows? They'll never be linked to it, but their fingerprints are all over it. Iran needs allies to pull off their Middle Eastern power play and Russia needs weapons in their fight to regain their lost bloc. China can provide that to both of them. Is the Chinese delegation all out there?"

"Yes. I saw them," Maggie answered.

"All of them?" Hunter asked. "Sometimes sacrifices must be made to keep attention off of you. The Chinese government and the Chinese people are two different entities with different levels of respect for human life. The government will do what it needs to advance its power and their human rights violations tell you all you need to know about how they treat their citizens. We already know Iran, Russia, and Belarus don't have their full teams out there."

Maggie glanced at the screen where the camera was panning the delegations. "I was paying more attention to Iran, but while the China team is large, I don't think that's all of them," Maggie admitted.

"Iran and Russia aren't innocent in this either, but I think China is calling all the shots. They need a bigger foothold in the Middle East and Iran can give them that while China can give Iran the weapons and money they need to stay in power," Hunter said. "Our time is almost up. We need to figure out who is holding the detonator. It won't be China. They won't risk proof of their direct involvement. That leaves Iran or Russia. I think China would trust Iran to get the job done. First, Russia doesn't have an official delegation here. And two, Iran has the most to gain behind China. Either way, I guarantee one of them will be leaving soon with a phone in their pocket that will detonate those bombs."

"We also don't know if there are any more bombs. We found four, but there could be more," Kane said. "A failsafe plan if something went wrong. You don't set up an attack like this without one."

"I still don't get why they target the Olympics. What do they get out of this?" Gage asked.

Maggie saw Hunter scan the stadium from their enclave in the holding area. "People that abuse power thrive during chaos, and bombing the Olympics with all these dignitaries and athletes here will create chaos. China can swoop in and offer aid in this time of need. Iran will scare off their challengers and no one will be watching Russia make a push for more land. All of Iran's adversaries are here. They've set up proxy forces in several countries. They wipe out the leadership in those countries and Iran's proxies can rush in to fill the power void. Syria, Lebanon, and Yemen are split. Syria's leadership is pro-Iran, while their opposition is backed by Saudi Arabia. Lebanon has pro-Iran Hezbollah, but the Sunnis are pro-Saudi. Then in Yemen, the government in exile is pro-Saudi but the Houthi rebels are pro-Iran. Iran and Iraq are allies, trying to bring the others to their side while Saudi Arabia, Egypt, the Emirates, and Bahrain are trying to stop them. Take out those leaders and their countries will focus inward instead on trying to contain Iran," Hunter explained.

Kane nodded in agreement. "It's actually perfect. You have mercenaries from Belarus who will most likely get economic support now from China and enter trade deals with Iran, former soldiers from Bolivia who will be helped by Iran's proxies to get back in power, rebels from Crusina with both Russia's and China's help to take over once again, and a bomber from Yemen who can name his price for putting this together."

"Hamid!" Maggie gasped as the United States got closer and closer to being called out.

"We'll worry about him later," Hunter said, turning to talk to the group.

"No, he's there," Maggie whispered, trying not to point.

Behind them was a bank of private elevators for dignitaries. Hamid looked upset. He must have discovered the bombs had been disarmed. He flashed a badge to security and they pressed the up button.

Maggie saw Hunter move so quickly that she didn't have time to ask him what his plan was. Kane saw it too, and moved to back up his brother. Hunter held up a badge to the security guard who nodded. Hamid turned, locking eyes with Hunter.

Maggie gasped as the elevator opened and Hamid jumped inside. He didn't pull a weapon. He pulled out a cell phone. Hunter dove into the elevator behind him. Maggie struggled to see what was happening as the doors closed. The guard looked confused, but Kane shoved past him, sticking his hand between the almost closed elevator doors.

Maggie took a step toward Hunter, but Grant grabbed her and shoved her to Gage. "Don't let her move," Grant ordered, the playfulness gone from his voice as he charged forward.

The elevator door opened, and over Kane's shoulder, Maggie saw Hunter and Hamid locked in battle. The sound of the elevator doors opening caused Hamid a split-second distraction and that was all Hunter needed. His forearm slid across Hamid's throat. Hamid struggled, but Hunter's headlock held.

Kane was talking to Hamid as Grant grabbed the cell phone from Hamid's hand, but then the doors closed and they were gone from view.

.   .   .

Hunter loosened the pressure on Hamid's neck as Kane began his interrogation. Hunter shouldn't have expected a confession but was still disappointed when Hamid refused to answer any questions about who was behind the bombings.

"Blood will be spilled whether you kill me or not. I'll never talk."

"You already told us what we need." Kane rolled his eyes.

Grant stepped forward and smashed his fist onto Hamid's chin. His eyes rolled back and Hamid went slack in Hunter's grasp.

"There's still a bomb," Grant said as the elevator opened on the suite level. "I'll get this guy out of here. You find the person running it all."

Hunter dropped his hold on Hamid, straightened his jacket, and walked off the elevator as if nothing had happened.

"What's the plan?" Kane asked.

"Find the cell phone and kill the person holding it."

"Simple, yet effective. Let's go."

The suite level was completely different. Secret Service and military protection lined the halls from the various countries. Hunter and Kane were stopped every ten yards and had to show their credentials. It was going to take forever to get to the Iranian delegation.

"Gentlemen, they're with us. Let them by."

Hunter turned to see a young woman with brown hair perfectly coiffed in navy blue pants, a white blouse, and a red jacket walking toward them with Dalton and Elizabeth flanking her. "Madam Secretary," Hunter said, nodding quickly.

Security let them pass and finally they could pick up

their pace. At thirty-three, Secretary of State Sutton Ramsey was the youngest person to ever hold the position. There were rumors that when President Birch Stratton's term was up in two years, she would be the leading candidate for the next presidency.

Sutton was new to the office and this was her first real test of diplomacy. She was technically here as part of the US delegation as a former Olympic athlete herself. Two games ago, she'd been on the fencing team. She'd fenced during her time at the University of Kentucky, where she'd earned her master's in political science with a focus on foreign relations. She'd been elected to the House of Representatives a year after hosting a podcast that explained politics, the economy, and foreign relations in a way that everyone could understand. She continued her podcast while in the House of Representatives, easily winning three straight terms and climbing the ranks in the foreign relations committee.

She gained national prominence when she joined President Birch Stratton at a global summit on foreign economic development and helped him broker a new trade agreement between several smaller countries that would not only supply a niche market for the United States but would help those smaller countries pull themselves out of poverty.

When the previous secretary of state resigned due to a health crisis, President Stratton had tapped Sutton Ramsey. She'd been in office for less than three months, but so far Hunter heard nothing but good things from those who actually dealt with her.

"I'm in a rather interesting position," Sutton said as they walked down the hallway. "Birch called and told me to do this and to not ask any questions. I'm not supposed to ask why the First Lady's best friend and husband are here. I'm not supposed to ask why I'm leading someone who's obviously a soldier to the Iranian suite. And I'm not supposed to stick around and find out. Here's the thing. I didn't get to where I am by blindly following."

Sutton stopped and Hunter saw Elizabeth and Dalton share a glance. "I'm not moving until I'm filled in."

"You need to take that up with the president," Hunter told her. "Right now, I don't have time for a temper tantrum."

Sutton's eye flashed, but she remained calm. "You don't have a say, soldier." Sutton pulled out her phone and made a call. She stepped away and Hunter saw her remain calm as she spoke into the phone.

"She's smart. She'll put it together," Elizabeth said with a sigh.

"Might be a good thing. She could be our boss," Dalton replied.

"We'll be retired by then, so it's not our problem." Elizabeth looked over at Dalton with a look that told Hunter Elizabeth was still weighing that decision.

Sutton hung up the phone and turned to them. "So, you disarmed four bombs seven minutes ago that were rigged to blow up the stadium. You believe the Chinese government is pulling strings with their Belt and Road Initiative to expand their power and control outside of China while having Iran and Russia doing the dirty work in a quid pro quo. We have at least one more bomb that's unaccounted for and we believe the cell phone that can detonate it is in the Iranian suite. What do you need?"

"Who is in the Iranian suite that would be powerful enough to be trusted with this, yet not so high up that they could be thrown under the bus if this goes FUBAR? The supreme leader would need deniability."

. . .

"Farhad Raza," Sutton answered after a moment's contemplation. "He's a general in the Islamic Republic of Iran Armed Forces who, at first and even second glance, is a midlevel military man. However, what's not on record is that he works with China on matters involving the Belt and Road Initiative. He's who Iran sends in to take property from the citizens for Iran's new initiatives with China."

"It has to be him. He's not attached publicly to these countries and is far enough down the political ladder that the government could hang him out to dry without getting their hands dirty," Hunter said to Dalton, who agreed.

Hunter could see Sutton's mind worked as she nodded. "Got it. Get rid of any weapons. Let's go."

"You're not to be there," Elizabeth protested as Hunter dumped all the weapons he had into the nearest trashcan.

"Then stop me."

Sutton didn't wait. She walked off down the hall leading to the suite. Hunter didn't have time for political bullshit. He had a target and never missed his shot.

"United States Secretary of State Sutton Ramsey and my assistant to see Ambassador Nazeri," Sutton told one of the guards.

"The men?" the guard asked.

"My security. They go where I go. Just like you do."

The guard went inside and a moment later came to hold the door open. Sutton was allowed in, but the guards frisked Elizabeth, Dalton, and Hunter before letting them in.

"Farhad Raza is the man closest to the door with the scar on his face," Sutton whispered to Hunter before plastering on a political smile and making a show of greeting their ambassador and his wife.

Elizabeth flanked Sutton to block the view of the more powerful members of the delegation from seeing Farhad in the back row. Dalton and Hunter stepped forward until they stood behind him.

Hunter pulled out his phone and dropped it.

"Whoops," he said with a smile as Farhad glanced to see who had dropped the phone by his feet and then quickly dismissed him. "Sorry about that. I'll get it."

The guard who had been watching turned back to watch Ambassador Nazeri as Hunter walked into Farhad's row and took the seat next to him. Hunter bent down, picked up the phone, and then turned to the man who held the trigger to the bomb in his hand. The cell phone was right there. Farhad's thumb moved to absently touch the screen. The screen activated, displaying a countdown. All Hunter had to do was get it.

"Nice phone," Hunter said, nodding to the cell phone. "Is that the latest model? Mine is a couple of years old and I guess since I've dropped it so many times it runs slow. How's that one?" Hunter held up his phone, hoping Farhad would do the same.

Farhad turned his scarred face to look at Hunter. Hunter saw the moment recognition hit him, which confirmed Sutton had been right. This was the man pulling the strings on behalf of the government. Hunter knew time was up.

Hunter moved at the same time Dalton did. Hunter had Farhad's arm in his hand trying to get to the cell phone as Dalton slid his arm across Farhad's neck, turning his head so the man couldn't look at his phone as he yanked the man from his chair. It was then Dalton saw the guards converging. A taser was pressed to Dalton's neck and a guard grabbed Hunter's shoulders and yanked him back.

"Bomb!" Hunter shouted as the guards dragged him out of the row of seats, literally kicking and screaming.

Everyone was up. People were screaming. Elizabeth was climbing rows of seats to make it to Farhad but was going to be too late. Hunter watched as Farhad unlocked his cell phone and pulled up his contacts list where eight numbers were listed. They'd been wrong. There were four more bombs unaccounted for.

27

Maggie and her team followed behind the swimmers. The towering basketball players strode behind them. This was a special moment in her life, but Maggie couldn't focus on enjoying it. Instead, she kept scanning the crowd, looking for Hunter.

The crowd was cheering. Way up ahead, the flag bearer proudly waved the stars and stripes. In the infield of the stadium, the Italian military was putting on a drill display with flags of all the countries present on the ends of all the rifles. Her brother reached out and put his arm around her shoulder. "It's okay, Mags. Let's just enjoy this."

"Bomb!"

Maggie's head instantly spun at the distant sound of Hunter's voice. It didn't matter that music was playing or that the crowd was cheering. She was so in tune with his voice that she'd know it anywhere, even if it was half a stadium away.

"What is it?" Gage asked.

Maggie didn't answer. She was too busy scanning the crowd. "There!" she pointed to the box where Hunter was being dragged backward and the blonde he'd been with was jumping rows of chairs as guards were coming after her. Maggie's immediately spotted the man Hunter was trying to reach. "Three o'clock, about fifty degrees up. He has a cell phone."

Maggie looked around frantically. She had to help. She had the handgun, but the accuracy at that distance wasn't great. Maggie spun and sprinted to the nearest drill team member, tossing the rifle with the flag of Grenada on it.

"I need to borrow this," Maggie said, catching the rifle midair as the woman in her dress uniform looked momentarily shocked.

She yelled in Italian, but then Gage was there stepping in with a smile trying to placate the woman and the attention Maggie was now gaining. "Take the shot, Maggie. I got your back."

"Whoa!" A basketball player gasped as Maggie raised the rifle to her arm, the colorful flag dangling from the barrel. There were no scopes on drill rifles. She'd had to eyeball it.

"Keep everyone away from me," Maggie said to the basketball player as the whole team towered beside her. They seemed to want to ignore her, but then Gage pulled his gun and everyone screamed and ducked for cover as Maggie pulled out her lucky bullet and slid it into the chamber.

Maggie wedged her elbow into her side. She took a target stance as opposed to a tactical one since she only had a single bullet to shoot. She lined up her shot. The man was about to press a button on his phone. Everything slowed. The man's hand seemed to freeze in place. Hunter's shouts seemed to fade away. The panicked people running disappeared.

Her finger moved to turn the safety off and then rested

on the trigger. Maggie had the target in her sights. She didn't think twice. She pulled the trigger.

Hunter was sure this was it. He couldn't get to Farhad. Three men were dragging him back. Sutton was shouting at everyone to stop Farhad, but the Iranians weren't listening. Instead, they were accusing her of an assassination attempt. Dalton was behind Farhad, on the ground, shaking with several thousand electrical volts, and Elizabeth was being blocked by everyone in the stands as she tried to fight her way to Farhad.

Farhad turned to Hunter, held up the phone and smirked. He dramatically lifted his finger and was lowering it to press the call button when suddenly he wasn't.

His hand exploded at the wrist and he fell back, landing on top of Dalton. Blood covered the guards who had been tasing Dalton and everyone froze in shock as Farhad screamed in pain, holding his wrist where blood was pouring out. Where had the bullet come from?

It was then Hunter heard the screams coming from below. He turned to see security rushing the field. Maggie dropped a rifle and placed her hands behind her head, waiting for them to arrest her.

Ambassador Nazeri was screaming at Sutton, who was screaming back.

Elizabeth shoved a woman aside, punched a man in the face, and leaped up to where Farhad had dropped his phone. "Stop! This is a trigger for a bomb, and unless you want to be accused of a terrorist attack, you will start complying or you will have to explain why every country here has a reason to overthrow your government. Do you think the innocent people of Iran would approve of their government willing to sacrifice their athletes to gain the favor of China?"

"What are you talking about?" Ambassador Nazeri asked.

"I believe this was yours," Grant sauntered into the room, holding up his cell phone with a picture of a giant Holy Cannoli on the screen. "Found it on my way back from turning Hamid Saeed over to authorities." Hunter almost smiled. *Authorities* would most likely mean an American-run black site, or at the very least, be locked up in the American embassy awaiting pickup to said black site.

"A life-sized stuffed mascot? Am I missing something in our translations?" Ambassador Nazeri asked.

Grant turned to the next picture. The cannoli had been cut open, revealing a small ANFO bomb inside with a cell phone attached. "Turns out my wife is one hell of a bomb sniffer. She found three of these on the way out of the stadium. Some men named Gator, Turtle, and Skeeter helped her cut the wires after she flagged them down as friends of yours." Grant reached into his pocket and pulled out a cell phone with wires hanging off of it. "How much do you want to bet the phone numbers on that man's phone calls these phones?"

"There's still one bomb unaccounted for," Elizabeth said quickly to stop anyone from thinking twice about calling any of the numbers on it as she glanced at the contact list.

"Your decision, ambassador. Your supreme leader was willing to sacrifice your life as a favor to China," Sutton said calmly.

The ambassador's face fell as he leaned closer to Sutton. "You mean, those bombs weren't on timers?"

"No, sir," Hunter answered. "I disarmed them and there

were no timers. Apparently, athletes weren't the only ones to be sacrificed for global domination."

"Are you willing to sacrifice your life for your leader? Which is it going to be? Hero with amnesty in the United States or international war criminal?" Sutton asked as if she were asking him if he wanted pickles on his burger.

"Notify the Italian authorities that we've uncovered a terrorist plot with the assistance of the United States," Ambassador Nazeri ordered as guards went running to do his bidding before turning to Sutton. "I've always heard Arizona is a nice place to retire."

"Grant," Hunter whispered, looking toward a screaming Farhad. Grant instantly knew what Hunter wanted. They couldn't risk anything happening to Farhad. He was the evidence they needed to prove the Chinese government's involvement with Iran.

Grant grabbed Farhad, claiming to get him medical assistance and whisked him away.

"Do you have this Madam Secretary?" Hunter asked. "I need to get the woman I love out of an Italian jail," Hunter said, nodding down to where Maggie was being hauled off in handcuffs as Gage and the rest of the shooting team tried to stop them.

"I believe Ambassador Nazeri and I can assist with that on the way to the airport. Can't we, sir?" Sutton asked as the ambassador nodded.

The ambassador looked defeated as if he'd just been told his hero wasn't real. And he wasn't. Their leader was just a man who was lust-driven for power and money. "Let's go thank her for saving our lives," the ambassador said as he clasped his wife's hand. "I was told I needed to stay for the entire ceremony. I'll talk, but I want assurances, in writing, from your government."

. . .

Maggie took the shot. She knew she hit her target. The second she did, she set the rifle down and held up her hands. "Drop your gun, Gage," she said as the realization that she'd be going to jail set in. She'd just shot the hand off of a diplomat in front of the entire world. There was no getting out of this. The only bright spot she could find was that they probably had really good food in Italian jails.

Guards surrounded her as her arms were yanked back and zip-tied. Maggie heard her name being screamed as she saw the entire section of Shadows Landing in the stands. The Townsends looked ready to take on the entire Italian police force. For that matter, they all did. Olivia Townsend-Fox and Ryker Faulkner were yelling into their phones along with Ryker.

Maggie would have a lawyer soon. She knew that much at least. All that mattered though was that people were safe and Hunter was alive.

"Don't say a word, Mags," Gage told her as they were hauled to their feet.

Suddenly, the combination of soldiers and police put their hands to the coms units in their ears. The K-9 officers looked at each other and there was a burst of Italian spoken so fast that Maggie couldn't catch any of it. The guards with the dogs took off running.

"What's going on?" Gage whispered as suddenly their guards seemed more interested in their surroundings.

"I don't know."

"Ladies and Gentleman. Please return to your seats and stay seated until we notify you," the official stadium announcer said in multiple languages.

Maggie cast one last look at her friends and family

before she and Gage were escorted off the field and into a holding room.

Maggie and Gage were shoved into chairs next to each other in a windowless room. Two officers stood guard across from them, and then nothing. They weren't questioned. They weren't told anything. They were just left to sit.

An hour passed and the door finally opened. Olivia walked in and instantly demanded their zip ties cut. "They're heroes, not criminals."

The door opened again before the guards could question Olivia. Maggie and Gage both looked surprised as the head of the Olympic committee, the American Secretary of State, and several other diplomats walked in with Hunter right behind them.

"Get those ties off them!" Hunter ordered. The guards jumped forward to do his bidding and Olivia rolled her eyes at her brother.

"I was getting that done, Hunter."

"Not fast enough. You still have things to learn, little sister." Hunter winked at her and rushed to Maggie's side. He kissed her in front of everyone as the guard cut the zip ties and she was able to fling her arms around his neck and kiss him back.

"You're alive," she whispered as tears filled her eyes.

"Thanks to you." Hunter kissed her again and she clung to him. "I never want to lose you, Maggie. I was stupid and took too long to see how perfect you were. For that, I'll never forgive myself. But while I might do some dumb things, I am not a stupid man. I know I'm the luckiest man in the world to have your love. I want to spend every day showing you how much I love you. I'm sorry I don't have a ring, but, Magnum Bell, will you marry me?"

Everyone in the room seemed to hold their breath, even the guards.

Maggie didn't keep them waiting. "Took you long enough to ask," Maggie teased. "Yes! I'll marry you. I love you, Hunter. And I vow to always help you remove your foot from your mouth, to love you every day, to stand by your side, to keep the home fires burning, and to spend the rest of my life loving you."

"*Amore!*" one of the suited men called out as he clapped his hands. "I am President Serro. I owe you a big apology. Our intelligence didn't show any of what you were telling us. We found the last remaining bomb and it has been removed. The building has been searched high and low. It's been a delay and not the opening ceremony we wanted, but it shows the spirit of the games with resilience, teamwork, and determination. However, I think I have a way to make it up to you. Mr. Townsend, you come with me while they get all this business done."

Maggie had a hold of Hunter's hand and didn't want to let it go. But when the president walked out of the room, leaving Hunter no choice but to follow, she reluctantly released him.

"What's happened?" Maggie asked Olivia before Olivia introduced her to Secretary of State Sutton Ramsey and the Olympic committee.

"There was an unknown plot organized by several disenfranchised groups who have been removed from power. They were led by a traitor to the Iranian government who was hoping to gain power by instilling an opposition leader to power in Iran." Sutton Ramsey locked eyes with Maggie and rolled them. That told Maggie all she needed to know. One, this was the official talking point. Two, she really liked the new secretary of state.

"To thank you for saving so many lives, we're bringing you out to publicly thank you during the close of the opening ceremony," the head of the Olympic committee told her.

"That's not necessary," Maggie began to protest.

"Yes, it is, Miss Bell," Sutton cut in. "The villains were defeated. We need a hero and everyone saw you take that shot."

"But there were others—" Maggie began to protest thinking about Grant and the other team of Americans who had helped them.

"True. There was your brother, your friends and family, and your fiancé." Sutton stared her down. The point was clear. The others who had helped were never here. "We'll bring them all down to join you. They are already restarting the ceremony. Let's get you cleaned up and back with your friends and family."

Maggie and Gage were whisked from the room and into a larger holding room. "Your coach gave me this," Sutton said as she handed Maggie and Gage US Shooting Team polo shirts. "You have to sell this, Maggie. I've talked to the president. Unofficially, we know this was a money grab and a power move by the Chinese government to expand their New Silk Road plan by bribing current leaders, promising favors, promising money and infrastructure, and working with rebels to overthrow those countries that won't get on board. With the Iranian ambassador's intelligence and our hackers, we have a paper trail of bribes, favorable treaties, weapons deals, and more all going through Iran and Russia and leading right to China."

"They were going to install allies in power to those countries who said no?" Gage asked.

"That's right. Hamid is talking and so is the Iranian

ambassador who is now a political refugee requesting amnesty. However, with the current political environment, we can't say what we all know because it would lead to war if we actually called China, Russia, and Iran out on it. Instead, this knowledge will be used behind closed doors to pressure them on nuclear weapons and expansion of power. So, Maggie Bell, the United States needs you to be the face of this story. The sharpshooting heroine who saved the day. You'll do all the press. You'll have to pretend to know nothing about the politics of it. And you'll be the feel-good story the world needs right now. Can you do that for us?"

"If anyone can be all sunshine and pink rainbows, it's my sister."

Maggie nodded. "I can do it, but on one condition."

"What's that?" Sutton asked.

"The US Shooting team gets more publicity and funding. We have an amazing group of people, many of whom serve our country, are financial managers, mothers and fathers, teachers, and so much more. No one ever hears about them and they should."

Sutton smiled then and held out her hand. "As a former Olympic fencer, I couldn't agree more."

"You fence?" Maggie asked with surprise.

"I do."

Then Maggie smirked. "I liked you before, but now I like you even more. I know a thing or two about knives and swords. Maybe you should visit Shadows Landing sometime and come to church with me."

"I don't know what church has to do with fencing, but I'm game." Sutton took her hand and shook it with a smile.

28

———

Hunter followed President Serro out of the stadium and into his motorcade. Hunter cast a glance to the happy president currently rambling on about *amore*. "Mr. President, where are we going?" Hunter asked.

"You saved my games. I must say thank you and nothing says thank you like diamonds." The motorcade came to a stop and Hunter looked out to see a woman dressed in black with her hair in a messy ponytail running to unlock the door to a luxury jeweler. "Your fiancée needs a ring, does she not?"

"Yes," Hunter said with a smile. "Yes, she does."

Hunter strode into the stadium seconds before Maggie was announced. The ring was tucked in his pocket as he slipped his hand into hers and they walked out to the cheers of the crowd. The talking points had been said, the story spun, and now it was all about public relations.

They didn't need words. Hunter looked down and smiled at his fiancée. Hunter reluctantly let go of her hand as Maggie stepped to the podium where she spoke briefly and waved to the crowd before stepping back into the arms of her friends and family.

"Where have you been?" Damon asked as the crowd cheered.

"On an errand with the Italian president. Turns out he's not such a prick after all, just an overly optimistic romantic."

"Is that a ring in your pocket or are you just happy to see me?" Kane asked as he and Hunter's brothers joined them in the last row of the festivities as athletes began to swarm Gage and Maggie.

"Yes, now be quiet about it. I want to give it to her when the time is right and that's not in the middle of this chaos."

"Nothing wrong with a big declaration of your love," Stone challenged.

Hunter shook his head. "This is Maggie's moment. I don't want to take the attention off her."

"That's sweet," his sister-in-law Natalie said, giving his arm a squeeze.

"So sweet I'm going to need to find a new room for the night. Again." Kane rolled his eyes but was smiling.

Hunter slammed his mouth closed as a tall blonde walked up behind Kane and tapped his shoulder. "Excuse me. You help tonight? You hero?"

Kane smiled and held out his hand. "I did. Kane Townsend."

"Olga Bjorklund. I'm a pole vaulter for Sweden. I would like to thank you for all you did so I could compete. Would you like to come celebrate with me tonight?"

Olga held out her hand and Kane turned back to Hunter with a blissful smile. "Don't worry about the room. I'll see you tomorrow."

Damon shook his head. "His days of being the jet-setting playboy are limited."

"And what of you?" Hunter asked, turning to his big brother.

"What of me?"

"Maybe you should find a wife and then your days of being the grumpy big brother controlling everyone's lives would come to an end," Hunter teased.

"No one wants to marry a boring old mechanic with hellions for siblings. Now, go get your fiancée. She's looking for you."

Hunter turned and saw Maggie glancing around the crowd for him. Hunter made a beeline for her and wrapped her in his arms. He kissed the top of her head as she talked to the Hungarian handballers who had tried to help her earlier. Hunter didn't push for her to leave. He didn't interrupt her conversation. He simply stood by her side as she shined and he wouldn't have it any other way. His fiancée was a rare diamond amongst bullets and she deserved to sparkle.

That night when they came together it was different. Each touch. Each caress. Each kiss. They seemed to linger with awe. They seemed to speak with no words. They seemed to love so deeply it made Maggie want to cry.

Maggie clung to Hunter as he moved inside of her. Emotion so deep and true was written across his face. He loved her. He cherished her. He respected her. He was proud of her. He'd told her all of this as he made love to her, but it was his touch that told her more than any words could. He worshipped her and she never wanted to let go of him. Maggie only hoped his spontaneous proposal was real.

But then Hunter lowered his head, captured her lips with his, and kissed her through her orgasm. All thoughts of what ifs fled only to be replaced with love.

~

It was the third day of competition. Maggie held her breath and then let it out slowly. She'd won gold for trap. Gage had won silver. Then she and Gage had won gold for mixed trap in a shoot-off. She'd won gold in air rifle 25 meters, but now it was down to the last shot for air rifle 50 meter three position. Could she make it four golds?

Allison was locked in at bronze. Now it was between Maggie and a woman from Poland. The woman took her shot and Maggie inhaled sharply. This was her chance to win. They'd been shooting shot for shot until now. Maggie needed a bullseye to win.

Maggie took a deep breath. She tamped down the excitement. Instead, she closed her eyes and swayed until she found her perfect balance. She took aim, made the adjustment Hunter had taught her, re-aimed, and pulled the trigger.

She kept her eyes on the target in disbelief even as she heard Hunter's cheers of excitement. She couldn't look away from the bullseye. She'd done it. All the work. All the practice. All the training. *Four gold medals.*

Maggie turned and shook hands with the silver medalist as her coach handed American flags to Allison and then to Maggie. The cheers were near deafening and that's when Maggie turned to look at the crowd. Her mouth dropped open in surprise. Yes, she knew there had been a crowd, but she didn't realize it was 90% Americans or that Sutton Ramsey was there cheering alongside President Birch

Stratton and First Lady Tate Stratton. But Maggie's eyes were on Hunter. He was cheering the loudest and the shine of his eyes told her he was just as emotional as she was. Pride and love for her was etched on Hunter's face as he smiled at her.

Next to him his brothers cheered and high-fived the Faulkners. Miss Winnie and Miss Ruby were jumping up and down, causing Granger and Kord a lot of anxiety as they spotted them. Gator was waving his South Carolina COCKS hat in the air and letting out several ear-splitting whoops. Turtle was jumping up and down. Skeeter high-fived the air. Timmons was weeping. Gage, wearing his silver and gold medals, and her father were hugging her mother who was crying happy tears as she cheered.

Maggie had never felt such love.

"The heroine of the Olympics, Magnum Bell, just swept the competition with four gold medals," the pretty female reporter known for being on a national morning show said as she grabbed Maggie for an interview before the medal ceremony. "Tell us about that last shot."

"I've been working really hard on my air rifle. I was close, but something was always just a little off. My fiancé actually taught me a little trick. In the end, it's what won me the gold."

"You're speaking of Hunter Townsend. He's Special Forces, correct?" the reporter asked and Maggie nodded. "Between the two of you, who is the better shot?"

"I am," Maggie said at the same time she heard Hunter yell, "She is!"

"You didn't always say that," Maggie called out to him, ignoring the reporter.

"A man can admit to being wrong, can't he?" Hunter was beaming at her.

Several women swooned.

The reporter turned to the cameraman, "Did you get that?" she asked as the cameraman nodded. "You heard it here first. A man has admitted he had been wrong. So, Miss Bell, you've won four golds, saved the Olympics, and are engaged to a man who actually admits when he's wrong. What are you going to do now?"

Maggie winked at Hunter and turned back to the reporter. "I better marry him then. And I'll need a copy of that tape."

29

Hunter and the rest of the Shadows Landing group disembarked from Ryker's private jet to the fresh smell of the Atlantic Ocean and the warm humid breeze of Charleston in the summer. The past ten days in Italy seemed a world away. As they sat in the warm Italian sun eating the best foods and drinking the best wines, the US military and CIA had been rounding up operatives, putting pressure on governments, and doing what they could behind the scenes to slow the power grab by this group of adversaries who were more formally allied than previously known. Eventually, this division would come to a head. For now, it was threats, tariffs, and sanctions. Diplomats and spies were doing all the work to keep the balance of power from tipping too far either way. That didn't mean countries weren't aligning as they had in past world wars. Deals were being made. Pledges of support were being signed on both sides. The only question was who would blink first in this contest for power. Yet, for now, Hunter and Maggie were home and global politics were a world away.

Waiting for them were the rest of Shadows Landing who

had not attended the Olympics. Reverend Winston and Melinda. Mr. Gann, Mr. Knoll, Miss Mitzi, and so many others. Lydia was pushing Landry in his wheelchair, surrounded by all the Langston children holding up signs.

Hunter hung back as the kids all rushed to hug her and Gage, and to see their medals. Maggie and Gage made their way, person by person, hugging them and talking.

A privately hired SUV pulled up and the door opened. Veronica's high-heeled leg appeared first. Then a driver got out and opened the trunk of the SUV and pulled out a wheelchair. Veronica walked around the SUV as she waved to everyone and opened the door. Hunter rushed forward to help, but Veronica waved him off as Blythe reached out and took Veronica's hand. Together they maneuvered out of the SUV and got Blythe into the wheelchair.

"Congratulations Maggie and Gage!" Blythe called out.

Gage and Maggie rushed forward. "How are you?" Maggie asked as she took Blythe's hand.

"Ready to go home. We wanted to wait until we saw you to tell you what a great job you did in Italy and to thank you and your town for taking such great care of me," Blythe said.

"We've been very spoiled by the town," Veronica added before hugging Hunter, Maggie, and then Gage. "I was getting up-to-the-second updates on how things went. I'm so glad it's over and now you're all safe to celebrate your wedding."

"To which, we want an invite. We fully intend to come back to visit. V told me Sutton Ramsey has agreed to come to the church weapons class and I can't wait to see that," Blythe said with a laugh.

"I might have failed to mention the weapons part," Maggie said with an innocent look that caused them all to laugh once again.

The town took an hour to say goodbye to Veronica and Blythe, as was the traditional southern way of farewells. Everyone broke up then, heading home to get refreshed before heading out to the Bells' for a big celebration. Both barbecue places from town, The Pink Pig and Lowcountry Smokehouse were catering while Wilder had brought in some of his bartenders from his nightclub to make drinks.

"I can't wait to take a shower," Maggie said with a cute little sigh. He couldn't wait to take a shower with Maggie. They'd partied nonstop at the athletes' village after her last gold medal. Hunter found himself accepted into the shooters' community as one of them. He met some great people from all over the world, but the best was having Maggie by his side and in his bed. The idea of dropping her off at her house and walking away every night actually hurt, so Hunter was going to make sure they always came home to each other from now on.

"Can we take a little detour before you go home to get ready?" Hunter asked.

"Hunter Townsend, do you have a surprise for me?"

"I have a score to settle with you."

∽

Maggie stared at the targets and burst out laughing. "Are you serious?"

"I figured we better make who the best shot is official. Three shots each," Hunter said as he pulled out his military rifle. "And the winner gets a prize."

"A prize, huh?" Maggie asked as Hunter set his rifle on the table at her outdoor firing range and reached back into his truck to pull out a giant three-foot by three-foot box. "What is that?" Maggie asked as she shook the box. It rattled and clanked and she was so curious the idea of letting Hunter win left her mind before it even fully formulated.

"Let's see what you got, Goldie. Ladies first."

Maggie sited her shot and fired. Bullseye.

Hunter sent her a wink and fired his first shot. Bullseye.

"Someone has been practicing," Maggie taunted before firing at the farther target and hitting another bullseye.

"Someone just underestimated me." Hunter fired again. Bullseye.

"Let's do a fun third shot," Maggie said, looking off into the distance. "See that peach tree about a thousand yards out?" Hunter nodded as he looked through his scope. "See the branch off to the right. There are two peaches hanging the farthest out. That's our target."

Maggie enjoyed the way Hunter cleared his throat in an attempt to hide his nerves. "Okay, Goldie. Let's see what you got."

Maggie lined up her shot and fired. The peach exploded. She smiled sweetly at Hunter, not bothering to tell him she'd used that tree for target practice since she was sixteen.

Hunter lined up his shot, fired, and missed. He shook his head and laughed. "Guess you win the prize."

He handed her the box and Maggie ripped the top off and frowned. "What is this?" Maggie reached into the box and pulled out two wrenches and a handful of pebbles.

"Part of the prize."

"There's another box in here."

"Then you better open it."

What was Hunter up to? Maggie reached in and pulled out another box. It made so much noise that she was afraid whatever was in it was broken. She opened it up and frowned again. There was another box inside of it surrounded by a bunch of . . . "Marbles?"

"Yeah, we could play marbles sometime."

Maggie shook her head and smiled. She didn't ask this time. She just ripped into the next box and pulled out a stuffed Olympic mascot. "It's Augie, the Holy Cannoli! What a great prize," she laughed. Only Maggie stopped laughing when she turned it around and saw that it was wearing an engagement ring on one of its puffy pastry arms. "Hunter," she gasped. When she looked over at him, Hunter was on one knee.

"I know I've already asked you to marry me," Hunter said, pulling the ring from Augie's arm. "But you deserved more than a spur of the moment proposal and President Serro agreed. This was the errand we went on. He wanted us to have a piece of *amore* from Italy. I saw this ring and I had to get it. It's a pink sapphire," he said with a smug smile and waggle of his eyebrows that had her both laughing and crying. "I promise to love you every day, Magnum. I promise to support your hopes and dreams. I promise to always be there for you, even if I'm deployed. And I promise to always carry you in my heart. I even promise," Hunter took a deep breath and looked up at her with more seriousness than she'd ever seen before, "to wear pink on our wedding day if it will make you happy. Because all that matters to me is that you're happy. I love you, Magnum. Will you do me the honor of marrying me?"

"Yes!" she said as he slipped the ring on her finger. "But I have some promises too. I promise never to make you wear pink. But salmon is a different story. I promise to always support your career in the military. I promise to never ask you to stay home when you're called up. I promise to always be proud of you and to always keep things running at home, waiting for you to return. However, there's one promise I need from you."

"Anything for you."

"I want you to promise that we're never apart from this day on. I want to work at my parent's place, but I want every night in your bed and to awaken every morning in your arms."

Hunter rose to his feet and wrapped her in a tight hug. "Then maybe I should have asked you this, Magnum, will you move in with me . . . tonight?"

"My bags are already packed." And then he kissed her. He kissed her with so much love that Maggie forgot all about the party they ended up being very late for.

30

Hunter laced his fingers with Maggie's as they walked into the Bells' backyard. The brick porch was full of people. The pool was filled with kids. Music was playing softly on speakers and the food and drinks were flowing.

"Oh my gosh!" Maggie gasped as she saw Tinsley and Paxton sitting on the couch. In Tinsley's arms was a newborn baby. "You had your baby!"

Tinsley smiled serenely and Hunter instantly saw the content and proud look on Paxton's face. Hunter's gaze turned to watch as Maggie knelt down and ran a finger over the baby's downy hair. That could be them someday. The idea used to make Hunter consider a vasectomy. Now the opposite was true. He could hardly wait to get to his house tonight to start practicing.

"Who is this?" Hunter asked, bending down next to Maggie to see the newborn.

"Tyler Kendry. Ty was born the day after you all left for Italy. He's been a good boy, even if he gets a little fussy sometimes," Tinsley said as Ty began to make that crinkly face meaning he was about to cry.

"May I?" Hunter asked, holding out his hands.

"You want to hold a baby?" Paxton seemed surprised.

"I do have a lot of experience, you know. There are nine of us," Hunter said, nodding his head to where a group of his younger siblings were laughing.

Tinsley slid Ty into his arms and Hunter moved him into position and began to rock. It was crazy how it all came back to him—the hours and hours he'd rocked his younger siblings. The baby's face relaxed instantly. Tinsley looked shocked. Paxton looked relieved. Maggie looked very turned on. Maybe they wouldn't be waiting very long to start a family of their own after all.

After handing a sleeping Ty back to his parents, Hunter took Maggie's hand and escorted her closer to the food.

"Here. Have a plate of the town's favorite barbecue," Earl, the owner of Lowcountry Smokehouse said, handing Maggie a plate of food.

"Here," Darius, the owner of the rival Pink Pig said, shoving a plate at Hunter. "Have a better plate of barbecue."

The two men were famous for competing over whose BBQ was the best. In fact, at church every week, blind samples were put out and donations to the church were put in the basket in front of your favorite barbecue. Whoever had the most was that week's winner and was flooded with after church diners.

"Thank you," Hunter told them. "We'll share them and enjoy them both . . . equally."

Earl, who looked a little like Santa Claus huffed. Darius had long ago shaved his head and was now shaking it. "Youngins," Darius muttered.

"Can't make a decision to save their lives," Earl said as they both walked off.

"Don't mind them," Miss Ruby said. "Darius is my second cousin's brother-in-law. He's always been a grumpy old man, even when he was a teenager."

"And Earl really gets his panties in a twist if you don't instantly praise his food. They'll get over it," Miss Winnie added.

"The important thing is you two finally made the most important decision. When is the wedding?" Miss Ruby asked and suddenly they were overrun by questions from everyone around them.

"She's the event planner," Hunter said, trying to deflect some of the questions.

"Are you really throwing me to the wolves?" Maggie whispered, wide-eyed.

"I sure am, sweetheart. I just love watching you do your job."

Maggie rolled her eyes and then smirked and Hunter's smile faded. Uh-oh. "Hunter wants us to elope."

"Oh, that's mean," Hunter gasped as the wolves turned on him.

Maggie smiled sweetly, gave him a little wave, and sashayed her way to the bar. Oh, he'd make her pay for this tonight in the best possible way. By having her scream his name, begging him for more.

Maggie took a drink from the bartender and laughed to herself as Hunter had his hands up as if defending himself from the matrons of town.

"So, you're going to be my new sister. About time my

brother got his head out of his ass and asked you to marry him."

Maggie jumped at the voice coming from behind her at the bar. She turned to find Penelope Townsend, the youngest of the Townsends, sipping a cocktail and staring at Maggie with her grey eyes. She looked very similar to Damon—jet black hair and those smokey eyes that didn't seem to miss anything. However, the biggest difference was Penelope smiled.

"I'm excited to gain two sisters."

"And how excited are you to gain six brothers?"

Maggie laughed. "Well, when you put it that way . . ."

"Penelope!" Hunter called out as he extricated himself from the matrons and swooped his baby sister up in a hug.

Maggie stepped back as all the brothers rushed Penelope and started giving her crap for not letting them know she was coming. Hunter kissed his sister but quickly moved to put his arm around Maggie.

"How is the wedding planning going?" Maggie teased.

Hunter smiled and Maggie's eyes went big as his eyes sparked with mischief. "Great. We're getting married next week."

"What?" Maggie gasped.

"They thought you were serious about me wanting to elope so they bribed me with a quick wedding to convince me to do it here. You better get to wedding dress shopping, sweetheart."

"I don't need to. I'm wearing my grandmother's dress just like my mother did. Are you actually serious?"

"You did say you didn't want to be apart."

Hunter's family stared at them with shock and a little bit of fear. They were waiting for her to go off on Hunter, but instead, Maggie tossed back her head and laughed. "I can't wait. I'd do it tonight if I could."

"No!" her mother screamed. "A week is enough to about kill me. There are flowers and invitations—"

Timmons threw his arm around her mom's shoulder. "Don't worry, Mrs. B. Maggie's dress will drip. She'll slay as a bride and the wedding will be lit, no cap! We understand the assignment and are ready to give off wedding vibes."

Maggie almost laughed at the look of confusion on her mother's face. "Don't worry, Mom. I'm a professional. I'll have it planned in no time."

"I'll help too," Olivia said.

"Me too," Penelope added. "And if it's really next week, I can stay for it."

Maggie was quickly pulled into wedding talk and instead of being overwhelmed, she was so excited she could barely contain herself. Hunter didn't run this time. He stayed with her, his hand on her waist, as he helped as much as he could.

"I'm just saying, having a shooting contest for the wedding guests would be cool," Hunter said.

"I couldn't agree more," her father added. "It's a family tradition, but now I have Hunter on the guys' team. We might finally win one."

"Hey," Gage grumbled for a moment but then reared back and high-fived Hunter. "Yeah, we will!"

～

Damon leaned against the bar and watched his family. Hunter kissed the top of Maggie's head and held her close as they teased each other about wedding ideas. They were the great couple Damon knew they would be.

Stone and Natalie joined the conversation to try to help out, but Stone just ended up siding with Maggie and teasing Hunter that he should wear a pink tuxedo. Timmons declared it to be aesthetic AF.

Olivia got in on it too, adding a purple paisley bow tie before high-fiving Maggie. Soon Penelope joined in along with the Bells, and Hunter dished it back to them as best he could, but he was outnumbered. Good. Hunter needed a woman like Maggie to keep him on his toes.

"He looks happy," Kane said, taking a swig of beer as he joined Damon.

"He does. And so do Stone and Liv. I like seeing my family happy and settled," Damon said pointedly.

Kane rolled his eyes. "You're worse than Mom and Dad. They're calling in for a video chat soon, but I get at least two texts a week that some granddaughter or other of one of the retirees is single and a nice young girl."

Damon chuckled. Their parents were in a retirement village in Arizona. It was hard on them to travel, so they whole family had flown out to see them right before Stone's wedding. "You don't need a nice young girl. You need a smart woman who is your intellectual equal. Otherwise, you get bored."

Kane took a sip of beer and shrugged. "True, but it's not as if the perfect woman just falls into your lap like Maggie did for Hunter."

"She didn't fall into his lap. She knocked him upside the head for being a dumbass. The lesson is, don't be a dumbass when you meet the right woman."

"No one has ever accused me of being a dumbass."

Damon looked at his brother and held his eyes. "Even smart guys can do stupid things. You know that better than anyone. Look at how many smart people you've had to rescue."

"And how many spoiled ones?" Kane grumbled. "I've been on a streak lately of kidnapped heirs and heiresses with nothing in their heads except family money."

Kane's phone lit up in his hand and Damon saw it was the office. Kane sighed and set down his drink. "I have to take this."

Damon watched his brother walk off to the corner of the yard and answer the phone. Kane needed someone to settle him down and have him appreciate the good things in life once again. He'd seen too much darkness in the FBI BAU and was now dealing with kidnappers and rescuing people from criminals. There was no brightness in his life. Kane needed a woman who didn't give into the darkness but would help pull him from it.

Damon took another drink and went back to watching his family. He would never have this, but he could make sure his siblings did. Especially Kane. He needed love and soon. The rustling breeze and the feel of someone pinching his ass told him Anne Bonny agreed.

~

Kane answered the phone with a sharp, "Yeah?"

"Mr. Townsend, we have a diamond level client who is being held for ransom," his assistant said.

"Who?"

"Tiffany Ambers, heiress to the Ambers Leather Goods company. She and her friends thought going to Africa without telling anyone would be a good idea since the royal family did it. The trouble is they didn't have the royals' protection detail and they flashed their money all over town."

"Who has her?" Kane asked, rubbing his hand over his face.

"Our old pal, Bokamoso."

"Well, that makes it easy. My brother is getting married in a week. Book me on the soonest flight to South Africa and tell the Ambers to have their private jet meet me there. It won't take long to negotiate this. Boka's last two hostages ransomed for a hundred thousand in under three days," Kane told her.

"I'll make the arrangements and text you."

Kane hung up and turned back to the party. Hunter hugged Maggie to his side. The bastard was smiling as if he'd just hit the jackpot. And he had. Maggie was perfect for him.

Kane glanced around and saw Damon walking toward him. He nodded his chin to the group of happily married Townsends and then pointed at Kane as if to say he was next. A cool breeze sent a chill up Kane's spine, but he shook it off as Damon joined him.

"Will you make it back in time?" Damon asked.

"I should. I know who is holding her for ransom. He's easy to work with, treats the hostages well, and isn't overly greedy. Should be in and out."

"Wouldn't it be nice to come home to a woman waiting for you?"

Kane shook his head at Damon. "For a man in his thirties, you sure act like a meddling old lady."

"It'll happen, Kane. If you let it," Damon told him.

"I'm not falling in love with a nineteen year old heiress," Kane said.

Damon's face softened as if he knew something Kane

didn't. "Didn't say it was this case, just that you will fall in love if you open your heart . . . or have it pried open by a very determined woman."

"Yeah, that sounds romantic."

"Look at Hunter and Maggie. That wasn't romance. That was a shot to the head."

Kane gave himself one moment to pretend he could be that happy and in love, but then his phone buzzed. His flight was leaving Charleston in an hour. He didn't have time to think about love. He had a damsel in distress to save. Again. Maybe someday he'd have a woman save him. Kane shook his head as he strode toward his car. Damon was getting in his head. There would be no happily ever after for him. He had a job to do.

What happens when Kane falls for a woman he's sent to rescue? Find out in RESCUED when smart and feisty Waverly is kidnapped and Kane is sent to rescue her. What starts off as another job turns into a battle for their lives and their hearts.

ALSO BY KATHLEEN BROOKS

Endless Shadows

Fading Shadows

Damaged Shadows

Escaping Shadows

<u>Shadows Landing: The Townsends</u>

Face-Off

Targeted

Rescued (coming October 2024)

<u>Women of Power Series</u>

Chosen for Power

Built for Power

Fashioned for Power

Destined for Power

<u>*Web of Lies Series*</u>

Whispered Lies

Rogue Lies

Shattered Lies

<u>*Moonshine Hollow Series*</u>

Moonshine & Murder

Moonshine & Malice

Moonshine & Mayhem

Moonshine & Mischief

Moonshine & Menace

Moonshine & Masquerades

ABOUT THE AUTHOR

Kathleen Brooks is a New York Times, Wall Street Journal, and USA Today bestselling author. Kathleen's stories are romantic suspense featuring strong female heroines, humor, and happily-ever-afters. Her Bluegrass Series and follow-up Bluegrass Brothers Series feature small town charm with quirky characters that have captured the hearts of readers around the world.

Kathleen is an animal lover who supports rescue organizations and other non-profit organizations such as Friends and Vets Helping Pets whose goals are to protect and save our four-legged family members.

Email Notice of New Releases

https://kathleen-brooks.com/new-release-notifications

Kathleen's Website
www.kathleen-brooks.com
Facebook Page
www.facebook.com/KathleenBrooksAuthor
Twitter
www.twitter.com/BluegrassBrooks
Goodreads
www.goodreads.com

Made in the USA
Columbia, SC
03 May 2024

35182846R00181